The Dressmaker's Parcels

Silvano Stagni

Perpetuum Mobile Limited

Cover graphics by Jason Arias

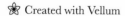 Created with Vellum

To my children

The Families

The family trees of the Mendes and Modiano extended families should help the reader navigate the large families mentioned in the book.

The Mendes Extended Family

Samuele Mendes (born 1870), **Fiamma Andrade** (born 1873)

- **Raffaele Mendes** (born 1895), married to **Antonella Levi - Children:** Carlo Mendes (b. 1923), Fiamma Mendes (b. 1926), Andrea Mendes (b. 1928)
- **Gabriele Mendes** (born 1897), married to **Rachele Modiano - Children:** Emma Mendes (b. 1924), Anna Mendes (b. 1926). Diana Mendes (b.1929), Leo Mendes (b.1932), Davide Mendes (b. 1934), Mila Mendes (b. 1943)
- **Emanuele Mendes** (born 1902), married to **Gemma Mustaki - Children:** Mario Mendes (b. 1932), Paola Mendes (b. 1934)
- **Myriam Mendes** (born 1905), married to **Michele Bolaffi - Children:** Enrico Bolaffi (b. 1930), Gloria Bolaffi (b.1936)
- **Roberto Mendes** (born 1913)

The Modiano Family

Baron Davide Modiano (born 1860) married to **Esther Coronel** (born 1866)

- **Greta Modiano** (b. 1885), married to **Michele Treves - Children:** not mentioned in the book
- **Michele Modiano** (born 1887), married to **Stella Basevi - Children:** Maximilian Modiano (b. 1912), Paola Modiano (b.1915), Alex Modiano (b. 1919)
- **Sarah Modiano** (born 1888), married to **Hans Basevi - Children:** not mentioned in the book
- **Celeste Modiano** (born 1890), married to **Maximilian Attard - Children:** not mentioned in the book
- **Daniele Modiano** (born 1891), married to **Perla Oppenheim - Children:** not mentioned in the book
- **Ricardo Modiano** (born 1894), married to **Hannah Sarah Cohen - Children:** not mentioned in the book
- **Rachele Modiano** (born 1898), married to **Gabriele Mendes - Children:** listed in the Mendes family tree
- **Barbara Modiano (born 1900), married to Herbert Cohen - Children:** not mentioned in the book

Figure 1- Map of Kingdom of Italy in 1935 - Courtesy of
Gundan, CC BY-SA 4.0, via Wikimedia Commons

Introduction

Emma Mendes Sonnino's four grandchildren were in Venice at the same time. She loved it and thought it was the best part of turning 90. It was not the exact date of her birthday; she had decided that her granddaughters should not miss school. School was too precious for her; at 90, she could still get emotional about being forced to leave her school by Mussolini's racial laws 76 years earlier when she was 14. She decided to celebrate her birthday when school in the United Kingdom had half-term holidays.

Emma could make her presence felt by just being in the room, and she was never loud or flamboyant. Somebody who could show her approval, or disapproval, with a look but whose smile could light up the night and make you feel loved and supported; she was a woman of substance, not a woman of noise. Many people had helped organise a celebratory weekend with forty guests, but nobody made a big fuss about it. They knew it was not her style.

That Thursday afternoon, Emma was enjoying being in the same room as her four grandchildren; they were all doing their own thing. Roy, her eldest grandson and his partner were working, Jonathan, 25, was reading, and Yael and Lisa were looking at old travel magazines.

Her son walked into the room with the mail. He gave the letters to his mother, thinking they were just birthday cards from her many cousins scattered around the world. Her youngest grandchild, Lisa, looked at the letter Emma had opened and put it on the coffee table next to the armchair where she was sitting.

"Grandma, why are you invited to a ceremony for the seventieth anniversary of the liberation of Rome?"

Emma picked up the letter again, read it, and then turned to her granddaughter.

"Well, they say here that they want to celebrate the Italian Jews who fought in the resistance and are still alive."

Roy, her eldest grandson, lifted his head from his laptop.

"Am I the only one who knows you were in the resistance? I can't believe you never told them."

Emma smiled; she gestured for her grandchildren to come closer and sit near her. Roy, his partner, and Jonathan sat on the floor, Yael and Lisa in the other two armchairs.

"I was not the only one in my family. It all started when my mother, your great-grandmother, found out she was pregnant with your aunt Mila eight years after the birth of her fifth child…."

Chapter One

1942-1943

Venice September 1942

It was love at first sight when Gabriele and Rachele met one Friday night in 1920. Twenty-one years of marriage and five children later, they could still feel better just being next to each other. Walking together around Venice improved their mood; they could face everything together. The war, racial laws, the need to re-invent themselves professionally when they lost their jobs because they were Jewish, and being concerned about their children's future had not changed how they related to each other.

They had been walking in total silence for the past twenty minutes. Silence between them was never uncomfortable; they were trying to absorb what they had heard half an hour earlier. It was not early menopause; Rachele was expecting their sixth child. They had arranged to see their closest non-Jewish friends, Paolo and Sofia Mondani, for pre-dinner drinks. It was a mild September late afternoon, and the oppressive heat and humidity of the summer were long forgotten. When they reached the Rialto fish market,

Rachele stopped, turned to her husband, and broke the silence.

"A child at our age with everything that is going on. What do you think?"

Gabriele took some time to organise his thoughts. He had not yet come to terms with the need to use different names for the hospital appointment. The racial laws prevented Rachele from seeing a non-Jewish doctor; it was not an emergency. The appointment was made under Sofia Taiman Mondani instead of Rachele Modiano Mendes. At that moment, he was just enjoying being next to his wife. The only thing on his mind was that twenty- two years earlier, he got lost in the green of her eyes, and he could still get lost in the green of her eyes.

"I am excited and angry at the same time; excited because of the new life we have created, angry because we had to see a friend of Paolo's at the hospital who knew very well who we were, but kept calling us Paolo and Sofia. However, when I stop thinking about those things, I am excited and worried about you."

At that moment, Rachele was more worried about the lingering smell of fish that was playing dirty tricks on her stomach. She put her arm around Gabriele's and pulled him towards their friends' home.

* * *

They had waited until after dinner to tell the rest of the family, and the general excitement had delayed everybody's bedtime. Rachele could not sleep. She did not want to wake up her husband. She quietly got up and walked to the kitchen, making as little noise as possible, hoping a hot drink would help her fall asleep. They kept mint on the kitchen windowsill; mint tea was infinitely better than any coffee or tea surrogate they had tried in the past. Somehow, she was not surprised when Anita joined her. Anita was their live-in housekeeper and her most loyal friend and confidante. The third most important adult in their household, the woman their children loved and called 'aunt.' They had shared a hot drink in the kitchen and their concerns several times in the middle of the night. Anita asked Rachele why she could not sleep. Usually, Rachele was not very talkative, but that night was different.

"I am fed up. Today was the final straw. I had to pretend I was Sofia. The doctor knew I was not, but he also had to pretend. I want to use this time to think about what I can do to change things, whatever contribution I can make to end this mess, so I can start when the baby is eight months."

Anita had not heard such fighting talk before; she did not know what to say. Rachele continued.

"I have had enough. We have been trying to adjust for four years. First, our children could not go to school with non-Jewish children, then we lost our jobs and had to invent another way of making a living, then we had to protect our home. By the way, I am eternally grateful for your help. I won't do anything now, but I will take this time to figure out what I can do."

Anita nodded. They both drank their mint tea, sighed, and spent some time in silence, then Rachele stood up.

"Good night Anita; thank you for listening. You and Gabriele are my rocks. I think I'll try to catch some sleep now."

Venice November 1942

Alvise Cantoni and Gabriele Mendes had been friends for a long time. When Alvise met Rachele, one of the few women to practice law in the Kingdom of Italy, they bonded immediately over their shared professional interests. They began working together when they lost their jobs due to racial laws. Rachele's law firm had found a way to make use of them. They were preparing cases and checking legal documents. It was a mutually beneficial arrangement. Alvise and Rachele could still earn money; the law firm used two experienced lawyers as glorified legal secretaries. They were getting their experience at a considerably lower cost. When war broke out, their workload increased. With most young men in the armed forces, Alvise and Rachele did all the work except discussing cases in court or publicly meeting clients. They were working independently but occasionally met to discuss cases. That morning, Alvise noticed Rachele was very annoyed.

"When I was expecting Davide, this was the time I stopped accepting new cases. I did not want to leave anything unresolved before I had the baby. Now there is nothing to leave unresolved. We are doing the boring part of our job. I miss dealing with clients and being in court. I am fed up. Once this baby is eight months old, I need to start doing something to change all this."

"Well, talk to me when you are ready. I might know somebody who is in a position to help."

Rachele smiled at Alvise's caution.

"Great, because at the moment, I even miss being mistaken for my secretary."

Venice, February 1943

Venice Jewish schools did not go any further than middle school, and Emma and Anna did not want to stay with their uncle in Milan or their mother's cousin in Geneva to continue their education. They had taken a few days off work to help sort out the nursery. Emma worked for one of her father's clients, Mrs Toffolo; she had just been promoted from apprentice to junior seamstress. Anna was learning to be a master baker. They had been cleaning the small room next to their parents' bedroom for a while when Anita appeared with mint tea and some biscuits made by Rachele the previous day. She was all dressed up; the two young women started teasing their honorary aunt. They noticed Anita's face and stopped. Anna was the first to ask what was wrong. Anita did not usually share "grown-up problems" with the children, but Emma and Anna were nineteen and seventeen, old enough to understand.

"Usually, I try to forget the war, those stupid laws, and everything else and just think of what needs to be done on the day. Today, what I have to do reminds me of what I usually try very hard to forget."

Emma stopped emptying a chest of drawers, turned back, took one of the small plates from the tray, and started putting biscuits on it.

"Where are you going?"

"I meet the court officer who has to agree to my guardianship of the unborn baby, who will be delivered by a woman that does not wish to be named but whose identity is guaranteed by Giorgio Falier. To maintain client confidentiality, he will be at the hospital during birth to confirm that the baby in question is the one for whom I have guardianship."

13

Anita also told them she was trying not to discuss it with their mother; she was sure Rachele knew all about it, but she was due two weeks later, and she needed to be as calm and relaxed as possible, given the circumstances.

Venice, March 1943

Rachele had already given birth to five children. She knew what to expect and was not keen to go to the hospital. However, this time, the doctor kept mentioning her age and potential complications for her and the baby. The Jewish midwife who saw her every week thought that the baby might be in an awkward position. She agreed with the doctor. In the end, Rachele was convinced, but the ruse they had to put in place for her to go to the hospital made her even more determined to be a proactive agent of change as soon as possible.

She hated the 'confidential' arrangement generally used by women who wanted to hide that they had a baby. In her case, hiding her identity was a way to protect her and the doctor. A non-Jewish doctor could not treat her, and her hospital admission was not due to an emergency. They were in clear breach of the racial laws. She hated Gabriele could not visit her or be in the waiting room. Giorgio Falier was there to confirm that the baby born from Rachele was the one mentioned in Anita's guardianship papers; Anita was there as well.

In the end, everything went smoothly, and a baby girl was born. They called her Mila, and the court gave her a last name until somebody filed adoption papers. Gabriele had to stay away to keep up with the "mother who does not wish to be named" story. Officially, Anita had come to take the baby away; nobody pointed out that she had left the hospital with Rachele. Too many people knew she was a friend of Doctor Paolo Mondani.

* * *

Gabriele's youngest brother, Roberto, was helping Emma make sure that the nursery was ready for the new baby; Emma was nineteen years older than her new sibling. She always considered Roberto as an older brother more than an uncle. In her eyes, he had always been considerably younger than the "other grown-ups." She could not hide her frustration from him.

"I am fed up with adjusting and just surviving, hoping that the war will end and those stupid laws will not exist anymore. I wish I could do something; we should all be doing something."

Roberto was smiling inwardly; he was not ready to tell his niece that he was indeed "doing something."

Emma could not stop venting her frustration.

"I remember how different things were when Davide was born. The Modiano grandparents came from Trieste. They did not need permission from any authority; they just bought the ticket and came. It was not secretive at all. Now my youngest sister does not even have my last name. Also, I should be studying hard for my *esame di maturità*[1] looking forward to studying law at the University and becoming a lawyer like my mother. Because of all those stupid laws, I must be grateful to work at Mrs Toffolo to make clothes for ladies who are not supposed to know I am Jewish. Uncle Roberto, I have really had enough."

Emma's outburst surprised her uncle. He lifted his head from the cot he was cleaning.

"I thought you enjoyed working with materials; I remember fondly your spending hours in the family warehouse, gently caressing those rolls of printed silk."

Emma stopped putting the baby's clothes away; she put down the tiny shirts she was holding, put her hands on her hips and assumed a very determined and confident pose.

"I love it, but I also love reading and studying. Mum loves baking, but she practises law; I thought I would practise law and work with materials as a hobby. I may not end up studying law, but I want to do something to change where the country is going. Will you help me?"

"Well, I know somebody who could help. Let's leave it for a while; think about it for three months. If you still want to do something by the end of June, I'll talk to my friends."

"His friends" were none other than himself, Emma's honorary uncle Paolo Mondani, his daughter-in-law Carolina Rinaldi Mondani, and Alvise Cantoni, her mother's unofficial business partner and her father's close friend. Roberto was just not prepared to share that with his niece yet.

Chapter Two

1936-1938

July 1936

There were only a handful of women practising law in the kingdom of Italy, and none of them had five children! Gabriele loved starting the day walking to work with his wife. Her heels made their relatively small height difference even smaller, her green eyes looking at him each time she stopped walking to make a point. They left earlier than usual to enjoy the relatively cool air before the summer heat and humidity made walking unpleasant. It was their private time.

Rachele's office was past the Rialto bridge, near the Fondaco dei Tedeschi. She had been working there since she got married and moved to Venice fifteen years earlier. Her good mood ended after her phone rang for the umpteenth time that morning.

"Could you put me through to Avvocato[1] Modiano, please? I asked to speak to him and not to his secretary."

"I am Avvocato Modiano," replied Rachele in a stern tone of voice. The caller 'regrouped' after a brief silence; the conversation was very productive, and he apologised.

She met her husband by the Rialto bridge to walk home for lunch. Fifteen years and five children later, his smile could still improve the worst of her mood. Gabriele noticed she was annoyed.

"Challenging day at work?" he said after kissing her on the cheek

"Somebody mistook me for my secretary yet again."

Rachele let off steam during their walk home. She knew that she and her sisters were an oddity, women who kept working even after they got married and had children. They were even more of an oddity because they did not need to work. She was grateful that it did not matter to Gabriele that she earned more money than he did. As they approached Campo San Giacomo dall'Orio her mood improved. She felt privileged that she and Gabriele were a true partnership, two individuals who choose to be together every day.

They climbed the two flight of steps to their front door. When they opened it, the aromas of lunch hit them. Leo, Diana, and Anna raced to hug them. Anita came out of the kitchen to greet them, saying that lunch would be ready when Emma arrived back from school. Gabriele smiled, Rachele smiled back. It was the life they wanted; everything else did not matter.

October 1937

Emma and her parents had gone to the station to meet the train from Vienna. Her aunt Barbara, her husband, and their three children would spend two nights in Venice before boarding a ship to Australia. Emma was there to allow the grown-ups to talk away from younger people's ears. She convinced the other children to follow the porter whose cart had all the luggage.

Rachele asked her sister what their plans were; it was her tactful way to figure out why they had picked Australia. Barbara was expecting the question; she had the same conversation several times in the previous months. They were going to sail to Alexandria, wait a day there and board another ship to Singapore. After a few days, they would board another ship to Brisbane, their final destination. Barbara started working at the hospital as head of their laboratory two months after they arrived.

Rachele saw a way to find out what she wanted to find out.

"How did you get the job?"

Barbara was delighted to change the subject

"I am not sure whether I was more surprised when they offered me a job, or they were when they read that the most senior researcher at the Imperial College in London had recommended a woman."

Rachele had used the diversionary tactic she often used in court. She then moved to what she really wanted to find out.

"So, you are moving to Australia for your job...."

By now, Barbara had figured out what her sister wanted to know.

"Herbert did not get his promotion because he was Jewish. When I received the letter, I replied I would come with a husband and three children if they were still interested. Six weeks later, they answered me they were. The following day, I almost beat David up on his way home from school. We started the paperwork two days after receiving the letter offering me a job. Herbert resigned. We sold our home. I am excited; it is a new adventure."

Rachele was quiet for a while, taking in what her sister had said.

"How did Herbert's parents react?"

"They think we should have made alyah[2] or go to the United States. They consider Australia a rough place, full of convicts and at the edge of civilisation."

"And is it?"

"I hope not; we have already contacted the Jewish community in Brisbane. They have painted a fairly civilised picture. It is as far away from Europe as we can go. I want these few days to be happy and serene. God only knows when we'll see you and our parents again!"

They were approaching the last bridge leading to Campo San Giacomo Dall'Orio. Rachele noticed Emma was busy showing the children how the porter was manoeuvring the cart with the luggage up and down the steps crossing a bridge.

When they arrived outside their home, Gabriele noticed that Anita had sent down the young (and pretty) maid to wait for them; she probably reckoned that the porter would not allow a good-looking girl to carry the luggage to the first floor flat and would do it himself.

When they entered the flat, the conversation stopped. The guests had to be shown their accommodations; Anita had prepared something nice to eat with tea or coffee and drinks for the children. Once you walked into

Gabriele and Rachele's home, you left the outside world outside.

The following morning, Davide and Esther Modiano, Rachele's parents, arrived from Trieste. Anita had been Gabriele and Rachele's housekeeper for over ten years, but she was still amazed by how Esther Coronel Modiano could enter a space and dominate it. Her posture and the way she walked matched Anita's ideas of a sovereign inspecting her land. And yet, Esther would not hesitate to wear a pair of rubber gloves and do the dishes or sweep the floor if that was she felt she had to do. Anita loved her pragmatism, her common touch, and her class. She usually referred to her as "a woman of presence, not a woman of noise"; somebody who treats everybody in the same way, from the Emperor to the porter walking with them from the station. Her Italian was fluent, but her German accent was still very strong after fifty years.

"Anita, good morning; how nice to see you. We woke up very early to catch the first train to Venice, and I can barely keep my eyes open. Can I make coffee?"

Anita still admired how Baroness Esther Modiano could waltz in and immediately pick up what had to be done, or, in this case, what she needed most to be done; leaving her husband to pay the porter, sort the luggage and walk to the guest bedroom with the maid. Barbara appeared in the hall and welcomed her mother, which gave Anita some time to organize coffee and biscuits. Esther stopped to greet her daughter and did not walk into the kitchen to look for an apron and make coffee, probably still wearing her coat and hat.

Barbara and Herbert were now at the mercy of Esther's inquisitive mind. They were sitting in the large sitting room, the one with a view of Campo San Giacomo

Dall'Orio, sipping yet another cup of coffee with the biscuits that Rachele, Anna, and Anita had baked the previous day. Esther knew no subtlety when she wanted to know something.

"So, what is the real reason you are moving to the other side of the world?"

* * *

Later in the day, people started arriving for dinner. Herbert and Barbara were overwhelmed by how many had come to Venice to wish them well. Barbara's siblings had arrived from

Trieste and Milan, some of their cousins from Rome, Trieste, Geneva, and Spalato.

* * *

It was time to leave Europe. They were not due on board until five. Herbert, Gabriele, and their father-in-law had gone to the station to collect the two steamers' trunks sent from Vienna. Before crossing the Grand Canal, Herbert stopped and turned to his father-in-law.

"Baron Modiano, Gabriele, I never expected such a crowd. It was very moving that everybody came to Venice just to say goodbye to us."

Baron Modiano stopped for a moment and put his arms on Herbert's shoulders.

"Herbert, we are used to people in other parts of the Mediterranean, but you are going to the other side of the world, almost literally. By the way, Haifa is your second port of call … Gabriele, what are the names Greta and her husband are using now? "

"They are Ruth and Chaim, Baron Modiano."

"All right, Ruth and Chaim (what was wrong with Greta and Michele?) will be at Haifa harbour to take all five of you to lunch."

The three men walked in silence until Herbert stopped and turned to his father-in-law.

"Baron Modiano, I am sorry I am taking your daughter and your grandchildren so far away."

"Herbert, anything involving a Modiano woman can only be a joint decision. The two of you are taking my grand-children to the other side of the world! But tell me, why Australia? Wasn't the Holy Land far enough?"

"We are just following an amazing job opportunity. It was coincidental that the job offer arrived the day before we decided to leave Vienna, and indeed Europe."

Baron Modiano turned to Gabriele and whispered, "We better act as if we believe them!

Early April 1938

Rachele was concentrating on a contract with her door open when she felt observed. She raised her head to see the senior partner in the firm standing at the door. As he walked inside the room, he noticed a magazine on top of her handbag.

"I had no idea you read that magazine."

"I don't; I just saw a headline that grabbed my interest and wanted to see what they were writing."

Rachele had asked him if he had time to discuss a contract with her, there was something that was not right, but she could not pin it down. Her boss could not help notice the title on the cover of the magazine. He asked her what she thought. Rachele told him it reminded her of her brother-in-law Herbert who had been bypassed for promotion in Vienna the previous year because he was Jewish. Herbert, her sister Barbara and their children now lived in Australia. Her boss reacted using a reassuring tone of voice, or so he hoped.

"You know I would do nothing like that. I hired you, watched you grow professionally and personally; you are safe here."

"It is not that. Barbara and Herbert emigrated because they stopped feeling safe in Vienna. After they left, I had a conversation with my older daughters about how safe we felt in Venice. Will we still feel safe in Venice next month? Yesterday Gabriele overheard a stupid comment about their Jewish legal counsel. Somebody mentioned that Alvise Cantoni was not a real Venetian."

"The son of the *Doge of the Ghetto,* not a real Venetian? They do not know what they are talking about."

Rachele smiled at the last comment; she stood up to pick up the magazine.

"Still, it is not relevant. I have not read the article yet, but I am beginning to wonder what would make me, or a member of my family, stop feeling safe in Venice."

"Venice is a bubble, the *Ponte Littorio*[3] is yet another evidence that Venice only has a tenuous link to the mainland. Therefore we are free from whatever stupid and dogmatic idea is fashionable there; you will always be safe here."

24

Rachele sat down again, it was nice to hear those reassuring words from the person who had faith in her all those years ago, but that was not entirely her point.

"Thank you, but I have started wondering, and I dislike it. I dislike the idea that my children might grow up with a sense of insecurity, that they might feel that they do not fit in the place where they were born. But you are here to discuss this contract; let's see if two heads are better than one."

Their discussion of the contract revealed Rachele's doubts; her boss said she could probably use a break from it. She ordered a coffee and read the magazine for ten minutes. The article intellectually annoyed and emotionally concerned her. Rachele rang her husband to say she needed fresh air and would leave the office early.

She loved the springtime weather in Venice. She walked to clear her head, wandered aimlessly, but was not lost, her surrounding slightly out of focus like an impressionist painting. It was just a longer route home. She turned left after Rialto Bridge, walked along the Grand Canal for a while, then turned right through countless narrow streets, bridges crossing narrow and wider canals. She found herself in Campo San Polo and arrived outside the front door of her home in Campo San Giacomo Dall'Orio about an hour after leaving the office. Rachele still had not decided how to react to the article that annoyed her so much, but had figured out what to do about the contract she had been reading for most of her day. She would discuss the article with Gabriele in the privacy of their bedroom, or they would take one of those after-dinner walks they both loved so much.

15 April 1938 - First night of Passover

It was a long-standing tradition that the Mendes clan would gather the first night of Passover. Gabriele's eldest brother, Raffaele, and his wife, Antonella, were the hosts this year. At the end of the Seder[4], they told the family they had decided to leave Italy.

Gabriele and Rachele were enjoying the walk home. Anna was walking silently between her parents until they were crossing the Ponte degli Scalzi.

"Will we leave Venice as well? Last year it was Uncle Herbert and Aunt Barbara, this year it is Uncle Raffaele, Aunt Antonella with Carlo, Fiamma and Andrea. Are we going as well?"

Rachele and Gabriele looked at each other; she nodded, so he answered.

"Would you like to leave?"

"I love my world as is, and I love living in Venice. This evening Grandpa said that our ancestors had been involved in printing and dying silk for almost four hundred years. Venice is our home; why should we leave?"

Gabriele hoped he was going to sound reassuring.

"People move because their job takes them elsewhere, they want to explore new possibilities, or they want to be with the person they love."

"Like mummy moved from Trieste to Venice."

"Exactly," continued Rachele, "and when you are an adult, you may decide to move for any of those reasons."

"During the centuries our family has lived in Venice," continued Gabriele, "there have been hard times and easy times, but we were never forced to leave or to stop being Jewish. It is a privilege compared to other parts of Europe. We may visit your Modiano grandparents in Trieste, or spend some time in the mountains, or go to the beach, or go somewhere else, but we shall always come home, back to our Campo in Venice."

Chapter Three

1938

Venice, Lido Tuesday, 6 September 1938

Gabriele and Rachele had as many nephews and nieces as possible in Venice for a few days before the Jewish High Holidays. A day at the beach was the highlight of this family gathering, and usually, the 'local' cousins would join the visitors. Adults, children, and teenagers congregated in different groups on the beach.

Anna was frustrated she had to stay with the children. She was sitting on a deckchair in the shade, reading a book, looking longingly at the group of teenagers playing volley-ball. Emma and their cousin Carlo running past her to get to their parents, brought her back from daydreaming. Carlo was holding a newspaper.

"Mum, did you see this? Does it mean that we can't go back to school?" asked Emma.

Rachele looked at the paper, her smile quickly replaced by a worried look.

"You may not be going back to your regular school. Carlo, take this paper back to whomever you borrowed it from, ask a waiter if we can buy one off the hotel, and then we can talk about it."

Gabriele gave his nephew the money to buy a newspaper, and Carlo was off on his errand. While he was waiting for his nephew to come back, he looked at his children, nephews, and nieces. You could hardly tell them apart from non-Jewish Italian; some of the Modiano cousins looked more like Slav. Emma, for instance, looked very much like her mother and several of her cousins, tall, slim, with a very light complexion and high cheekbones.

Some of her older cousins were sitting on the sand near Anna's deck chair. She was happy to be around them. Diana and some of the older children had stopped whatever they were doing and had gathered as well. Her brothers and other cousins close to them in age continued building a sandcastle helped by her Aunt Sarah. Anna realised that whatever she was about to hear would not be pleasant.

Carlo was back with the paper; Gabriele took it. The mood of the group was not playful anymore; any bantering had stopped. Sarah Modiano had taken it upon herself to shield the younger children from whatever serious conversation was about to happen.

Gabriele passed the paper to his wife. Anna noticed that her mother's demeanour had changed as she took the newspaper from her husband. The relaxed woman having fun with her extended family was gone; the professional was back. Instinctively, Rachele looked around to assess who else was within earshot. It was a Tuesday, so there were no locals. It was September; most people around them were not Italians. Still, she was careful with her choice of words.

"They will separate Jews from the rest of the population in the school system, from the teachers to the school staff, from the primary school pupils to new university students. Those near the end of their degree will still be able to finish University. Anybody else will not be allowed in their old school anymore unless it is a Jewish school entirely staffed by Jewish teachers. I read the law when it was published yesterday, and in the afternoon, I discussed it with Alvise Cantoni and other Jewish lawyers. The Jewish community will start schools, so you may still go to school, but not your old ones. It will probably take a week before we know of any plan in Venice. Alvise is briefing the communal leadership this afternoon."

All the cousins silently took in what Rachele had just told them; the first to break the silence was Carlo, who strangely smiled.

"Mum and Dad were going to tell you tonight that our visas arrived yesterday. We are leaving for Canada in November; we are going at the right time."

Carlo and Emma had always been very close. He was four months older, but she thought of him as an older brother. Emma was now trying to take in the future separation from her cousins and the forced change of school.

Alessandro Modiano, the youngest son of Rachele's oldest brother, said that his dream of becoming a lawyer had gone. Another cousin said he would start working with his father. Then they all started talking at once, asking questions or making comments. Rachele clapped her hands; everybody stopped talking and looked at her, wondering why she did it.

"Now, if you ask your question one at a time, we may try to answer them. If you all speak at once, I only hear a noise, and I cannot react to noise."

One of the teenagers muttered (or at least he thought he muttered).

"Aunt Rachele in her best impersonation of General Radetzsky."[1]

"I heard that!" said Rachele with a smile.

Trieste, 23 September 1938

Gabriele always approached Trieste with some trepidation; after almost twenty years, the Modiano baronial palace still intimidated him. He could not help address Rachele's parents with their full titles when he was there. He was fond of them, and he knew they had grown fond of him, but the big mansion was still intimidating. This time he could not stop thinking of the fiercely antisemitic speech Mussolini had delivered slightly more than a week earlier in Trieste's main square. He sat in silence most of the train journey, fully aware of Rachele's concerned glances. When they arrived, it surprised him to notice that all his children were still presentable. He quickly inspected them as they walked along the platform to meet Baron Davide Modiano and his driver. Everybody looked neat and tidy when they greeted their grandfather, who enjoyed every second of being at the centre of his grandchildren's attention. Gabriele let his wife and younger children go with the Baron in the family car, following them in a taxi with their older daughters. The Baron's butler led them through the thick door into the vast atrium; he noticed Baroness Esther Coronel Modiano coming down the marble staircase framed by two large doors into the garden. Her calm but enthusiastic entrance contrasted with the staff's fast pace, bringing their luggage inside and taking it upstairs. They were soon at the centre of the informal, engulfing, warm welcome that the Modiano household bestowed on friends and families. Gabriele never failed to admire how his parents-in-law could dance from one grandchild to another, making everybody feel special. Davide Modiano looked overwhelmed by the grandchildren, but, in reality, he was in complete control, getting everybody where he wanted them to be.

The relationship with his in-laws did not start in the most positive way. They hoped that their young daughter would marry the son of a Jewish aristocrat from Venice, but he was accepted into the family very quickly. As Barbara put it, "Once my father saw the way you were looking at his daughter, he immediately welcomed you."

It was clear to both Gabriele and Rachele that her father wanted to talk to them as soon as possible. He looked at his daughter and son-in-law, excused himself, and headed for his study. Rachele noticed that her mother, the house-keeper, and the butler were taking their children to the rooms they would use; she used her eyes and a tilt of her head to tell her husband that they would have to follow her father through the large double doors into his study. Baron Davide Modiano almost looked defeated when he started speaking.

"I am not sure whether Mussolini planned such a strong anti-Semitic speech the week before Rosh Hashanah, but it happened. I doubt it was an isolated episode or that he let himself be carried away by his own rhetoric. More restrictions might come our way, and I'm afraid they will come for our assets. You need to be thinking of a way to protect your home and your savings."

Gabriele knew Rachele's father well enough to see through his matter-of-fact tone of voice. He was convinced that the situation was serious, and it deserved their attention. Rachele noticed her husband's concerned look; she was far more pragmatic in her reaction.

"Do you know whether something else is being put together?"

Davide Modiano seemed to recover his natural posture; he almost replied matter-of-factly.

"It is only a gut reaction. I will come to Venice for the day next week once I have figured out how we may protect our home and the business."

Father and daughter were now pragmatic and business-like; they had something to plan. Gabriele could see that their emotional reaction had shifted. Unfortunately, his emotions had not, or at least not yet. He always admired his wife's pragmatism.

"I think you should also discuss it with Daniele; he is the stockbroker in the family."

"I need to discuss it with Michele and Celeste first; after all, they are very active in the family business. Sarah, Daniele, Ricardo, and you have built professional lives outside the business. Michele and Celeste have invested their energies in it. You have shares in the company and will inherit more; they are running it."

Gabriele was always ill at ease when the Modiano family business was discussed in his presence. He still remembered the words one of Rachele's aunts used to compare Modiano's coffee trading and coffee roasting international company with his family "being in textile."

"Baron Modiano, thank you for your concern. I agree with you; I think Rachele and I must talk about it and maybe discuss it with you when you come and see us in Venice. Meanwhile, if you do not mind, I would like to leave you and Rachele to discuss the world of coffee; I need to get changed."

Davide Modiano smiled and excused his son-in-law. Gabriele left the room. He thought he had, yet again, found a balance between the interest in his wife's family business and the 'no interfering unless asked' policy he had adopted since his first visit all those years ago. He hoped to find somebody who could tell him which room his in-laws had assigned to him and his wife; Gabriele was sure that he would find everything unpacked and put away in the wardrobe and drawers by the efficient Modiano household staff.

Venice, 18 October 1938

Rachele was staring at her cup of coffee as if drinking it were a major life-changing decision. Children's voices around the breakfast table were like a concert masterfully conducted by Anita, who undoubtedly was the core of the family. Gabriele interrupted her morning thoughts.

"Are you drinking that coffee, or are you looking at that cup as if it were a Canaletto painting?"

That line had Diana, Leo, and Davide laughing. Emma and Anna looked at one another and then at their mother. The more vocal of the two, Anna asked her mother whether she was all right. Rachele smiled, took a sip of her coffee, and stopped; it was cold. Anita appeared at her side with a fresh cup. Rachele got up and hugged her, thanking her for taking care of them.

On their way to work, Gabriele re-started the conversation that sleep had stopped. Emma was their main concern. Venice had no provision for a Jewish high school, and they were reluctant to send Emma to Milan. Maybe if they gave up on one of the two maids, they could afford private tuition for her

Rachele had always thought that her daughters would go to University as she and her sisters did. She made a remark about "this nonsense" not lasting forever. Gabriele instinctively looked around to see who might have overheard his wife.

Once they crossed the Rialto bridge and reached Campo San Bartolomeo, Gabriele kissed his wife on the cheek, wished her a good day at work, and continued walking to his office. For the first time, he wondered whether his beloved city might turn against him and his family.

* * *

Baron Davide Modiano wanted to make sure that his home and assets and those of his children were protected. He had taken the first train to Venice to have the confidential opinion of his daughter, the lawyer, meeting Rachele at her office to show her what his lawyer had suggested to protect the family business and assets if there were more laws against Jews. He had paid frequent visits to Venice since his daughter married her Venetian soulmate, but still found the city wonderfully bizarre. The unfamiliar noises that met a traveller just arrived from "the real world" still surprised him. He took the waterbus to Rialto, the *vaporetto,* as he knew the locals called it; he knew the way to his daughter's office from the bridge.

Rachele's boss knew she was meeting her father during office hours; Baron Modiano had sent the law firm many clients. He passed through reception when Davide Modiano arrived and led him to Rachele's office. They stopped at the door.

"Here we are, Baron Modiano, this is the office of the best lady lawyer in Venice," he said with a smile; this was an old banter between him and Rachele, who promptly replied with a smile.

"That is not correct; I am the best lawyer in Venice, who happens to be a woman," she said smiling, as she stood up to greet her father, "welcome to Venice, dad, do you need a coffee?"

"A Modiano never says no to a coffee."

Said the Baron with a smile as he hugged his daughter and kissed her on the forehead.

A secretary appeared with coffee and some biscuits. Father and daughter sat at the table in Rachele's office, and Baron Modiano took several paper from his briefcase.

Three hours later, it was time for lunch. It might have been a business trip to Venice, but Baron Davide Modiano had no intention of missing lunch with his Venetian grand-children.

They had gone through all the papers. Rachele had taken copious notes, made some suggestions, and promised she would reflect on some points overnight and call him the following morning. They left the office in time to meet Gabriele. The conversation was generic on their way home; the tone changed when they arrived at Campo San Giacomo Dall'Orio. They stopped by the back of the church in the middle of the Campo. Rachele looked around to see if there was anybody within earshot. She then asked Gabriele if he could discuss "their situation" in her office Monday or Tuesday of the following week. Gabriele agreed. He opened the building's front door, and they climbed the two flights of steps to their flat. All three of them were looking forward to being engulfed by the "Mendes bubble."

Venice, 31 October 1938

On his way to have lunch with his siblings, Gabriele was thinking of what he and Rachele had agreed earlier in the week: turn some of their capital into gold and jewel, open a bank account in Switzerland, make a fictitious sale of their home to Anita, and transfer some of their investments in her name. He wondered whether it was enough or they had to follow in his older brother's footsteps and leave Italy. He got off the vaporetto and walked towards the restaurant. When he saw his brother Emanuele and his sister Miriam, he wondered how he could find the right moment to ask them whether they had discussed the possibility of leaving Italy as well.

After lunch, Roberto wanted to discuss something sensitive with Gabriele. They started walking together to the *vaporetto* stop. They rode in silence; Gabriele knew his baby brother well enough not to break that silence. They got off the *vaporetto* and started walking towards Gabriele's home. When they turned into Campo San Giacomo Dall'Orio, Gabriele invited his brother for coffee. His brother accepted.

Once the children heard the door open, they rushed to meet their father; Leo and David reached him first and started screaming that their Uncle Roberto was there. Diana's face lit up, and Rachele and Anita joined the group in the hall to welcome the guest. For a while, Roberto enjoyed being engulfed by "The Mendes bubble," well-organized chaos that made you forget the outside world existed. However, his outside world did exist, and he wanted to share some of it with his older brother. Rachele figured out that her brother-in-law wanted some time alone with her husband.

"We need to leave dad and Uncle Roberto alone; they have something important to discuss."

she said as she removed Davide, who was happily playing, sitting on the floor between his uncle's legs.

Anita appeared and said she had taken drinks and a cake in the small sitting room where they would be removed from the family chaos and could talk. The two brothers stood up and left the room. Roberto became more talkative.

"What is the secret behind your household functioning like a well-oiled clockwork?"

Gabriele smiled as they entered the sitting room

"Anita is in charge."

They sat down and kept bantering as they were eating the cake. Gabriele realised his brother was getting ready to share what he wanted to share. Once Roberto had tasted the cake, he was ready to talk.

"I love being here. I have always loved visiting you and Rachele."

"You always loved Rachele's cakes. But I am sure you are not here to sing the praises of your sister-in-law's baking skills."

"I have been singing the praises of Rachele's baking skills almost every day since you married her."

Roberto stopped, smiled and blurted out in one breath,

"I joined a clandestine political party."

"Please do not share any detail. The less I know, the better. Protect our parents, their home, and their business from your political activities. I am proud of you, but I must protect my family, my home, and our parents. That is the battle I want to fight."

Gabriele hugged his baby brother, who looked relieved as he left. A concerned Gabriele went looking for his wife.

Venice, 5 November, 1938

Gabriele's parents, Samuele and Fiamma, had all their children and their families for lunch after morning service in the synagogue. It had been as close to a regular Saturday lunch as one could get. They talked about people in the congregation, how the children were doing in their new school, the early fog, and their health.

Gabriele, Rachele, Anita and the children were walking home after lunch; Gabriele at the rear end, as usual, surveying their family, Emma and Anna walking together talking, Diana holding hands with Leo and Davide watched by Rachele and Anita. The children were laughing, and Anita and Rachele were laughing with them. Gabriele was walking with his hands in his coat pockets, head bent down so much that the hat almost hid his face. The familiar route and the voices of his children were the only two things that kept him from falling into a canal. After crossing the *Ponte Degli Scalzi*, Rachele slowed down, moved to his side, and put her hand into his coat pocket. They walked in silence, the fog almost embracing them. After a while, Gabriele stopped and turned to his wife.

"Nobody mentioned the increase in antisemitic articles in the papers. Should we be thinking of leaving as well?"

Rachele nudged him to continue walking. She was a lawyer and could only work where they practise Italian law; he was a civil servant. They did not have job opportunities abroad like her sisters Barbara and Greta, or enough capital to buy a partnership in an existing business somewhere like Raffaele had done after they got their visas for Canada.

"We have followed my father's suggestions. Where would we go? What would we do once we were there?"

"I think we are sleepwalking into something bad for our children. Look at them now; Emma and Anna are probably talking about boys they saw from the ladies' gallery. Diana, Leo, and Davide are laughing with Anita; I have the gut feeling it will not last."

"It will not last. They will grow up. Remember your Venetian history. In the days of the Most Serene Republic, a Doge would issue edicts against Jews, but things went back to 'normal' after a few years. Racial Laws will not last forever. You'll see."

Gabriele put his right hand in his coat pocket and held Rachele's left hand that was already there.

"I hope we shall outlast them, and our children's future will not be permanently ruined."

Gabriele and Rachele continued to walk in silence, side by side, reassured by each other's presence. Emma and Anna joined them. Emma was annoyed that Anna kept teasing her about a boy sitting next to their cousin Carlo in synagogue. Rachele told Anna to stop teasing her sister. Diana joined them and started teasing Emma, which prompted more comments from Rachele and made Emma more annoyed. Gabriele smiled for the first time since they left his parents' home. The present was a nice place. The future will wait for them on Monday.

Chapter Four

1938-1939

Venice, 11 November, 1938

Rachele had worked through her lunch break. The afternoon edition of the paper lay unopened on one side of her desk near the tray with the remnant of two sandwiches, water, and an empty coffee cup. Her boss walked into her office without knocking; he had a very sombre face. He was holding his copy of the afternoon edition of the paper and asked if she had read it.

Rachele was mentally going through everything she was working on to see which one could attract the attention of the press. Her boss closed the door, sat down, pushed the paper in front of her saying, "we need to find a way to keep you working for this firm after January."

Rachele read the headline.

"The cabinet has approved the laws to protect the Italian race, no mixed marriages. The definition of Jew, discriminations and entry in the official personal records...."

She started taking notes as she was reading; her boss sat in silence watching her. When she lifted her head, he had very reassuring words for her:

"Slightly less than twenty years ago, a client introduced me to this young lady who told me she had graduated from law at Trieste University. You told me you were the only woman in your year. I would see you as an oddity or a bet, but you were a bet I would win. I never regretted taking that bet. We have up to the end of January to think about how we can keep your skills and your brain."

Rachele was very touched, but her "lawyer brain" was working at full speed.

"I have too many things going through my mind, my husband, my children, my whole extended family, my job. Give me time to study the law, and I will have some ideas."

Her boss sounded firm, reassuring, and caring at the same time.

"I have a better idea. You are too close to this one; who is the colleague you would trust with your worst secret?"

"You, of course, but if I have to name somebody else… Giorgio Falier. Meanwhile, I should not take any new cases that might end up in court; I hate the idea of not being able to follow things to their very end. Now, if you excuse me, I have to call Gabriele."

"Whatever is going on in your husband's office, tell him I am on his side."

Gabriele was having a completely different conversation with his boss. The person who had been promoted over him was a party faithful, who, allegedly, marched to Rome with Mussolini in 1922.[1] His boss strode into his office, dumped the paper on his desk, told him he would be gone by the end of the year, turned around, and left the room.

Gabriele sat at his desk, staring at the paper without really reading it. Gabriele felt somebody had transported him to a parallel universe where everything had become hostile. He could not think pragmatically. Images of his wife, children, Anita, his parents, siblings, nephews, and nieces were all chaotically coming to his mind. He wanted to shelter everybody from this hostile world. The phone brought him down to earth. He hoped it was his wife calling him. He picked up the phone and immediately felt better. It was his wife. Rachele sounded concerned and as deflated as he was. Gabriele did not hide his state of mind.

"Well, the *Fedelissimo*[2] came to my office simply to tell me I have a job till the end of the year, not a day longer. How are you?"

"I am at my fifth page of notes, and my to-do list already has ten items in it. I had a completely different reaction. My boss asked me who should look into the law to see if there is a way for me to keep working for them.."

Rachele might have sounded deflated, but she knew what to do; Gabriele did not. Talking to each other reassured and calmed them. Rachele, always pragmatic, was the first to say goodbye. She had to attend to items on her to-do list before the end of her working day. They would meet later to walk home together.

* * *

Anna was always grumpy when she felt she was considered one of the younger children. She sensed that something had happened; she was eagerly waiting for Emma to arrive home to see if she had any information to share.

Anita's mood and her "let's wait when your parents come home" were not good signs. Annoyed and nervous, she retreated to her room; she closed the door sat by the window, hoping to see her parents walking across the *Campo*.

Anita looked at Emma's face when she opened the door. Emma had obviously read the papers, or at least somebody had discussed the content of the front page with her. Unfortunately, there was more.

"Aunt Anita, can you look at the back of my jacket, please? Franco Cantoni, Deborah Abulafia, and I were walking home past our old school when two older boys, wearing the Fascist uniforms for students, started throwing things at us. We ran, but they hit me in the back at least twice. I do not know what they hit me with. Franco looked, but I asked him not to tell me."

Anita looked at the coat and realized that those boys had been throwing eggs at them. She took the jacket and promised to give it a good clean, hugged Emma, reassured her it was not a big deal, gently guided her into the kitchen, sat her down at the big table, gave her some water, and tried to calm her. Once Emma left the kitchen, she let off steam, talking to Maria, the maid, but really talking to herself.

"I do not understand those boys; they do not have political views; they are thugs. Why did they have to throw eggs at three Jewish teenagers? They were just walking past. I wish I could do something more than be mad."

Maria tried to calm her down.

"There is nothing you can do. Those boys are members of the youth wing of the Party; the police will always protect them against Jews and non-party members. Sit down, have some water, calm yourself down before Mr. and Mrs. Mendes arrive home. I'll take care of what's cooking."

Maria's husband was not a party member. The black shirts regularly took him and forced him to drink castor oil whenever anti-Fascist graffiti appeared at Castello.

Anna saw her parents walk across Campo San Giacomo Dall'Orio. She quietly moved to the front door to talk to them. Anita appeared from the kitchen; she briefly explained what happened to Emma without explaining why and suggested to Anna that she ought to see how her sister was doing. Anna understood her parents needed to know the entire story before they talked to Emma. She decided she could speak to her parents later, turned back, and went looking for her sister. Maybe she could get out of her what was worrying Anita.

Anita opened the door and stepped out onto the landing. She wanted to make sure she caught up with Gabriele and Rachele before the children ran to hug them, as usual. She was an impressive sight from the bottom of the last flights of steps. Gabriele felt she was looking like a sentinel watching over their home and that, alone, reassured him that everything would be all right in the end.

When Gabriele and Rachele reached the landing, Anita greeted them and whispered.

"Emma came home shocked. Members of the Fascist youth pelted her and Franco Cantoni with eggs. Anna has not seen the paper but senses that something has happened. You need to talk to Emma and Anna."

Venice, 25 November, 1938

Gabriele now hated his job and his office. On his way to meeting his wife, he was thinking of what he could do to earn money. They had a large and expensive household to run.

Rachele was in a pensive mood. She kissed her husband, and they started walking towards the Rialto bridge. The fog was embracing them like a cosy blanket. They crossed the bridge in silence, holding hands like teenagers, both of them lost in their thoughts, both of them reassured by the occasional touching of their shoulders. When they walked past the market, Rachele looked around to see if anybody was too close to them and started speaking in a tone of voice that was just slightly above whispering.

"I think that what they have in mind might work. I shall structure and analyse cases from home. Giorgio will deal with clients and with the court if necessary. It will mean less money, but it is better than no money at all."

Gabriele's voice showed all the frustration he had built up since the eleventh of November.

"The moment I figure out what to do, I resign. I cannot stand the 'Ghetto' jokes and the sudden pointing out that I am not one of them."

Rachele was hoping to sound reassuring…

"Well, my income will not change until the end of January. If things are so dire, why don't you leave at the end of the month?"

…without much success…

"To do what? There isn't much use for my experience outside my department of the city's civil service."

47

…but it did not mean she gave up.

"Yes, but in eighteen years, you have managed budgets, controlled projects, and worked with suppliers. There may be a lot of small businesses that need help with that."

Venice, 18 January 1939

Gabriele did not like bookkeeping, but he was good at it. He found his first clients one week before leaving his job and now had five clients. He was happy that Emma could continue her lessons and Maria's salary could be covered, but constantly monitored how much they had to dip on savings to run their households.

Rachele still had a job, so he continued walking to work with her and meeting her outside her office to walk back home. It was an essential part of the day for both of them, something from the old life as they were adjusting to a new normality.

Gabriele and Rachele were walking hand in hand, feeling cocooned by their physical proximity. They did not look any different from other Venetians. They had just crossed a bridge on a narrow canal and were now in the *Campo* between the market and the Rialto bridge. Rachele stopped to look at a shop full of Murano glass objects. Gabriele was lost in their reflection on the shop windows. It was a clear sunny winter day; they were wrapped up in their coat. Gabriele looked at his wife as if she were the most precious thing in the world. Rachele brought him down to earth.

"Today, we discuss how they will pay me once I officially stop going to the office."

"I am seeing three potential new clients today. One of them wants a Jew on his side because we have a strong business sense. A year ago, I would have made a very rude comment and left. Nowadays, all I can see is another retainer. Annoyingly, he is the most likely to sign. "

Rachele sounded pragmatic, loving, and exasperated at the same time.

"My boss was asking me if I knew any other Jewish lawyer who needs work. He reckons they can save money, and we can still earn a good living. I have already mentioned Alvise to him. They will pay us as experienced legal secretaries, less than I earn now. We need to have a pragmatic and unemotional discussion of our finances today. Our maid officially works for our housekeeper, who is officially our landlady, but we still need to pay them, and our children's schooling, and put food on our table, and keep our very large home warm, etc."

Gabriele still felt romantic.

"I'd rather spend time with you in another way, but I agree. We need to look at our finances; I hope I have more clients by lunchtime."

They had reached Rachele's office. Gabriele hugged her, kissed both her cheeks and started walking towards the vaporetto stop. Rachele watched him, wondering how much of his relaxed and confident attitude was an act he put on for her sake.

Venice, 20 February 1939

Rachele had gone back to doing what she was doing during the early years of her career. It was not the part of her job she loved the most, but it was a way to earn money, structure her day, and keep the brain working. It frustrated her she could not do the job she was qualified to do just because she was Jewish. She was happy she had time to bake.

In the past, her family and career did not leave enough time to bake every day; now, she could use her skills as a master baker. Alvise Cantoni arrived with his share of files. He was not in a good mood. He complained they had to do the boring part of their job so some junior, Aryan, lawyer could do the exciting part. Rachele pointed out that they earned money. Neither of them felt any better. The doorbell rang as Anita walked in with coffee and biscuits. Rachele left the room to open the door; Anita fetched another cup of coffee and more biscuits

Giorgio Falier usually met Rachele and Alvise on his way to work. Once Rachele had cleared away the coffee and biscuits, they started on the files. Giorgio enjoyed this part of his working day; Rachele and Alvise hoped to get used to it one day.

* * *

Gabriele had just spent the morning doing the books of a seamstress. Spending time amongst reams of material reminded him of his childhood when he visited his father in their warehouse. His client was in a chatty mood.

"*Do* you know of a Jewish girl who wants to come and learn the trade? You know you can trust me, and you are here once a week to check. Let me know."

"Thank you, Mrs. Toffolo, and thank you for coffee and *baicoli*[3] Would you consider sharing the position between two girls? Would you be happy for them to go home early on a Friday afternoon and stay home during the Jewish holidays?

"I have no problems; I am sure that they might agree to help if I have to dress a bride on a Sunday."

* * *

Gabriele and Rachele used to enjoy their private time when walking between home and their offices. They replaced it with a walk every evening before dinner. Their new ritual was a walk to the vaporetto stop in *San Stae*, then take a vaporetto to the Accademia, walk to the Zattere on the Giudecca Canal, and then walk back home. It was a walk that allowed Gabriele to be in the Venice he loved, the sudden views across a narrow canal, the small openings, the openness of the Giudecca Canal. They would walk along the *Zattere* in the darkness of a winter evening and then walk back home through narrow streets, squares, past big churches like the one in *Campo Dei Frari*. They would discuss their days, the children, or just be silent together like they used to do on the way home from the office when they were going to an office. Rachele was concerned about the cost of their children's education, given their reduced income.

"Emma is the most expensive; three families pay four tutors to prepare their children for exams that will happen next year for 16 hours a week. I hate the idea of stopping our children's education, but we have five children, and we should take all of them at least through the end of middle school."

Gabriele shared his conversation with Mrs. Toffolo; Rachele smiled.

"I learnt to be a baker when I was in high school; I started at her age. My parents wanted us to have a trade to cope with anything life would throw at us. I think she may like the idea. I just would like to put it to her the way my parents put it to me. It is good to have a trade in one's pocket."

"Please do. I wish I had a trade in my pocket. This is the first time neither of us has a guaranteed salary at the end of the month. We need to sit down and look at our finances at the beginning of each month."

Rachele tightened the grip on her husband's arm, determined to sound full of enthusiasm.

"A family board meeting, I like the idea."

They had now reached the point where they would turn right, away from the Giudecca Canal, on their way back home; they stopped talking and just enjoyed walking next to each other. It was a clear, chilly night, and they were walking along narrow alleyways that were protecting them from the cold wind. They were tucked into their coats and scarves. This evening their city felt very romantic, and they embraced the romance.

Emma and Franco Cantoni had known each other all their lives. They were born two weeks apart; their parents were close friends. They had a lot of friends in common. They had just left a party near Ca Rezzonico. Emma was annoyed.

"I hope I did not drag you away earlier than you had planned. You did not have to walk me home."

"Yes, but I realized that somebody said something that upset you. I know you too well, Emma Mendes, probably better than I know my sister."

They had just crossed the bridge over Rio Ca Foscari; Emma stopped to look at a shop window, then caught up with him.

"Your sister is ten; we have known each other all our lives! I am annoyed. I was talking to Marco, and I overheard Angela mention Jews, so I made a point of listening to what she was saying, paying less attention to what Marco was saying. "

"You mean something distracted you from your blue-eyed dream?"

Emma punched him lightly in the arm before continuing.

"I could not see whom Angela was talking to because I could not turn my face, but I heard her say to whomever it was that her parents told her she should stop seeing former Jewish schoolmates."

They had now turned into a narrow street, and Franco looked around and lowered his voice.

"I heard that too. The irony is that Angela was talking to somebody who was Jewish until last January."

Emma answered with an equally low voice.

"You mean she was talking to Chiara Levi? My parents know her family. One week after they became Catholics, they said it was not prudent for them to be seen with us."

They were now crossing another bridge on a narrow canal. Franco stopped to look at a delivery boat floating past; Emma had stopped because he did. They both leant on the railing. Franco lowered his voice to a whisper and shared his frustration with his lifelong friend and honorary twin.

"First, we could not go to our old school, then our parents lost their jobs, now we are being isolated. I hope it ends here."

"I don't know. I love Venice and always felt safe here. When I visit my grandparents in Trieste or my cousins in Milan, those cities are too noisy. My grandfather keeps saying that Venetian Jews had restrictions in the past, and they never lasted long. Our parents found other ways to earn money. We'll survive, you see."

Emma straightened herself and started walking. Franco followed her, a smile on his face.

"You will not be able to marry your blue-eyed, golden boy! He is an Aryan, whatever that means!"

"I am too young to think of whom I am going to marry. And I could always marry you!"

Emma smiled when she said that, clearly teasing Franco back.

"That would be the closest thing to incest I can think of!"

Emma agreed; they were walking past the Frari church. That brought the conversation to a lighter level as they crossed bridges across narrow canals, walking along narrow streets until they reached Campo San Giacomo dall'Orio.

"Thank you for walking me home, Franco. You did not have to, but I am happy you did."

Chapter Five

1943

Venice, 11 April 1943

Paolo had volunteered to support the Jewish midwife who was checking on Rachele. He was a cardiologist, but everybody trusted the midwife; a doctor was not strictly necessary. It was more of an excuse for him and Sofia to come and inspect the baby. They had been wondering why their friends had chosen a relatively unusual name for the baby. While he and the midwife were with Rachele, his wife Sofia was in the nursery with Gabriele, holding the baby. It was her chance to find out.

"If I remember correctly, she looks very much like Emma. Paolo and I have been wondering why Mila, it is such an unusual name."

Gabriele picked up the baby from her cot and handed it to Sofia.

"We chose a new name for both our families and a short one. Mila was Rachele's closest school friend; they lost touch. Her Hebrew name is Hadassah. It reminded me of

'Hadash,' new in Hebrew. I took her birth as a sign of renewal, a harbinger of new things to come. Emma, Anna, and Diana call her 'surprise'; a practice that Anita and Rachele are trying very hard to stop."

The consultation with the midwife was finished. Anita came to see her out. Paolo wanted to have a confidential conversation with Rachele. He was not sure how to start without revealing more than he wanted to; he chose the direct approach.

"I am a member of an underground non-Fascist party; we are trying to stop people from being called as reserves giving false certificates of exemption. So far, I have created false histories of heart disease, but I am worried somebody might notice this outbreak of heart conditions and start looking into who signed those certificates. Would you mind looking at the rules for exemption and coming back with some suggestions?"

Rachele's enthusiasm surprised Paolo.

"Not at all, you just gave me a great idea. I am fed up with being discriminated, of trying to find loopholes to keep our way of life. I have been thinking of ways to fight back; create perfect counterfeit legal documents could be my way to fight back. Of course, I'll look into the law. Give me a week to come up with a solution; in the meantime, if you have any urgent need to create an exemption, let me know. I just need you to organise a copy of the military rules so I can study them."

Later that evening, Rachele mentioned to Gabriele that she had agreed to look into something for Paolo, giving no detail. Talking to Anita when she was feeding the baby, she said she might have found her way to do something "to end this nonsense".

Venice, 16 May 1943

Emma was sitting outside in the vaporetto; it was a perfect spring day. She had just delivered a dress to a client. She had finished work for the day and was on her way to visit her grandparents. A woman sitting near her was reading the paper; the view of the palaces along the Grand Canal was a striking contrast with the war described on the front page. Venice was a bubble, and the conflict felt very remote. Another passenger with a child made her think of her younger siblings. She loved her job but missed school; and yet nobody could stop her from reading and pursuing her interests. She hated all the restrictions and was determined to figure out what she could do to change things. She got off the vaporetto and started walking along the narrow roads that led to her grandparents. She could not tell them she wanted to fight back. She already had some practice in smoothly changing the subject whenever her grandparents mentioned young men or getting married. She may not be her mother, but was good at keeping things to herself.

She almost bumped into a woman carrying a parcel. Emma apologised and picked up the box; the woman thanked her and went on her way. Outside her grandparents' door, she realised what she could do. She had a legitimate reason to walk around Venice, running errands for Mrs Toffolo, and could deliver messages or parcels or other things, and nobody would pay any attention. She had to discuss it with her uncle. They would have to make sure that her actions did not affect her family. Once they were protected, she was not afraid of running risks.

Figure 2 - Front Line in Sicily, July 1943 (Map by
Gene Thorp © 2007 Rick Atkinson)

Venice, 25 July 1943

It was a working Sunday for Emma. She loved working on
bridal dresses. The client had brought a lot of white silk.
Nobody asked questions, but Mrs. Toffolo, in private, had
been saying that she suspected it was from at least one
parachute, if not two. On her way home for lunch, she
noticed a lot of excited passengers in the vaporetto. They
were holding the afternoon edition of the papers. She
looked at the front page and became excited as well. She
bought the newspaper from the newsagent by the Zattere
stop, read it on her way to the San Stae stop, then walked
home as fast as she could, ran the two flights of steps,
opened the door, barged in holding the paper, and shouted.

"They arrested Mussolini; the war is over, the war is over."

Anita was right behind her, closed the door, mentioned that
she heard it on the radio. The radio she kept in her room
because racial laws prevented Jews from owning a radio.
Anita also pointed to the room overlooking a canal where
people on boats shouted the same news Emma had just
shared.

"This has been going on since 9 am when the radio announced the arrest. We know. Lunch is in half an hour. Your uncle Roberto brought something special from friends in the countryside, something we have not found for a while. We have made something you have not eaten in a while! Your uncle is in the sitting room talking to your parents."

Emma rushed to the sitting room. She was very fond of her "baby uncle," who was closer to her in age than her new baby sister was. Roberto was holding Mila, the latest addition to the family, trying to get her to react to his funny faces. She kissed her parents on the cheek and then greeted her uncle.

"I am so happy to see you. What did you bring us? Anita dismissed the arrest of Mussolini but could not stop talking about your mysterious gift."

Roberto Mendes did not have the opportunity to answer. Rachele could not hide her excitement anymore.

"We have been hearing people celebrating the arrest of Mussolini the whole morning. We have not had fresh eggs and real flour for several months! Anita, Anna, and I have been making fresh pasta, baked a cake, and done other interesting things we are all going to try soon."

Roberto handed over the baby to his sister-in-law and hugged Emma. Diana, Leo, and Davide entered the room. Diana announced that lunch was almost ready, and Leo mentioned he was looking forward to the cake.

Roberto whispered to Emma, "I need to talk to you in private. I'll walk you back to Mrs. Toffolo after lunch."

The family sat down to eat fresh pasta. Diana proudly announced that she helped Anita make the vegetable sauce. She also revealed that Anna had prepared a savoury cake using some of the herbs planted on the terrace. They would use it as bread that night. Anna had not seen that many eggs in a long while, even in the bakery where she worked three mornings a week.

After everybody from Anita to Davide had thanked Roberto for the flour and eggs, they reverted to the family habits of each sharing what had happened to them. Gabriele had paid a visit to his parents, Rachele had been working at a complex brief due the following morning, and Mrs. Toffolo had tasked Emma to cut the material for a jacket. Anita and Rachele congratulated her; Emma explained why it was such a big step and a delicate job to her father and uncle. They congratulated her as well.

It was an unusually lavish lunch; only Davide ate all his portions. The others either did not finish what was on their plate or just had pasta. Anita and Anna were busy discussing what they could do with the leftovers. As they were clearing up, Diana followed Emma.

"Could you ask Mrs. Toffolo if she has a place for me to come and learn something? I do not want to go to Milan for high school; I'd rather stay here with all of you and learn to be a seamstress. You are earning money now. Maybe one day I shall be able to earn money and help."

"Diana, it took me three years to earn anything more than pocket money; let's hope that the war is over before the next three years. Maybe you can go to a regular school after all."

Diana was not discouraged.

"For the moment, I want to stay here and learn to be a seamstress rather than moving to Milan to stay with Aunt Sarah just to go to the Jewish high school."

"I'll talk to Mrs Toffolo then. She is paying us Jews less than what she pays her Catholic staff; she says it is because she cannot write off the cost of our salaries. Mrs Toffolo will not pay you for the first six months and very little per hour for the rest of the first two years, but she is willing to employ Jews. Some of our clients are the wives of high-ranking Fascist members. Her introduction is her way of warning us. If she just says Emma rather than Emma Mendes when I walk into a fitting to take notes, I know that the lady's husband must not know that Mrs. Toffolo employs three Jewish girls, and hopefully four soon!"

Diana could not reply because their uncle interrupted them.

"Emma, if you are going in the next fifteen minutes, I will come with you. I need to take the same vaporetto that you take to go to Giudecca."

Emma and Roberto left together shortly after. On the way to the vaporetto stop, Roberto started looking around to see how crowded the street was and if anybody could over-hear them. When they arrived at the Riva, there was enough space around them that Roberto felt confident that nobody could overhear him or the echo of his voice. Narrow Venetian streets amplify noise even when they are not bordering a narrow canal.

"Emma, if you have not changed your mind about fighting back, I might have something for you. You told me your job sometimes takes you around Venice with parcels."

Emma was beginning to be excited; she had had enough of being a second-class citizen. She was ready to do whatever her uncle asked her to do.

"Yes, sometimes we deliver dresses to Mrs. Toffolo clients, not just in Venice. Tomorrow I go to Mira; I could go further if I had papers with a different name and without the note "member of the Jewish Race." You know we cannot leave the province of Venice without permission from the Police."

Roberto kept his voice very low.

"Would you be available to deliver other things to different addresses? At the moment, I cannot say more than that."

Emma took the hint from her uncle and whispered her reply.

"Of course I am; if I had different papers, I could go even further than the province of Venice."

"Thank you. Let's leave it at that for the moment. I will do everything I can to prevent you from running unnecessary risks."

During the afternoon, Emma was concentrating on work. It was her first time cutting material for a dress. It would have been a stressful afternoon, even during regular times, because of the costs involved in getting it wrong and starting again with a new batch of material. Wartime rationing was making things worse. As Mrs. Toffolo said, the white silk was probably coming from a parachute. They knew their client was supposed to marry a pilot; Emma's colleagues wondered whether the parachute belonged to a downed allied airman or had been "requisitioned" from the warehouse at Treviso Airport. Those working that Sunday afternoon also listened to the radio, given the morning's event. Everybody stopped when they announced a speech from the new Prime Minister, Badoglio. When he said, "the war continues," they felt disappointed. They felt so excited during the day, so full of hopes for the future; after that speech, they all came down to earth.

On her way home, Emma noticed people tearing down posters with images of Mussolini; she wondered what would happen, whether joining her uncle's organization still made sense. She remembered the tales of her mother's brothers in World War I. In those days, Trieste was still part of the Austrian Empire, and the Modiano clan was mainly in favour of their city becoming part of Italy. When Italy joined the war against the "Central Empires"[1], two of her brothers reached Italy by way of Greece and volunteered to fight in the Italian Army. She remembered the pride in her grandfather Davide Modiano's voice as he told her how they had entered Trieste with the Italian Army and how her grandmother Esther had burst into tears seeing them after more than three years. That memory strengthened her resolve; if the war continued, her fight should also continue. Actually, it should start. She was sure that she or her uncle would tell her parents. She was equally confident that they would keep her secret. Her mother would be proud, and her father would be worried and proud.

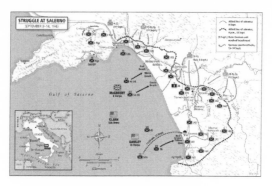

Figure 3 - The landing at Salerno 9-11 September
1943 (Map by Gene Thorp © 2007 Rick
Atkinson)

Venice, Friday, September 10th, 1943

It was easier for Samuele, Fiamma, and Roberto to come
to Friday night dinner. The curfew for Jews meant they
could not have dinner and walk home, so it was easier for
them to be accommodated by Gabriele and Rachele than
it would have been for them to accommodate a family of
eight and Anita.

Anita, Anna, and Fiamma's preparation for Friday night
dinner usually started on Sunday. They all looked out for
something they could buy with their ration cards to make
the meal special. That week they had found vegetables
from Sant Erasmo island, and the fish market in Rialto was
well stocked. So dinner was a soup, grilled fish, vegetables,
and the best cake they could come up with using cornflour
since they could not find any real flour either with their
cards or at a price they were willing to pay in the black
market. Everybody agreed it was an excellent meal for
wartime standards.

The conversation that evening had all been about the
Armistice announced two days earlier. They were trying to

figure out what signing a separate peace with the Allied forces meant for Italy and what it meant to them as Jews. Gabriele was worried that the Germans had turned from allied into occupiers overnight. The front line had not reached Rome yet, and they were far away from Rome. Rachele wondered what tactics the Germans would use to delay the Allied Army. Emma expressed her concern at Hitler's reaction to the about-face Italy had just made. She felt the Fuehrer would plan some form of punishment for Italy and the Italians, not just for the about-face but also for the scene of jubilations that had followed Mussolini's arrest and the news of the Armistice.

Gabriele and Rachele noticed Emma was exchanging glances with her uncle during the dinner conversation. They both felt that her daughter and Roberto knew something they could not share with the others. They discussed it as they were going to bed; Gabriele wanted to talk to his brother, but Rachele insisted they should ask Emma. She was their daughter; Roberto was an unmarried young man who had the right to do what he wanted without interference. They decided to ask Emma that night. They left their bedroom and knocked at their eldest daughter's door.

Emma was reading a book and was surprised by her parents knocking at her door. It never happened, especially not at that time of night after dinner.

Rachele was the one who suggested talking to their daughter, so she started.

"We have noticed that you and Roberto were exchanging glances at odd times. Your father told me that his brother is engaged in some form of anti-Fascist resistance. Are you working with him? You can answer. As a lawyer, I am sure you know I am used to knowing confidential details I cannot discuss. Your father kept the secret of his brother being a militant anti-Fascist for years until I confronted him tonight."

Emma smiled; she had experienced her mother's "discrete" questioning before.

"And you have experience interrogating people, mother. We all know that. I do not exactly work with him, but he introduced me to his organization."

"May I ask what you are doing?" asked Gabriele

"Not much at the moment; I simply carry things from one place to another, mostly with the cover of delivering dresses or collecting material or buying things for Mrs. Toffolo's workshop. No, dad, it is not weapons. I think they are both training and testing me. I know that uncle Roberto has an important role in the organization. Still, I only work with three ladies. We do not use our names, and I do not know anybody else beyond them and Uncle Roberto, of course."

Her father was the first to react.

"Thank you for trusting us; what you told us will never leave this room. I am proud of you, very worried, but also proud. You are doing what I would love to do if I did not have to think of my children, and, as you know, we still have young children."

So far, Gabriele had the reaction Emma expected; she was curious about her mother.

"I am very proud of you. You remind me of my brothers who fought for Italy and against Austria in World War I, although technically they were Austrian citizens and would have been executed had they been caught. They followed their ideals as you are following yours."

Emma smiled inwardly. She had correctly guessed her parents' reactions.

"Funnily enough, Mum, I thought of them when I asked uncle Roberto if there was a way I could join him."

"When the war is over, I have to tell them and your grandparents they will be very proud."

"Yes, Mum, but be patient and wait. Meanwhile, let us all try to survive until then. Any chance we could continue the conversation another time? I am exhausted."

Gabriele and Rachele reacted as if they were suddenly aware they were in their eldest daughter's bedroom in their pyjamas and nightdress. They hugged their daughter, kissed her on her forehead, wished her goodnight, and went to bed.

Gabriele could not sleep; after five minutes of silence, Rachele asked if he was proud of their daughter. His answer did not surprise her.

"From tomorrow morning, I'll wonder if I shall see her again every time she leaves our home. I'll never have a moment of peace until this is over, but I am so proud of her and of my brother I could burst."

Rachele hoped that now that Gabriele had voiced his concerns and feelings, he could fall asleep.

"Please try not to burst until the war is over; I'd like to celebrate with you. Good Night."

She kissed her husband, and soon they were both asleep.

Chapter Six

1943

Venice, 18 September 1943

Before the war, Saturday morning breakfasts were special. The family was getting ready to go to synagogue. Gabriele would go first, then Rachele and the older children, and, last but not least, Anita would take the younger children aiming to be there half an hour before the service ended. The entire process was presented to the children as a privilege. You had to be grown-up to go with daddy, big enough to go with mummy, and if you were still a baby, Anita would take you there. Now, they were all trying to make a special occasion out of what they could find.

This week they were not very successful in their food shopping. Anna's apprenticeship in a bakery meant they had some flour, but they did not find many eggs. So, the "special" part of a special breakfast was more in the way they had laid out the table than in the food on the table. The Mendes clan was a close-knit family, and they always turned a meal into a noisy occasion. They all stopped talking when they heard the doorbell; they did not expect anybody.

Gabriele and Rachele were aware of Emma's rebellious[1] activities, so they were not surprised when Emma stood up and went to her room. Anita went to check who was ringing the bell on a Saturday morning from the window in the study. She recognized the callers, made some gestures to wait, went back to the dining room, told everybody it was Alvise and Franco Cantoni and went to open the door.

Gabriele and Rachele looked at each other, wondering what was going on, told Anna to tell her sister to come back. Anita was visibly worried when she entered the dining room, followed by the visitors. Diana looked at her and decided to take her baby sister and her brothers to the playroom, saying she would read them a story as a reward for being well-behaved at the table.

Emma and Anna walked back into the dining room at the same time as the younger children were leaving. They immediately noticed Franco's serious face; he looked like he had been fighting tears. Alvise waited a few minutes to make sure that the younger children could not hear.

"Professor Jona[2] killed himself yesterday! Angelo Fubini told me. Earlier this week, he was asked to hand over the list of the Jewish community members. He was sure that it meant trouble. Why would they want the list when the police has all our records? He struggled for a few days to find a way not to do it. When he realized he had no alternatives, he killed himself. "

Alvise barely caught his breath as he was saying it. Emma immediately thought of contacting her Uncle; Rachele hugged Anna simply because she was standing next to her.

Gabriele crashed down on his chair and started shaking his head.

"Paolo Mondani and my brother are right; it is time…."

The bell interrupted him; whoever was ringing was in a hurry, or on a mission, or both. Anita gestured to everybody to stay where they were and went to check who was ringing the bell.

Rachele collected herself while waiting for Anita to come back; she sent Emma to fetch two cups and saucers so Alvise and Franco could have some of their mint tea. Alvise and Franco sat on chairs previously occupied by one of the younger children. They all thought that it was taking Anita a long time to come back. When she saw that Roberto Mendes was the person ringing the bell so forcefully, she had immediately gone to open the door through the shortest route, without passing through the dining room and tell the others who was ringing,

Emma appeared with a tray holding two cups and saucers when Roberto marched into the dining room, followed by Anita.

"Shabbat Shalom, everyone. If Alvise and Franco are here, they probably told you already. I am relieved that the younger children are not in the room."

Emma and Anna looked at each other.

"Diana decided it was reading time in the playroom and disappeared with them when Franco and his father arrived."

Roberto was too tense to even think of sitting down; he could not even stand still.

"Diana is a very smart lady! So, we are all here. We might as well discuss what to do. It is time to think of an escape route. People I know who regularly listen to the radio told me that Hitler is planning a big punishment for Italy. I wonder what the Fascist Republic is planning to do. Alvise, I will take care of my family, but if you need any help. I'll do what I can."

Gabriele stood up as if pacing around the room helped him think. Rachele, the lawyer, spoke first.

"I still do not understand who asked for the list; we are all registered with the police. All, except Mila, who, technically, is the daughter of unknown parents under Anita's guardianship. What was the purpose of asking for the list?"

Alvise was about to answer, but Roberto spoke first.

"Rachele, think about it; if they are coming after us, they would have to go to each local police station and demand to see their list of Jews. If they have the list of the Jewish community members, they could find us more easily. It will also be easier for them to tick each name as they go. So, for instance, if they come and you and Anna are out, they can come for you another time."

Rachele was annoyed that she missed the obvious, was she too shaken to think clearly?

"Of course you are right, Roberto. I guess I am still shocked. I helped Professor Jona with his will three days ago, and he did not mention anything. I did not know he was living that nightmare. I wonder, Alvise, if they had any legal right to ask him to hand over the list."

Alvise was trying very hard to be a calm and controlled legal professional.

"Do you think it matters? I do not know who asked him, but I sincerely doubt that, nowadays, anybody in uniform cares about legal rights. We have to leave now; we have other people to tell. Please do not come to synagogue later; very few people will be there; the rabbi is aware of what is going on. Take good care of yourselves. Thank you for the tea. Come on Franco, let's go."

He and Franco stood up and followed Rachele to the front door.

Roberto quietly told Gabriele.

"I know Emma told you she is working with me. If need be, she can be my link to all of you." then louder "I still have to tell Emanuele and Miriam, our parents and I found out this morning on our way out they may appear in the afternoon. Dad even said he was ready to ring the bell due to the circumstances."[3]

After he left and Rachele and Anita reappeared. Emma told Anna to wait before telling Diana and their brothers and sister to come back. They still had something to discuss.

Venice, 20 September 1943

Emma had just delivered a dress to a client. In Mrs. Toffo-lo's workshop, her position had progressed; she was in charge of the final fitting before delivery. Her clients lived in Castello[4]; therefore, she had the perfect excuse to go home by way of whatever route she chose. She was given the task to pick up an envelope from an office and deliver it to a shop. She did not know whether she was tested and was better off not knowing what was in the envelope. The standard cover story was that she was running an errand for Mrs. Toffolo.

After her delivery, she went to a café to meet her uncle. She found him sitting at a table, wearing an air force pilot's uniform.[5]

When he was wearing a uniform, they behaved as if they were a couple. There was no improper public display of affection, but they often held hands and stayed very close to each other. Roberto had an important message for Emma's parents. He looked as if he was whispering sweet nothings to his girlfriend's ears, but the conversation was quite different.

"Hitler vowed to punish Italy for its betrayal of Germany. So far, Mussolini never allowed the deportation of Jews from Italy; I am afraid this will change soon once the Germans take charge of Italy north of the front line. We need to convince your parents to leave Venice. Your lives may be at risk. I will organize fake identities for all of you. But you need to help me convince them to leave town."

Emma was not sure her uncle knew he was preaching to the choir; she just nodded, so he continued.

"Many people from other Italian cities have fled to the country to escape air raids; you will be just another family that moves to the country."

Emma had inherited her mother's pragmatism.

"As you know, we are already organizing Rosh HaShanah dinner. When do you think we should leave?"

"I do not think there is any immediate danger, but I know we need to start organising your temporary move out of Venice. I'll look for accommodation for a large family, but you need to help me convince your parents. They are lucky; Anita's loyalty to your family is unquestionable; she will protect your home no matter what."

"Technically, it is her home; we are her tenants."

"Exactly, trust me, you need to leave."

Emma was concerned that her clandestine activities might end so soon after they started.

"Do I have to stay in Venice?"

"No, you can leave with them. You will work from another base. I can't tell you what it is now; you will find out before the end of the week."

They stood up and walked out of the café, hand in hand. At the vaporetto stop, Roberto kissed his niece on the cheek. They hugged, and she boarded. On the way home, Emma wondered what the new assignment could be and how to tell her parents what her uncle had told her. When she arrived in Campo San Giacomo Dall'Orio, she looked around and wondered when they would leave the place she loved. She hoped they could come back relatively quickly once they left.

Venice, 21 September 1943

A lot of and Rachele's non-Jewish friends had disappeared. Paolo and Sofia Mondani were two of the few who stayed in touch; they were very close friends. Paolo and Gabriele met in primary school; they became close and were still close. In their youth, sometimes Paolo would be invited for Friday night dinner by Gabriele's parents, and Gabriele would have dinner at the Mondanis when they served appropriate food. Paolo and Sofia met Rachele before Gabriele had picked up the courage to propose. When Paolo heard about professor Jona, he immediately sent a note to Gabriele and Rachele, inviting them to watch the sunset on their terrace overlooking the Grand Canal.

Paolo and Sofia's son, Arrigo, was a Prisoner of War in East Africa. Their daughter-in-law, Carolina, used to receive letters through the Red Cross. They had not received a letter in months. Rachele stood up and hugged Sofia, making encouraging comments. Paolo looked like he was looking at the view of the Rialto market, but he was staring at nothing when he said.

"I am jealous of your parents; they do not have to worry about Roberto being killed somewhere far away."

It was time for Gabriele and Rachele to go; they had to be home before the curfew. They all stood up and moved inside; Paolo stopped them when they were in the middle of the large living room.

"I have seen the posters on the street; I am seriously concerned about you and your family. You should think of a place to hide. Carolina's family has very close Jewish friends; she told me that her uncle is trying to get them to go to Switzerland, and he is also thinking of ways to hide them. She thinks we could easily hide your whole family between this flat and hers."

Gabriele smiled at his old friend, more like an honorary brother.

"Thank you, Paolo. Emma and Roberto have a plan for us, not sure what will happen, but we are thinking about what to do."

"Well, we thought about what we can do to help you, for as long as you need. A night, until the war ends, whatever you need. The allied armies are near Naples; this war will not last forever."

Gabriele and Rachele had been silent for most of their way home. Gabriele felt Rachele was considering an idea, a plan, something. He knew she would share it when she was ready. When they walked past one poster with some mandates from the newly formed Social Republic of Italy, the new puppet state of Germany in the Italian territory north of the front line, she stopped. Gabriele looked around, expecting one of his wife's tirades against those puppets of the Nazis, when she simply said,

"The Painting!"

"What do you mean?"

"We can use the almost Canaletto that Countess Pesaro De Bonfili gave us as a wedding present."

"Use it for what?"

"Use it to bribe somebody if we need to smooth our way out of Venice, but we need to be clever about it."

Gabriele looked around to see if anybody might overhear them.

"How do you plan to go about bribing somebody? Who do you think we should bribe?"

"I have not figured it out yet, but at least now I know what we can use. I shall share my thoughts with Emma and see what she thinks. Let's go now."

Rachele held her husband's hand but did not say another word until they reached home. She was trying to think of all her old clients, the ones she had before she was forced to leave the law firm, trying to figure out who was a party faithful, wondering who could owe her enough gratitude to help her or who was known to accept bribes.

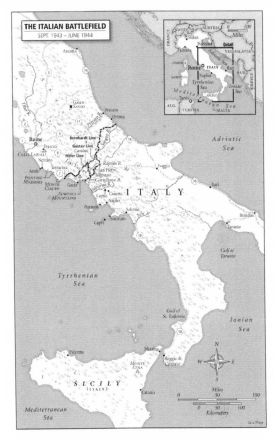

Figure 4 - Italian Front September 1943 June
1944 (Map by Gene Thorp © 2007 Rick
Atkinson)

Venice, 30 September 1943

Gabriele and Rachele decided not to attend synagogue.
Gabriele could blow the Shofar at home[6] for the family
and their lunch guests. The lack of availability of food
made it necessary that guests contribute to the food served
for lunch, something very unusual, especially when guests
were not part of the extended Mendes clan. Gabriele's two
brothers were there, Emanuele with his family Roberto

with their parents; their sister Myriam was already on her way to Switzerland with her children. They had invited Alvise Cantoni and his family. The mood was not festive. Rachele knew Alvise was making plans to leave Venice, so were they. Running for their lives was in the mind of most adults, but nobody discussed it. The conversation was artificially light-hearted, and nobody dared discuss the elephant in the room.

Before lunch, Gabriele had blown the Shofar for the benefit of everybody. People gathered in circles of peers; the younger children played together, the teenagers talked in the small sitting room; the adults were in the large sitting room, and Samuele and Fiamma took a nap in the guest bedroom. You could almost forget that there was a war until Anita came in from her room, where she was listening to the radio, and said something to Roberto; they went to collect Emma and went back to Anita's room.

The teenagers continued their conversation; the grown-up did not miss the meaning of that gesture. Gabriele and Rachele knew Anita would not have summoned Roberto and Emma to listen to the radio on one of the holiest days of the Hebrew Calendar without reason. Their conversation stopped; they all looked worried and were waiting for Roberto or Emma to come back. Instead, Anita reappeared to take Franco Cantoni away from the teenagers. The grown-up looked at her with questioning faces, but nobody spoke. After what Gabriele felt was a long time, Alvise broke the silence.

"I wonder what Anita heard that was so important to call them. It must have been crucial if she summoned Franco as well."

Gabriele and Rachele looked at each other; Alvise's comment about Franco made it clear that he knew his son was working with Roberto and Emma. Finally, Roberto came back.

"Things are looking up. According to the BBC, Naples is rebelling against the German occupiers; they may throw the Germans out."

The mood changed immediately. Everybody started smiling; the allied army was making inroads north. They were still south of Rome, but sooner or later, they would reach Venice bringing safety and freedom with them.

Chapter Seven

October 1943

Venice, 2 October 1943

Gabriele, Rachele, and their children had gathered around the table for the ceremony that ended Shabbat. It was Emma's turn to hold the candle. The light of the candle fascinated Diana; Leo was looking forward to a small sip of the wine used for the blessing. Standing opposite Emma, Anna held Davide, trying to stop him from grabbing the glass cup that their father was using. Once the ceremony was over, Gabriele asked them to sit down because they had something to discuss. He felt he had to keep a matter-of-fact tone to reassure his younger children.

"We have just finished the ceremony that marks the separation of Shabbat from the other days of the week. We shall soon have another separation. Tomorrow we shall start getting ready to leave Venice. It may become too risky for us to stay here. Uncle Roberto has organized a place for us, somewhere he trusts; we shall know more when we see him."

Then he turned to his younger children.

"Leo, Davide, it is important that you never contradict your parents or your older sisters in the next two days. Uncle Roberto will have new names for us we shall use until we return to Venice. You need to learn those names and use them whenever it is necessary. It will be a big adventure for all of us."

Davide was looking at the ornate glass that was now empty.

"What about school?"

Rachele smiled and tried not to sound condescending.

"You will go to a new school. You must learn a new name very well because that is how they will call you in the new school."

Leo seemed to be lost in his thoughts until something clicked in his head. Suddenly, he looked worried.

"I noticed that my sisters have been working on some of the family's clothes for the entire week. Is that related to us leaving Venice?"

Gabriele was not sure how much it was prudent to share with his younger children, but he felt he had to share something.

"Yes, and whatever happens, you have to be careful not to tear them until we reach the new home that uncle Roberto has organised for us."

Emma, Anna, and Diana went back to their improvised workshop in Anita's office. They had to finish adjusting the clothes for the following day. They had taken off the lining of the skirts the women of the Mendes family would wear, hid cash, and put the lining back. Their mother's jewellery was hidden inside jackets that Gabriele, Rachele, Emma,

Anna, and Leo would wear. Diana had more cash hidden behind the lining in her coat. Emma added an extra internal lining to her parents' briefcases to hide more money and documents. Gabriele, Rachele, and their older daughters would have their original papers sawn into their clothes.

Emma and Anna went to bed. Diana could not; she felt her home was too quiet. She found refuge in her parents' study with all the lights switched off, looking outside at Campo San Giacomo Dall'Orio. Rachele found her sitting by the window, the room lit by the moon.

"I wonder when we shall see our home again. I am afraid of what might happen to us."

Rachele tried to be reassuring.

"Diana, we all are. We will be back. I cannot tell you when, but we will. I have to think that we will; otherwise, I could not bear the level of uncertainty we have to face. We need to trust the information Roberto gives us. The war will be over; the Kingdom of Italy has already revoked those stupid laws. As your grandfather would say, once again, Venetian Jews will have outlived a period of discrimination. We always do."

Rachele was not sure whether she had reassured her daughter. She was worried, but put up a reassuring front for the sake of her children and her husband. She had shared her concerns with Anita. Rachele had grown to consider her one of her sisters. Anita was fiercely loyal and fiercely protective of their children. Anita knew. They had met in the kitchen too many times, both unable to sleep because they were too worried about what the future might bring. They had reassured each other, preparing a hot drink, hoping it would make them sleep. Her ability to cope without Anita was one of the several things that worried Rachele.

Figure 5   Map highlighting the position of Stra

Venice, 3 October 1943

Roberto had secured accommodation in a country estate owned by the parents of 'somebody he knew' along the Riviera del Brenta.[1] It was a house in the estate that was previously used by the family of their eldest son when they visited during the school holidays. Roberto's contact was pretty confident that his older brother's family would not be coming until the end of the war. If they appeared, the main house was huge and could easily accommodate them, his parents would be delighted by the idea of having their grandchildren around. They would be unspecified relatives who wanted to escape the air raids in Verona.

Paolo and Sofia Mondani had offered to help them leave Venice; they also volunteered to help them stay in touch with Anita through Sofia. Besides Roberto, they were the only three people who would know where the Mendeses were; Gabriele and Rachele trusted them with their lives. Anita would not be left alone in their large home;

Rachele's parents would hide in plain sight in the flat. They were supposed to arrive a few days later once their new papers were ready. A cousin of Rachele from Trieste and his family would also move in. Last but not least, Roberto would also move there using the assumed name of Roberto Cunin, a lawyer from Padua exempt from military service because of poor health.

Anita had gone with a porter to the station left luggage to store four suitcases that Gabriele and Rachele would retrieve the following morning. She took the vaporetto home; Roberto boarded the same vaporetto, sat next to her, and gave her an envelope with the false papers the rest of the family would use to leave Venice. They were supposed to leave home at different times and meet in the third compartment of the first class coach.

They all had rehearsed their story. Gabriele and Rachele's story was that they were an accountant from Padua and his wife from Trieste fleeing the air raids that had plagued Trieste together with their daughter and son. Anna was a young girl who had just visited her grandparents. Emma was the wife of a pilot, joining her husband with their two children; Gabriele and Rachele's two eldest daughters were all carrying false papers that made them about seven years older.

The first to leave, with a suitcase, was Emma. She was wearing two layers of clothes and a jacket on top of the dress. The 'filling' in the skirts made them heavier. Gold sowed in the hem of the dress, and cash hidden in the lining. She met a lady they knew in Campo San Giacomo Dall'Orio and claimed they had a police permit to visit their grandparents in Trieste.[2] It was the first thing that came to her mind. She hoped Leo remembered his instructions, basically never to contradict his big sister no matter what she said.

The walk to the Mondanis was relatively shortEmma did not have time to think or say goodbye to the place she loved. Her brother had insisted he could carry their baby sister all the way to Paolo and Sofia, but Emma was constantly checking that carrying a six-month-old baby was not too much for him. Despite the complication of finding milk, Mila was growing.

Sofia was waiting for them near their home. They had acted as if Emma and the children had got off the vaporetto from the station. Emma did not know what Paolo and Sofia had told their neighbours. She knew that their daughter-in-law Carolina was active in a clandestine political party, and she trusted the judgment of people she had known all her life as Uncle Paolo and Aunt Sofia. When they arrived at the Mondanis, Sofia immediately started fussing over Mila. She had found the right formula without ration cards at the local pharmacy. Paolo was showing Emma and Leo where they would sleep when Leo asked,

"Emma, now that we are with Uncle Paolo and Aunt Sofia, can we say that I am your brother and not your very tall son?"

Emma and Paolo looked at each other. Paolo realized Emma did not know what to say, so he replied.

"Until you reach the new home, you have to be consistent with that lie. It is a way to protect you, your brother and sisters, and your parents. From now on, you'll have to be very careful. Here you are in a safe space. Until you come back to Venice, you will have to pretend. Always follow what your parents and your big sisters tell you to do."

He looked at Emma, who had tears in her eyes. Paolo realized he had to say something that reassured her; his eldest honorary niece was just nineteen.

"Emma, if you are going to work with your uncle, you need to become good at pretending. Remember that everything we do will bring us closer and closer to the day you come back to Venice and your real selves."

Anna had gone to visit her grandparents; she had a small suitcase. She could easily have said that she was spending the night at her grandparents' if anybody had stopped her. Her suitcase had her overnight things and fresh clothes for the following morning (not the whole truth, she also carried cash, jewellery, and false papers). She was very happy she had "won" the draw to say goodbye to her grandparents. Samuele and Fiamma were reluctant to leave Venice. They knew that their youngest son had plans for them, but they had not yet agreed to go. Samuele kept saying that Venetian Jews had outlasted many challenging periods in their history. They were simply going through another one of them. They were happy to see their granddaughter. Her Uncle told Anna that she should not disclose where they were going. The only thing she knew was that it was somewhere on the railway line to Verona.

Gabriele and Rachele could not enjoy the time for themselves. They had dinner with Anita, and nobody mentioned the following day over dinner. Once dinner was over, they discussed details and went through the code they had discussed with Sofia Mondani to pass messages between them. They were not aware that Anita had a similar conversation with Roberto and Emma about what each name Emma would use meant. The name when everything was all right, the name when she had 'good' company, and the name when she thought she was followed. It was a mild October evening, so Gabriele and Rachele ended their day spending time on the terrace.

Venice, 4 October 1943

Sofia had laid out the best possible spread, given the circumstance. Emma felt very rested, despite everything. Her baby sister slept in the same bed. It took quite a while for Mila to settle into sleep; Emma did not know how to cope, and was grateful for Sofia's advice. Now, she was enjoying a moment of peace, looking at the Grand Canal from her hosts' terrace. Leo joined her; she hugged her brother. They spent a few minutes simply looking at the City they were about to leave.

Paolo and Sofia insisted on going to the railway station with them; they would not go inside for fear of breaking their friends' cover. Paolo wanted to make sure that a porter could help Emma with the suitcase. They were all concerned about saying the wrong things on the vaporetto, just in case they were overheard. Sofia was holding Mila; Paolo was distracting Leo, pointing out boats and other aspects of Venetian life. They left Emma alone with her thoughts. She was looking outside, trying to memorize as much as she could; she did not know when they would be back. Once they got to the train station, Paolo made sure a porter could carry Emma's suitcase to the train. They hugged Emma and Leo, kissed baby Mila, and left. Emma was the first to arrive. She followed the porter to the platform; then the porter followed her to the third compartment from the back. Emma felt compelled to explain to the porter that it was far enough from the door not to get crowded and close enough to manage with a baby when they arrived at their destination. Anna joined them shortly after; she took a seat near Leo and started making faces at baby Mila, who recognized her and smiled. There was nobody else in the compartment, but they were not taking any chances. Leo remembered his instructions. Emma and Anna talked as if they were strangers who had just met on the train. Shortly after Diana and Davide joined them, they only had a bag full of Davide's toys.

They all looked at each other when they heard the voice of their parents. Gabriele was talking to the porter that was carrying the suitcases on the train. They closed the door to the compartment. They still did not trust their environment to speak freely. Rachele was unusually calm and collected. Diana was the first one to notice; she felt free to say something because, in her false papers, she was still her mother's daughter.

"You look very calm, collected, and satisfied. Yours is the only relaxed face; why?"

"I know something that I will share with you tomorrow. It is the first step of something I put together, and it has worked. We are all on the train. Your father is used to my not being able to discuss things sometimes, and I am keeping everything to myself until I know everything worked."

They felt the train slowly moving. Gabriele stood up; he was relieved that the two compartments on both sides were empty. He thought the decision to travel first-class had paid off. Once the conductor checked their tickets, they could talk. He sat down, picked up Mila, and put her on his lap, smiling.

"Next stop… and next step, Stra."

Anita, Paolo, and Sofia watched the train leave from a side entrance of the station. Rachele hoped that somebody wearing the uniform of the Fascist militia would also be watching the train move. The next step of her plan would happen in Stra, a town on the Brenta Canal, not far from their final destination.

Nobody spoke as the train was crossing the bridge to the mainland. When there was no more water to be seen, Leo remarked they were running away to keep their freedom, and he had intentionally kept his voice very low.

Gabriele and Rachele exchanged glances with their three older daughters. They thought they had shielded their younger children from many concerns and anxieties over the past few months; somehow, Leo had been aware of what was going on all the time.

They did not speak much during the relatively short journey. There were other people on the train, and they could not be sure they wouldn't be overheard. Gabriele, Emma, and Diana had something to read; Anna and Leo played with Mila. Davide was sleeping. Rachele was going through her plan; she was worried that she had not shared more with Anita, who had a role to play in what would have followed their successful arrival in Stra.

When they were about to arrive at the small station, Gabriele organized his family; the grownups took down all their luggage and made sure it was near the door. Few people were getting off, and they were the only large group with several suitcases. Roberto noticed them immediately and came to help them. He was wearing the jacket of the uniform of the Italian Air Force over civilian clothes; there was another young man with him. Roberto introduced him to everybody once he had made sure that the train had gone and nobody was within earshot; he was Enrico Contarini, the younger son of their host. Emma wondered how they would reach their final destination: nine people plus a baby, five suitcases, and two bags. Roberto started carrying things and asked Emma to stay there with her brothers, the baby, and the rest of the luggage. Once they had removed all the suitcases and bags from the station platform, Emma was surprised to find a large cart with makeshift benches and room for the luggage pulled by two horses. Roberto laughed at Emma's face and cracked a joke about their fuel being easier to find. Leo and Davide were very excited, Diana was tired, Anna was puzzled, Emma was intrigued, and Mila was asleep. Gabriele sat on the front bench with Enrico Contarini and the driver. Rachele and Roberto sat behind them. Emma thought they were talking in riddles. She wondered what her mother had been up to and hoped she would share it with them in due course; after all, they were a family, not a group of people engaged in covert operations. Or were they? It had become difficult to tell.

They stopped at the City Hall, where they met two witnesses who were prepared to swear that they were a family who had lost all their papers in Verona during an air raid. They showed the (fake) police report that temporarily replaced their documents. Gabriele did not know how much the whole thing had cost his brother. They came out of the City Hall with authentic papers; only their names were different. They were the Conti family, originally from Padua, but former residents of Verona. The children all kept their first names; Gabriele was Gino Conti, an accountant; Rachele was Rina von Moden Conti, originally from Trieste.

After City Hall, they hopped back on the cart towards their final destination, a country estate near the Brenta Canal. They made a prearranged stop, officially, to allow everybody to stretch their legs. Roberto noticed a quizzical look on his older brother's face.

"Your new landlord officially knows Roberto Cunin, a young lawyer from Padua. He has no idea who the dashing pilot is; I had to change."

Gabriele's quizzical look had now turned into a smile.

"Out of curiosity, what is the name of the dashing pilot?"

"I have no idea; the dashing pilot comes out when I do not have to give my name to any official. He is very absent-minded and slightly shellshocked, so he keeps forgetting his papers at the airport."

"And he always comes out when the airport is sufficiently far that nobody would think of asking him to get them."

"Exactly"

"I gather Enrico knows the dashing pilot."

"Enrico knows a lot of things, including your eldest daughter's secret identities. He is one of the five who knows who she is."

They arrived at their new home until the end of the war. It was a lovely house, part of a large estate that bordered on the Brenta Canal. It stood past an unexpected turn in the driveway, was near the gate, but almost hidden from the main entrance. Gabriele and Rachele had expected a smaller place. The style differed from the gatehouse; it had been built relatively recently. Gabriele looked at his wife. They were relieved; they would not be cramped after all.

It was a nice place, but it was not Venice. The first thing Diana noticed was that the house was near the canal; Emma saw you could access the house from the main driveway, but it also had its small gate; Anna thought it was small, Leo liked the swings by the tree, Davide had never seen so much grass, Mila was asleep. Gabriele noticed the small gate and wondered whether Gino Conti could find some bookkeeping work in the village; Rachele was thinking about sending a message to her boss without disclosing the location.

Count Contarini was waiting for them outside the front door. Gabriele was not expecting that and was embarrassed that the family was not looking their best. The Count was smiling and welcoming.

"This is the place we built for my eldest son, Rodolfo, when he got married. He is in the Navy. He and his wife lived here after they got married until his wife's uncle got him a desk job in Rome, then they only came for holidays. Angelica and the children are now in Switzerland; she had complications with her last pregnancy. Enrico told me that a relative of his best friend needed a place to stay for a large family. I took the liberty of putting some things from our estate in your pantry. I hope you do not mind."

Gabriele was surprised; Rachele found her voice first.

"Thank you, Count Contarini, and thank you for renting us your place; it is a lifesaver."

Count Contarini bowed to Rachele, almost kissing her hand.

"I am sure it will be our pleasure. Now that our grandchildren are in Switzerland, my wife and I are very pleased that this house is again full of children."

Gabriele thought the Count looked familiar; he was sure he had met him years ago but did not remember the occasion.

"Count Contarini, thank you. We did not expect such a warm welcome…."

Then the proverbial penny dropped, and he stopped talking. He looked at his brother; Roberto nodded, so Gabriele continued.

"I am sorry, Count Contarini, but you looked familiar, and now I think I have just placed you. You were a guest at a wedding we attended in 1939."

Rachele, Emma, and Anna looked alarmed. Rachele made a mental note of telling her husband off; what was the point of fake identities if they stayed with somebody they knew? The words of Count Contarini reassured them.

"I know, I knew you were coming, and I also know that these days, the less we remember, the better. Don't worry; a few months ago, our son told us not to be surprised by anything; he told us we should have a party line and stick to it. We stuck to it when Enrico told his pregnant sister-in-law that she had three hours to pack and leave her home with her children to be whisked away to safety in Switzerland. We do not know where our son and heir is. We do not know what Enrico and his friend 'the lawyer from Padua' are up to, and I have just had the pleasure of meeting Gino Conti and his family. Nowadays, we use names as little as possible, and ask questions only when it is essential."

Rachele, Emma, and Anna relaxed. Rachele decided not to tell her husband off, after all. When the Count continued.

"Here, you are sheltered from the comings and goings in the rest of the estate. I regret to ask you not to remember some people you might see here, even those you know very well. And now, you must excuse me. I have to go back to my work. My wife and I thought we would give you a few days to settle in, and then we shall invite you to share whatever meal will manage to put together."

He bowed and made to leave; Gabriele and Rachele were about to say something when the Count turned back.

"Also, I wonder if Gino Conti is free to give me a hand in the estate's administration. My bookkeeper was drafted as a reservist, and now he is in the same prisoner of war camp as Arrigo Mondani."

Rachele was speechless; she looked quizzically at her brother-in-law, who looked like the proverbial cat who ate the canary. Gabriele recovered from the surprise.

"Thank you, Count Contarini, I will, and thank you again for your warm welcome."

The Count left, and they all went inside. It was larger than they expected. A dark wood-panelled entrance hall with two double doors led to a formal dining room on one side and a sitting room on the other side. The stairs leading to the upper floor were also dark wood. In the back, there was a playroom and a large kitchen. Anna marched into the kitchen and screamed.

"They gave us two loaves of white bread! I don't remember the last time I had white bread! Even at the bakery, we did not eat white bread! We also have eggs, milk, flour, and some vegetables. We have landed in paradise."

Rachele hugged her brother-in-law.

"Thank you, Roberto, thank you very much. Now, can you do me a favour? I need to make a discreet call to Venice, and I need to tell Sofia to pass a message on to Anita no later than tomorrow morning. You have performed one miracle getting all of us here; can you do another one for your sister-in-law?"

Stra, 5 October 1943

Rachele woke up very happy; her plan had worked. She was now hoping that her 'carrot' would have been big enough to leave Anita alone later.

Gabriele picked up on his wife's good mood; since they were out for their morning walk, he felt free to ask his wife why she looked so happy.

"Well, I was very nervous at the prospect of a family of eight leaving home in broad daylight, so I did my research. Alvise told me he thought my ex-boss' youngest son had deserted after September 8th.[3] I checked with Gorgio Falier and then called my ex-boss. He agreed to meet me and asked me to visit him at home. When I arrived, his wife greeted me loudly as if I had been calling on her, then my boss joined us in the sitting room, and after I asked for his help, his son appeared wearing civilian clothes."

Gabriele was getting impatient.

"His help for what, exactly?"

Rachele smiled and continued talking in her best professional voice, ignoring her husband's eagerness to understand what happened.

"Patience, let me make my entire case, and you'll understand. I needed him to contact a client that was eternally grateful to me, or at least to the law firm. I asked him to do it because I needed plausible deniability if the approach went wrong. I gave him money so he could genuinely say he was representing me and therefore bound by professional confidentiality."

"As if it mattered nowadays."

"Anyway, my idea was to find somebody we could bribe with our almost Canaletto painting. I know you are a close family friend of Countess Pesaro De Bonfili, but I am sure she understands the issue. She "loves you like a son," as she keeps saying every time we meet her, I am sure she would have no problem using that painting to save our lives."

"I have no problem either; why didn't you tell me?"

"Listen to my plan till the end. You are inherently honest, and I have been legally devious. To cut a long story short, I said I did not want to share my plans with Anita, which was not a complete lie. I only shared part of my plan. So, if we could board the train to Verona undisturbed and got papers from a City Hall using our false identities, they could help themselves to the painting with some excuse. Of course, I did not tell them where we were going. I did not know at the time, and neither did you. So I arranged to call my boss, which was one of the calls I asked Enrico to organize yesterday. That is why I went out with him again on the horse cart with the excuse of going shopping. We almost went as far as Padua, and I called from a phone in a post office. My boss did not ask for my location, and I did not share it with him. Then I called Sofia Mondani with a message for Anita. "

"And what was the message?"

"Well, in the next two weeks, somebody will come and help themselves to the painting. Anita knows she will have to go to the police and report the theft."

"Why?"

"This war will not last forever; I am betting that people heavily involved with the Fascist regime will be demoted if not tried in court if they had been nasty. We shall then claim that our painting was stolen and prove it with Anita's report to the police. There is some hope that we might get it back."

"How Machiavellian of you! You were right; a few years ago, I would not have approved; I am slightly more flexible now. Let's go back and have some breakfast with our children. We should not discuss this ever again, at least not until the war is over."

Everything was ready when they arrived home; Anna and Diana were all excited. Enrico had come with Giuseppe, a farmer from the estate, they had milk and eggs and flour, officially for the children, but Anna thought there was a lot for everybody. Diana had already boiled the milk for Mila; Anna had found mint leaves outside and was making mint tea for everybody. She had also requisitioned some eggs and some flour to make biscuits and a cake for breakfast. Emma appeared from the back door, and Leo walked into the kitchen; he had just got out of bed.

Whatever happened to the rest of the world, their world was still as normal as it could be.

Chapter Eight

October 1943

6 October 1943

Stra

When they arrived from Venice, Enrico and her uncle told Emma that she would receive messages through Giuseppe, who would bring them milk and eggs every day. That morning, he had forgotten the flour he was meant to bring them and asked Emma to come to the farm to get it. She had to wait half an hour because he had another delivery to make and would not be back in time. Nobody else knew which flour bag to give Emma.

So, after her parents left, she walked out of the back door in a different direction. She was cautious because she was not yet familiar with her environment; she was apprehensive; it was the first time she was summoned.

She arrived at the farm and saw Enrico, as expected. Enrico kept up the cover of giving her flour, so they went into one of the outbuildings past the stable. Emma followed him past a room that looked like a warehouse; he moved a rusty old cart to reveal a door; the door led to a room full of clothes, uniforms, and wigs.

"This is your excuse to come here most days; you are paid to alter clothes. We take donations and mostly turn them into men's civilian clothes to give to the soldiers that are going into hiding to fight the Germans rather than fighting with the Germans. We also have wigs and female clothes, and you need to make four for yourself and pick a wig. Those are the disguises you will use when you need to go to Venice. The name you will use will be Elena Giadrossi. Try to memorize it to react to it as if it were your name. We do not want Emma Conti to draw attention to the rest of the Conti family. You'll start tomorrow."

"Could my sister Diana help? She had been apprenticed to Mrs. Toffolo for a few months before we left Venice."

"I'd rather not have her here. She is too young; she could inadvertently blow your cover." He paused, smiled, and continued, "Your uncle told me that under no circumstance should I recruit anybody else from your family. Two people risking their lives is enough."

Emma didn't like the idea of her uncle forbidding Enrico to recruit anybody from her family; what if somebody volunteered? She tried to hide her annoyance.

"Well, as Jews, we risk our lives every day. I'd rather risk my life doing something else other than sitting and waiting for them to come and get me."

Enrico smiled; he knew what Emma meant.

"I can also see your uncle's side. I am the youngest, and I am worried that my two older siblings are also active. My father is involved in something he is keeping to himself.

Let's protect your family. Your uncle may have a bullet for me if something happens to them."

Emma appreciated not being patronized; Enrico still did not know the strength of the Mendes/Modiano women.

"'I understand, but never underestimate my parents, especially my mother. Can I at least take something home for Diana to do some work? I have to explain to her why I have to ask her to take my measurements."

Emma walked back with a bag of flour in her hands and carrying an army backpack with a parachute that "had been found" and could make excellent shirts. They had agreed that they would use the cover of altering clothes for the estate and people of Stra. Diana would help from home because there was not enough room for two people in the small space they had carved for Emma. The parachute was an "advance" for her work; the family could do with the silk whatever they wanted.

Venice

Roberto Mendes needed a place to stay that was not the house he shared with his parents. He thought of his brother's home simply because it had three entrances. Gabriele and Rachele had bought three flats and merged them, and they kept the front door of each flat. The study, the primary residence, and Anita's rooms and the kitchen had separate entrances. He had a false identity as a lawyer from Padua, Roberto Cunin, officially renting a room in what was technically Anita's property. He had many ways of going in and out, so Anita could genuinely say she did not know when he had gone, if he had come back, and how long he had been out. Roberto was talking to Anita when the doorbell rang. He jumped up from the chair and tried to figure out how to leave the place when Anita stopped him.

"Don't worry; they have rung from the main entrance; we are in my office. I can open the door, and if I do not come back in twenty minutes, you can leave from my door. The stairwell leads to a door that opens in a courtyard onto Calle del Tentor. Nobody could guess that you were here, and if you turn right, you will avoid Campo San Giacomo Dall'Orio, so whoever is ringing now will not see you. Wait twenty minutes unless I make a lot of noise; if you hear noise, leave quietly."

Anita went to the study to check who was ringing; she told the visitors to wait, ran back to the kitchen, reassured Roberto, and then ran back to open the door to Baron Modiano, his wife, and a porter. Anita was aware they were coming. She knew they were pretending to be her cousins from Trieste, but did not know what name they were using. Luckily, Baron Modiano was quick to react.

"Anita, thank you for letting us stay here; we were anxious about air raids in Trieste, and Venice was the obvious choice. Elsa, you have the purse with the money. Can you pay the porter, please, and don't forget to give him a tip."

Anita thanked the porter, closed the door, and told them that somebody else lived in the flat, a friend. They should join him in her office, and she will bring them a mint tea. Her other tenant would take care of their luggage later.

She preceded the couple into the office to find Roberto very close to the door. He relaxed when he saw her smile and completely relaxed when he saw whom she was leading into the room.

"Avvocato[1] Cunin, please meet the new arrivals, my cousins from Trieste…."

"… Mario and Elsa Modlich, a pleasure to meet you, Avvocato Cunin. We are not using our old names, just in case we inadvertently make mistakes. Nice to see another known face. We are only missing our nephew, who will arrive from Udine at some point this week; we are not sure when."

Roberto wished his parents were there; maybe Rachele's parents could convince them to leave home.

"I am relieved to see you, Mr. Modlich. I wish you could speak to my parents. They refuse to leave their home. I like your attitude about names; we shall all have to do a lot of pretending for some time. I hope you will not be shocked when your granddaughter will appear looking slightly different and with a different name."

"We shall do our best, shall we not, Elsa? I am sure Anita will point out an area of this huge place where we can speak freely."

Anita looked like she had just been dragged back to reality from her thoughts.

"Well, this room and the kitchen if we stay away from the terrace. The other three sides back on other rooms 'of this huge place.' Mr. Modlich, you know the way to your room, and I am sure that Avvocato Cunin will gladly fetch your luggage from the entry hall."

Roberto smiled and obliged.

Stra

Gabriele and Rachele had not given up on their two walks a day. They did not have Anita to mind the children, but their daughters were old enough to oblige. They were exploring, walking to the group of homes they had noticed when they arrived. They were very jealous of the two opportunities a day to be by themselves and have private conversations.

"Tomorrow, I have a meeting with Count Contarini to see how I can help him with the administration. I will not charge him my normal rates; so far, the estate sends us milk, eggs, and flour every day, they let us buy vegetables at a ridiculous price. We need to figure out how we can buy fish. I am almost embarrassed to be paid. If he asks me to work for him two mornings a week, I'll do it for free."

"We are going back to barter, aren't we? On the other hand, thanks to Anna we have fresh white bread. I can make challah for Friday night.[2] Mila has all the milk she needs. If I think of all the problems we had in Venice finding food, this is heaven; as Anna and Diana keep saying."

Gabriele was smiling; he knew they had been lucky his baby brother had sorted out their temporary home.

"Davide yesterday found the swings, so he is in heaven."

"I have been thinking. Your brother is very active, our eldest daughter is following him. I am fed up with simply trying to keep our way of life as much as possible. I think it is time to do something."

Gabriele did not expect the determination he heard in his wife's voice, but he was not surprised.

"What about trying to stay alive to survive the war?"

"That is not enough. I may not be going to bear arms, but I have to do something."

They had reached the houses, and there were other people around them; they thought they might be overheard and started talking about the children and kept calling each other Gino and Rina.

10 October 1943

Stra

Everybody was homesick. Even Davide said he missed Venice. The previous day had been a bizarre Yom Kippur;[3] it was strange not to be in synagogue. Anna and Rachele prepared meals for younger children who did not have to fast yet. Gabriele spent a lot of his day praying. At the end of the day, he blew the Shofar, and they had the post-fast meal. Thanks to the flower, milk, and eggs they received every morning, they had enough food for a dinner that was better than usual.

Emma had to go to work and did not have time to dwell on anything. She was impatient to do something more than disassembling military jackets to make skirts or organize the two older men who were supposed to dye the material to turn them into civilian clothes for men. She was sitting in her tiny workshop when somebody knocked at the door behind the rack with civilian clothes; she moved it and let Enrico in.

"Time for Elena Giadrossi to take a trip. Tomorrow you need to collect a person from a shop on the Lido in Venice and deliver him to a dentist in Venice. You will have to spend the night in Venice; your uncle tells me that your old home is a safe place, but you need to use the entrance to Anita's rooms, whatever that means. You are expected; your uncle will not be there. How is your English?"

"Very basic."

"Good, remember that you will have to speak Italian in public, and the person you collect will have to pretend he cannot open his mouth because his jaw is hurting."

Emma was excited and nervous. She had to remember everything that Enrico was telling her.

"You have not told me where I have to go."

"Your cover is to deliver clothes to a dressmaker you know, Mrs. Toffolo; she will tell you the address in the Lido. When you get there, they will tell you where you have to take your pretend husband. Wear the blonde wig. They are expecting a blond lady."

Emma was surprised to find out that her former employer was involved in clandestine activities. She had to figure out how to discuss her absence for two nights with her parents and what to tell her siblings. She will probably tell her mother; after all, Rachele was used to professional confidence. She finished what she was doing, picked up work for Diana, and went home.

Once she arrived, she was surprised that her mother had no problems keeping to herself why she was spending two nights in Venice and offered to help her with the 'transformation' into Elena Giadrossi, bar the blond wig. An hour after she arrived home, Enrico appeared with a horse-drawn cart to take her to the station; he was surprised to see how different she looked, just with a hat, padded hips, and more formal clothes.

Venice (morning)

Doorbells made people jump, even when they were expecting somebody. People were especially jumpy in the former Mendes household in San Giacomo dall'Orio.

Three out of the four residents had false identities, and the fourth knew everything about them. They were having breakfast. Anita still was not used to the Baron and his wife, whom she had to remember to call Mario and Elsa, having breakfast with her in the kitchen. She had known Roberto since he was a teenager, and she was used to being treated like family by the extended Mendes clan, but she did not have that level of familiarity with Rachele's parents. When they heard the doorbell to the main entrance, they all jumped. Roberto grabbed his mint tea and ran to his room, ready to leave from the back door; 'Mario and Elsa' stood up, left the kitchen, and went to their room.

Rachele's cousin, his wife, and their two teenage children had arrived. They introduced themselves as Carlo and Ginevra De Antoni and their adolescent children, Pietro and Maria. Anita had met them before, but she greeted them with their new names. She told them to leave the luggage in the hall for the moment and meet the rest of the residents. On the way to the kitchen, she knocked on Baron Modiano's bedroom, and she spoke with a loud voice so Roberto could realize that she was with "friends."

On the way to Venice from Stra

Enrico made sure Emma had memorized all the instructions on the way to the station. He also told her which train she had to take two days later; Enrico would be at the station to meet her. However, if she missed that train, he would go home, and she would probably have to walk all the way, and that would not be advisable. When they arrived at the station, Enrico helped Emma off the cart; she kissed him on the cheek, picked up her suitcase, and walked into the station to buy the ticket. She was nervous but also felt in control and concentrated on the next task to calm her nerves. Once she got on the train, she waited until it left the station and went to the toilet. There she put her blond wig on, brushed her "new" hair, and moved to a different coach.

Venice, later in the day.

During the train journey, Emma decided that Elena Giadrossi would be a taller and blond version of her mother. Rachele was medium-height, but her confidence, her demeanour, and her posture made her look taller; she could look down on anybody and "cut down" to size any opponent, especially in court. Emma made an effort to walk like her; she was alone in the compartment, so she took to pacing up and down to rehearse walking differently. Once the train arrived at the station, she had become Elena Giadrossi. She stopped for a moment to enjoy being home again, took the vaporetto to San Stae, to go to Calle del Tentor, and to the back door of her home.

Emma rang. She looked calm, but she was anxious, very conscious of her blond wig, and embarrassed to use a false identity with Aunt Anita. As expected, Anita looked down from a window.

"Do I know you?"

"Your sister from Asolo sent me. She told me you could put me up for two nights; she said you have a room with a back view I could use."

" Ah, yes. You must be Elena. Come in."

She opened the door. When Emma was safely inside, Anita took her to the kitchen and whispered. She was very nervous.

"It could be risky today. They can be here at any time. I have told the younger adults to hide."

"Anita, take a deep breath and start from the beginning. Who is here, and who can be here at any time? And how did you know my name was supposed to be Elena and not Emma?"

"Your uncle lives here, or better… Roberto Cunin lives here. He did not mention anything I am not supposed to know, but he did tell me that my sister from Asolo would send somebody I knew under the name of Elena Giadrossi. When I told him I do not have a sister in Asolo, I only have a brother who emigrated to Canada twenty years ago; he told me he was aware of that with a huge grin."

Emma did not know that Anita was involved in her uncle's activities.

"Did he involve you in anything?"

"No, not really. I am involved because I know that Roberto Cunin is not a lawyer from Padua with a heart condition. I also know that Mario and Elsa Modlich are not my cousins from Trieste, the ones I do not have. You know my other tenants, your mother's cousin with his family, except they are the De Antonis now."

Somehow, knowing that Anita also had some involvement in her clandestine world reassured Emma.

"Ok, so I understand why we are talking in the kitchen with the Radio on. Who can be here at any time?"

Anita was getting more and more anxious.

"Black shirts, they came here yesterday. They said that they wanted to requisition the flat. I said that I already have tenants and that my sister from Asolo was due to arrive any time, and then I would have no room left. They said they would be back to take something to help pay for their people lodging somewhere else. What can they take from here? I do not know. I am confused; what will your parents say when this is over, and you come back?"

Emma realized she had to sound calm, collected, and reassuring.

"Don't worry, just ask for a receipt so you can prove that they took something. Whatever happens, you then go to the police and ask for advice on what to do. If taking something means that they leave you alone, it is not that bad. By the way, how did you get an official letter confirming that your non-existent sister from Asolo is about to move in?"

Anita did not answer; she smiled despite her nervousness. Emma slapped her forehead as a sign she had figured it out and smiled back.

"Roberto Cunin, of course. You may be more deeply involved than I initially thought. Now I understand why you are worried."

Anita was back to her overprotective self.

"I am very worried. I am worried about everybody, and especially about you. Do your parents know what you are up to?"

" They are generically aware of it. Although I do not discuss details with them, in the same way, I will not discuss details with you."

Anita shook her head, a gesture that took Emma back to her childhood.

"You and your siblings are like my children. I can't stop worrying. Settle in your old room and re-appear for dinner in an hour. Remember, everybody here uses their new identity, except me; my old identity is my cover."

Emma went to her old bedroom and closed the door behind her. She took her blond wig off and changed. Shortly afterwards, somebody knocked at her door. When she opened it, her grandfather did not even give her time to react. He just hugged her; Emma's tension melted in that hug. Her grandmother followed with a hug of her own. Then they both gestured her to be silent, and, in a very soft voice, Mario Modlich said that they were using their new names all the time for fear of making mistakes when they went out.

The conversation at dinner was about strategies to find food the following day. Anita felt she had to stay home, just in case, but would be happy to give her ration card to whoever was volunteering with food shopping. Emma listened to them planning the trip to the shops as if it were a military operation and couldn't help thinking of Giuseppe. He came every morning with milk, eggs, flour, and sometimes with vegetables from his orchard. She decided she'd better avoid mentioning that particular aspect of life in the country; it would have been too much for her fellow diners.

11 October 1943

Venice

Emma slept very soundly, woke up early, left a thank-you note for Aunt Anita, signed Elena Giadrossi, just in case, and left. She would be back before the curfew, and Aunt Anita knew what to do if it was not safe for her to be let in.

She felt relatively confident in her impersonation of Elena Giadrossi, but was also careful, walked to catch the vaporetto at the Zattere, choosing a route that would have been unusual for Emma. The familiar environment did not distract her. She was concentrating on walking like Elena Giadrossi and carefully followed everything they had taught her to figure out whether somebody followed her. She was carrying a large bag with a parachute that Enrico Contarini 'had just found' and was more worried about that than about her trip to the Lido later. She had to keep up the pretence of delivering her work to Mrs. Toffolo. The reunion with her old boss was very emotional. She knew to expect a blonde Elena Giadrossi, but was aware that Emma would turn up.

Emma did not know what Mrs. Toffolo's involvement was; she was not surprised when her former employee kept her in one of the fitting rooms, well away from the rest of her staff. She gave her a message and a bundle of materials for the lady in the shop at the Lido. Mrs Toffolo noticed Emma's surprise and explained she had a nephew missing in Russia. The Germans had taken her son and many other soldiers from barracks in Bologna. She did not know where he was.

On her way to the Lido, Emma could not help thinking of Mrs. Toffolo, who did not know where her son was. Her uncle Roberto had told her that uncle Emanuele and aunt Miriam and their families had plans to hide somewhere as they did, but she did not know where they were. Once the vaporetto reached the Lido, she could not help thinking of the times she spent on the beach before the racial laws. Emma found the restaurant, entered and asked for Anna Falon. She was led into the kitchen, outside in a courtyard, and into a garage. She was alarmed because there were two men inside the garage. She was expecting at least a woman. One of the men had a bandaged head, and the other moved towards her.

"Don't worry; we are using the name Anna Falon as a code. Anna Falon was my mother; she died three years ago. Just remember me as Remo, you have a message for me, and I have an envelope for Mrs Toffolo and your parcel. I also have a hat and a light coat that should fit you; at least Mrs Toffolo told me they should."

"I did not know I was supposed to go back to Mrs Toffolo; I only know I am supposed to deliver the 'parcel' to a café near the Station and then go home."

"We need Mrs Toffolo to have this, and your cover will not be compromised. You brought something to Mrs Toffolo this morning and will collect something else from her to finish it wherever you live."

He gave her a thick envelope that was small enough to fit in her handbag, told her to put her jacket in the bigger bag and wear the coat and the hat. Once she had delivered the "parcel," she should change and walk out of the café wearing her suit jacket and no hat. He introduced her to "her parcel," a downed American airman who had escaped capture; he had been found by some "friendly farmers" and was now on his way south to cross the border. Emma changed her clothes as ordered, and then they walked out from the back. They walked to the vaporetto station at the Lido and took the line that was not going through the Grand Canal. Emma felt that a roundabout route would be less likely to have police or black shirts on board. She hoped to hide her anxiety, had to be calm, collected, and in complete control, or at least look as if she were. She did not know that her "parcel" was not an American airman, but a test to see if they could trust her.

* * *

Anita had been nervous the whole morning; she had told half her 'tenants' to go out shopping for food, she said to those who had not gone out to stay close to their room and be very inconspicuous if anybody rang. She also tried to clear Emma's room, made the bed, moved Emma's clothes to her room and the suitcase under her bed. She would put them back later.

At midday, they came. They rang and knocked at the door. Anita knew that the 'safe' cupboard was blocking the entrance to the baby's room, where the family had hidden many things they could not take with them. Nobody had thought of hiding the painting by the school of Canaletto. They came, they stormed the house. They did not look at the safe cupboard, but they found the picture in the living room. When they left, Anita did not have a receipt; she had a note saying that the flat was exempt from lodging refugees or soldiers.

Things had gone according to the plan Rachele had devised. Anita told Mario and Elsa Modlich, and Carlo and Pietro De Antoni they could come out. When Ginevra and Maria De Antoni arrived back from their shopping expedition, they were surprised to see that the "almost Canaletto" had gone; Anita calmly told them she would go to the police the following day.

Emma arrived back later than expected. She was more relaxed; her first time doing something more dangerous than delivering documents had gone well. They even walked past a couple of black shirts, and she kept calm. Anita quietly told her that the painting had gone. Black shirts came and took it and showed Emma the letter they gave her; there was no mention of the picture. Anita told her that Rachele would know whether it was genuine or fake. She would go to the police tomorrow morning after

Emma took her train back. Anita asked Emma to tell her parents.

Emma did not care about the painting these days. If they were going to leave the flat alone, it was a price worth paying. She and her parents will look for it when the war was over. A safe haven was much more critical now. Worrying about the painting was a peacetime luxury; she could not afford it now when survival was the only thing that mattered.

It was only after dinner, when she was back in her room, that Emma realized she had not told Anita which train she was supposed to take, but somehow Anita knew.

Chapter Nine

October–November 1943

13 October 1943

Stra

Emma woke up very relaxed; her first mission was over. It took her a long time to fall asleep the previous evening. She kept thinking of what she could share, but had no intention of sharing that Anita knew too much to be just an innocent bystander in what was going on, or that Mrs Toffolo was distributing fake papers from her workshop. She could share that Mrs Toffolo had given Diana some work to finish and that black shirts had 'requisitioned' the almost Canaletto they had in their living room.

She heard Giuseppe arrive with eggs, milk, and flour. She realized she had lingered in bed too long, time to get up.

Emma entered the kitchen when her parents arrived back from their morning walk. Gabriele would take Leo and Davide to school and then help Count Contarini do the estate's admin. Rachele would walk up to the farm with Emma and left it at that.

Emma told her mother about the painting as they were walking. She wondered why Rachele was so relaxed about it, more to the point why she smiled when she heard Anita had gone to the police the day she left Venice. Her mother did not ask her what she had done in Venice and why she had met Mrs. Toffolo. They parted company at the farm. Emma went to her workshop, and Rachele went to the main house; the Contarini had asked her for informal legal advice, Rachele's standard line, when she did not want her children to ask questions.

Rachele had just waved goodbye to her daughter and turned towards Count Contarini's home. She had an appointment with Enrico. The meeting had been arranged via Giuseppe. Rachele had figured out that he carried messages for Emma so we could see together her and Enrico only when it was absolutely necessary. The previous day, she had tested her theory and asked him if he could organize a discrete meeting with Enrico; she had the conversation standing beside her husband, so there was no doubt of what "discrete" meant. Giuseppe reported back that Enrico had arranged to meet her under a pergola, in the main garden of the villa, a bit cold, but nice.

Enrico was sitting where he could dominate the whole environment. All access points were in his line of vision, and he was near the gate to the tennis court area where, realistically, he could try to hide if something happened. He stood up when he saw Rachele approach.

Enrico's parents had always been despairing of his social skills. He always came straight to the point. He hated small talk. Not only was there no time to waste, but he could also be interrupted at any time, and, most of all, he was aware he might have to run for his life with no notice.

"Good Morning, Rachele; what can I do for you?"

"Good Morning, Enrico; I come with an offer to help."

"I assume you are not just talking about helping my mother organize the next party."

Rachele smiled at that line; Enrico did not have an exact measure of her. She began to wonder if her brother-in-law, Roberto, had talked about her at all.

"If that might help bring the end of this madness closer, I might, otherwise I'll leave it to Gabriele, Anna, and Diana, possibly helped by our sons, except somebody must look after Mila."

Enrico smiled at her reaction.

"If you are ever in trouble about that, ask my mother; she misses her grandchildren so much. Mila may even make her forget that I have not given her grandchildren yet."

Now Rachele thought Enrico was engaging in what he considered small talk. She decided not to play along and come to the point as fast as she could.

"I wouldn't count on that. Anyway, I have helped people in Venice prepare false legal documents. I will not use weapons. I am not capable of aiming at anything. I'd be a danger to myself; the others will be safe. I am not prepared to go anywhere. That rules out anything that takes me away from my husband and my children overnight."

Enrico's posture changed; he now became more serious, more business-like.

"I was hoping we could use your legal skills. We have people who could write excellent false legal documents or other paperwork, but we need to have plausible content to make them credible fakes; you will provide the text. I can get Rina Conti a part-time job as a legal secretary with the town lawyer. Would you be happy to go there three mornings a week? That would be your cover to move around the area, including Stra."

Rachele, the lawyer, was back. She was now taking mental notes; Enrico did not know he might have to answer short but pointed questions.

"Why would I need to move around?"

"It might be necessary to deliver papers somewhere, or it might be necessary to deliver messages. I promise I shall never ask you to deliver weapons. Your brother-in-law will kill me; he reluctantly assigned your niece, Emma, to me after he organized your accommodation in Rodolfo's home. I cannot possibly have him mad at me for two members of his family."

Rachele had no problems with anything Enrico had just told her.

"It does not seem much, but I can do that."

"Well, your friends' daughter-in-law Carolina Mondani is politically involved; I may ask her if there is anything else you can do."

Rachele wondered if they were back to small talk.

"I was not aware that you knew Paolo and Sofia's daughter-in-law."

"My eldest brother, Rodolfo, married her sister, but I would not acknowledge Carolina if we met in public."

"I see; any news of her husband?"

"I think Carolina knows he is alive, but the Red Cross has delivered nothing in months. Anyway, welcome on board.

You will hear from me in the same way Emma hears from me."

Enrico stood up, nodded, and left. Rachele lingered a few more minutes. She seldom had been on the periphery of things, but this is what she was asked to do. Gabriele was happy to survive until the end; she had to follow her eldest daughter and her brother-in-law and do something. If that were all she could do, she would do it without complaining.

Venice

Mario and Roberto were getting ready to listen to the BBC. That was illegal, a 'rebellious act,' even before you consider that Mario (Baron Davide Modiano) and Roberto (Roberto Mendes) were Jewish and technically could not own a radio (they didn't, officially it was Anita's). There was a radio in Anita's office, but that radio was hidden inside a cupboard in Roberto's room. Anita and Elsa were in the kitchen preparing dinner. Anita was still ill at ease with having Baroness Modiano help her in the kitchen, but she insisted. They had the radio at full blast and were singing along. They were always very noisy when Roberto was listening to the BBC.

Mario and Roberto were listening to the messages for the resistance in Italian; Roberto was taking notes. Mario tried his best not to notice what he was writing. Ignoring anything Roberto was doing was his 'price for admission' to listen to the radio. The news came next. The bombshell came after sharing what happened in the front line (that was not moving North fast enough).

"The Kingdom of Italy has declared war on Germany. The Italian ambassador in Madrid delivered the ultimatum at 3 pm today; we still do not know the response of the German government."

Mario and Roberto looked at each other, speechless. At the end of the news, Roberto switched the radio off, unplugged it, put it back in the cupboard, covered it with a blanket, and locked the door. Mario looked at him quizzically; Roberto had no better idea of what was going on.

"I did not know that it was coming; I know that there are several Italian soldiers in prison camps in Germany. They are now prisoners of war; I suspect that was the main drive; I cannot see what the official Italian Army could do to help the mighty Allied Armies. I am not sure what it means for us, though."

Mario sounded very concerned

"I am afraid things will get worse for us. Mussolini is nominally the head of the Republic of Italy, but the Germans really rule the country north of the front line. The Kingdom of Italy abolished the racial laws, the Republic may bring in stricter laws to appease the Germans. We need to hope that the front line moves north as quickly as possible."

Stra

Enrico appeared in the workshop with a bundle.

"More uniforms to turn into civilian clothes, put some ladies of the estate to work, they can help with the die and pay them with clothes. Your mother has joined the fight, and this is the only thing I am prepared to tell you."

Emma took the bundle of uniforms, hid them under a pile of other clothes, and prepared to close the workshop; Enrico offered to walk her home. It was getting dark, and although it was all inside the Contarini estate and therefore not affected by the curfew, the lamplights were not working. He had to report a message Sofia Mondani had left for Rachele when she rang his mother.

On the way, the conversation was very light-hearted; Emma had the feeling that Enrico was avoiding telling her something on purpose. In the short time she had been doing 'clandestine' work, she had learned not to ask irrelevant questions and not to question why somebody was not telling her something. She had learned from her mother what plausible deniability meant.

When they reached the house, Enrico used an excuse not to follow Emma inside; Rachele stepped outside.

"Good evening Enrico, how are you? What is the message from Sofia?"

"Sofia told me to tell you that Anita has gone to the police, whatever that means. "

"Yes, Sofia was not aware that you sent Emma to Venice. By the way, wasn't it risky sending her to San Giacomo dall'Orio? What if somebody saw her?"

Enrico felt as if his commanding officer had reprimanded him. He was beginning to realize that Roberto had not been embellishing the stories he told him about Rachele.

"She had a blonde wig and changed her posture by channeling you. Somebody might have seen a vague resemblance, but they would not have recognized her."

3 November 1943

Stra

Rachele had been working with the local solicitor for a couple of weeks; she spent most of her time writing false official papers. It turned out that her old law firm had trained Guido Orlando. That made for an interesting first meeting. Rachele was shocked to see him walk with a cane; she remembered him as a very sporty young man. Guido Orlando was surprised to find out that his new 'legal secretary' was the woman who trained him. After the first nice but awkward moment, they got to work. Two weeks later, Guido was still very deferential, still talking to his old boss, forgetting that he was officially the boss now and they would have to act as if she were the unqualified employee. He would never dare disagree with Rachele; she was tempted to say that the sun was shining on a rainy day to test Guido Orlando's reaction.

Guido Orlando's law office was in Stra's main square. Right by the front door of the building, there was a bike rack with an attendant. Rachele left her bike there, tipped the attendant, and was about to walk inside when she noticed her boss coming in from the police station with a young man. When they caught up with her, Guido made the introduction.

"Rina, meet police detective Umberto De Antoni; Umberto meets my assistant Rina Von Moden Conti."

The young man took his hat off and nodded. They climbed the two flights of steps in silence. Once they were in the office, Guido Orlando turned the radio on with the news. They moved to another room.

"Nobody can overhear us here. Rina, Umberto works with Enrico, and he has an urgent request."

Mentioning Enrico's name was his way of telling Rachele that Umberto could be trusted. The young police detective sat down, took a notebook out of his pockets, and tore out three pages.

"These are the notes I have to ask you to destroy. According to a source I trust, there is a plan to round up men between 45 and 55 for forced labour. They cannot be drafted into the reserves, so the exemption from military service would not work. I do not think the police will be involved, but we need to come up relatively quickly with reasons for exemption."

Guido stood up to look for the last legal updates from the Republic. He showed the relevant law to Rachele, who had been taking note; Rachele briefly looked at the page.

"How long do I have? I would like to study the law first. We need to avoid heart issues unless they are backed up by medical history. An epidemic of heart conditions would probably raise suspicion. I want to find half a dozen reasons for exemption, then write templates. We may need to involve different roles to sign them; I do not know yet."

"I am not sure how much time we have. If the police are not involved, we may have no advance notice at all. "

Rachele opened the bundle of legal updates.

"Give me an hour to study the law and then we can plan what to do."

The policeman left, saying he would be back an hour later. Rachele got to work. Guido took the notebook pages left on the table, tore them into small pieces, took out two large volumes from the bookshelf and retrieved two metal boxes, divided Rachele's notes between them, then he took out a box of matches and burnt Umberto's shredded notes.

8 November 1943

Stra

After a month in the country, Emma was getting used to the different morning noises. The chiming of church bells would usually take her back to how much she was missing Venice. She believed in what she was doing and loved the idea that she was doing something that might bring her old life closer. She thought of carefree ball games on the beach at the Lido with her cousins as she was getting dressed. She was younger then, and the war had prevented her from experiencing the same things later. Hopefully, someday she will be playing ball games on the beach again.

This morning, Giuseppe had two notes for her and one for her mother. The image of her mother, the underground fighter, was alien to Emma and her siblings.

Her instructions that morning were to get ready to go to Venice; she was supposed to stay out for three nights and spend one night in Rovigo, a guest of people she did not know. Roberto would have the details of the operation. Giuseppe told her that Enrico was not around, but he thought it was time she had some shooting practice, and he would arrange it for the following week. He informed her that one of his daughters would teach her. There was more than a hint of pride in his voice.

Figure 6 - Map highlighting the location of Stra
and Rovigo

Venice

Emma wondered why she would receive her final
instructions from her uncle during the entire journey to
Venice. She did not ask why, and Giuseppe did not volunteer the information. Her uncle welcomed Elena Giadrossi
at the door. He gave her ten minutes to go to her room,
freshen up, turn back into Emma, greet Anita and
whomever else she bumped into, and then meet him in
Anita's office by the radio.

Although they had no reason to believe that the flat was
bugged, when he talked to Emma, the radio in the office
was on, playing music.

"You have to take an escaped American prisoner of war to
Rovigo. The good news is that he is a blond American of
Sicilian origin who speaks some Italian. The bad news is

that his accent is horrible and would give him away the moment he opened his mouth."

Emma was going through her mental checklist.

"So, what is the cover story?"

"He is supposed to be your husband, discharged from a military hospital, still recovering from his wounds to his face. A wound to his jaw infected his gums. You have decided to visit a dentist in your hometown, Rovigo, a family friend you trust."

"Why? I need to have an answer to that question. Somebody might ask me what was wrong with the military hospital. What if I said that they had not noticed the infection and now I want him seen by somebody I trust?"

"That is a good idea. Here are your papers. I won't have to tell you to memorise your last name. The exchange with the other handler will happen on the train; I was concerned because it has never happened before, so Paolo Mondani has offered to assist you. "

"Why?"

"Because we are overprotective. Next time, you will be on your own. He will get off at Padua with the other handler and take the next train to Venice."

Emma was disappointed not to see Mrs Toffolo; she was fond of her and missed the witticism of the man she knew as "Anna Falon." She was also annoyed that her uncle thought she needed a babysitter, but was happy to spend time with Paolo Mondani, her honorary uncle.

9 November 1943

Venice, Rovigo and back to Venice

Anita told her that Aunt Sofia expected Elena Giadrossi for breakfast, and she and Uncle Paolo would go to the station together. When she got to their home near the Rialto fish market, Sofia welcomed Anita's niece at the door.

An hour later, Paolo and Emma took the vaporetto to the station. They bought tickets and boarded the train. Paolo knew where they were supposed to sit. She noticed the couple that was already sitting in the compartment. The man was wearing a hat, and his head was bandaged to fake a dressed wound, but his blond hair was noticeable, and his blue eyes could pierce the wall of the compartment. They sat opposite them; Emma apologized to the lady for blocking her space. The lady made all the right noises; Paolo smiled. They were seated opposite the right couple.

Emma noticed that the man also had a heavily bandaged arm held still by a scarf wrapped around his neck. She wondered whether it was part of the disguise or he was genuinely wounded.

They were alone in the compartment, but were sitting in silence. Emma was nervous; that was something new for her. Her honorary uncle was a reassuring presence, although she would never admit it to anyone. They sat without saying a word until the train crossed the long bridge from Venice to the mainland. At the next station, the woman sitting opposite Emma noticed that two black shirts and a German officer were boarding the train. Emma had the false papers showing that she was the wife of the other man. Paolo and the American quickly swapped seats. Emma had read and memorized the fake

127

documents in the morning. She was Elena Giadrossi, wife of Carlo Hertisch, born in Trieste. The papers showed an address in Rovigo, the city where Emma was supposed to hand him over to another handler. The train started moving again; they could hear the two Italians asking for other travellers' papers. Emma mentally went through all the documents she had in her handbag. Her husband was wounded when enemy planes attacked his ship in Pola. Emma also had a letter to a doctor in Rovigo describing shrapnel wounds in the head, and temporary brain damage that made it difficult for him to speak. She had learned from her mother that the feeling of being prepared was the best way to beat nerves or fear. She was nervous and afraid, but had to look in total control, ready to answer any questions when they were asked for their documents.

Paolo could see the three uniformed men from where he was sitting. They were at least four compartments away when a young man in civilian clothes that were too big for him walked past the door to the compartment. Paolo thought he was a soldier of the Italian Army who did not want to fight with the Fascist, or did not want to fight any more, and was trying to get home. The train was not far from Padua station, and probably the young man hoped that by going to the toilet or moving further away from them, he could reach the station and get off the train before they asked him for papers. No such luck. The German noticed him, pointed him out to one of the two Italians who shouted.

"Stop; where do you think you are going? We need to see your paper first."

Emma noticed the American was distressed. Paolo and the other lady tried to reassure him. The four of them made a point of not looking at the commotion in the corridor. The young man had started running. It was a mistake. The three uniformed men ran after him. They run past their compartment. They were only a few minutes away from Padua station; this would definitely be the wrong time for a red light, an attack on the train by fighter pilots, or anything that would go against the train reaching the station.

They heard the noise of the doors to the passageway between coaches being opened and slammed shut twice. Paolo and Emma looked at each other; they had skipped the request for documents. Paolo knew Emma too well not to notice that her face had relaxed; he could sense her inward sigh of relief. A few minutes later, the train arrived at Padua. Paolo and the other handler prepared to get off; Paolo hugged Emma and shook hands with the American. The other handler simply stood up and left.

When the train started moving again, they were alone in the compartment. Emma was silent for a while; she wanted to avoid other people accidentally catching them mid-conversation. When she thought that everybody who boarded the train in Padua had found a seat of their liking, she introduced herself (well, not her real self, of course). Either the American had seen the false papers and was sticking to the script, or his name was Carlo. He noticed Emma's quizzical look and told they named her him after his grandfather.

Emma realized his Italian was good, but his accent was not. He almost sounded like an Italian caricaturing an American trying to speak Italian. She pointed out that he did not sound like an Italian. Carlo laughed and told her that his father would agree with her. He appreciated that when other people were around, he could not speak. Emma smiled and pointed out that her papers said that he had problems with his speech following a shrapnel injury to his jaw; it was fine for him not to say a word.

The conversation made time fly, and they soon reached the next station, the one before their final destination. When the train moved again, they were still alone. Their instructions were pretty straightforward. They were supposed to go to a dentist close to the station. She knew how the dentist would signal if there were any trouble and what they had to do if that was the case.

The train slowed down as it approached Rovigo station. They stood up to get off; as the train stopped, they noticed two black shirts and a German soldier waiting to board the train. Emma was ready with her story. They were very polite. They helped her with the suitcase and helped Carlo negotiate the steep steps off the train since he could not use the bandaged arm to steady himself using the handrail at the back of the door. Emma thanked them, and Carlo even attempted a fascist salute with his left arm and faked an attempt to smile. The two black shirts answered with the same greeting. The German officer clicked his heel in a 'heil Hitler' salute; then, they boarded the train. Emma and Carlo walked away from the train; once they were at the bottom of the stairs of the subway leading to the exit, they looked at each other, sighed, and then laughed.

Emma remembered the directions to reach the dentist. It was not very far from the station; when they arrived at the door to the dentist's practice, she noticed a red tablecloth hanging from the terrace above the entrance. It was a sign that there was some problem and they had to come back later. Emma's instructions were to go to a restaurant nearby and ask for a table away from the road. Once they got there, the waitress looked at them and commented on Emma's bright shirt. Emma replied, according to her instructions. The two women smiled at each other, and the waitress took them to a table in the back, near the kitchen door. Emma had their fake ration cards. They ordered lunch; she helped Carlo eat. Halfway through a soup, an elderly lady joined them. She greeted Emma as if she were a family member. She helped Carlo eat, saying that Elena should eat the soup before it turned cold.

The waitress had kept the tables near them empty. There were better tables in the restaurant. It was a family scene; in reality, as the lady was helping Carlo eat, she talked in a low voice. She spoke about family members, but she was clearly explaining what was about to happen. After lunch, they would have gone to the dentist, and then Fabio, whomever he was, was supposed to come with a horse-drawn cart to take them home. When the waitress came to take the plates, she told the elderly lady that the red table-cloths were now dry and ready to iron. Emma took it as the all-clear for them to go to the dentist. The elderly lady went back to the kitchen, grabbed her coat, then walked out with them. They crossed the street, and soon they were ringing at the door to the dentist's practice. A woman opened the door and welcomed them in. She was a younger version of the elderly lady, clearly her daughter. She did not take them to the main waiting room but up a flight of steps to the dentist's home. In the living room, they found another lady wearing a blue skirt and a yellow shirt like Emma. Emma made a mental note to ask Enrico how they knew what she was wearing. She was just told to wear something bright and pack something grey or black.

The elderly lady turned out to be the dentist's wife. She left them alone; Emma noticed how the other handler could have been mistaken for her from a distance. Same height and the same blond wig, different hairstyle, but close enough. Both ladies were wearing green coats; Emma's was made from an Army uniform, and the other one was likely to have a similar provenance. Materials were scarce; anybody who knew how to sew could have a go at adjusting an old army coat.

The two handlers barely talked to each other and did not exchange names. They did not have to. Carlo thanked Emma and followed the other handler out of the living room. Emma was left alone for a few minutes, and then the dentist's wife reappeared, Emma could change in the living room, and then they would go to the station in time for her to catch a train that would take her back to Padua long before the end of the curfew. As she was changing, the dentist's wife tore Carlo's false hospital papers to pieces; then, she threw them in the fireplace. Her hostess was conscientious that everything had burnt down and was unreadable.

She left the building, wearing a grey suit under her coat and a grey beret.

She would have liked to go to the station on her own, but her guts were telling her it was all right. Her train was not on time; luckily, the earlier train was also very late, and she took that one. She said goodbye to the dentist's wife as if she had been a much-loved family member and boarded the train. She took out a magazine and started reading.

The train arrived in Venice early enough for Emma to take a roundabout route home. Instead of walking from the station, she took the vaporetto to Zattere. Before the racial laws, a café at the Zattere had been the first meeting place of her group of friends, the first taste of independence. Going somewhere to meet her friends without the super-vising look of a parent made her feel very grown-up; what she found out years later was that one of her friends was the nephew of the newsagent at the Zattere. The kiosk was within earshot and sight of the cafe. Once she got to Zattere, she took another vaporetto to San Marco and then to San Stae and walked home. Memories kept flooding in as she was unnecessarily turning into narrow streets and stopping to look at shop windows, checking that nobody followed her. It took her longer, but she was relaxed when she rang the bell. Still, she decided to discuss her unease with Enrico the following day.

It had been a long and tense day, her first "delivery" to new people out of town. Anita hugged her, and Roberto congratulated her; he told her he had something for her since she was back a day early. Emma had many questions for them, but she decided to enjoy the company of her grandparents. She was very careful to call them Mario and Elsa.

Chapter Ten

November-December 1943

17 November 1943

Stra

The fog was thicker than what Rachele was used to in Venice. She loved the idea of being embraced by soft cotton wool but hated not being able to see from a distance and only guess what would come towards her when they were close. She and her daughters were eternally grateful to the ladies of the estate, who had knitted wool stockings for them. It was not winter yet, but mornings were chilly. She was also thankful that Countess Contarini had given old winter pyjamas that used to belong to her sons when they were as old as Leo and Davide were. She might have to organize a trip to Padua to see if she could buy some for her husband, herself, and her daughters.

Her route to work had become so familiar that she could be miles away in her head and still get there. She locked her bike at the guarded rack in the square and went to work. Guido kept hot water in the kitchen and had mint tea ready for her. Today he was more attentive than usual. He was not simply deferential; he had the excessive kindness and tact of somebody who is about to give bad news.

"Good morning, Guido, what happened? Has Giorgio been arrested?"

Giorgio was the printer turned master forger to whom she occasionally delivered documents.

"No, this morning I received a bundle of new rules and decrees from the so-called 'Republic'[1] "

Rachele interrupted him

"Be careful how you talk, we are now in the jurisdiction of the Republic of Italy, the Kingdom of Italy is south of the front line."

Guido would not follow her advice

"Why should I? Who can hear me other than you? Why should I have any respect for something created by the Germans, just to say they are not occupying Italy? Mussolini has no power. He is a puppet of Hitler. Also, what sort of state has a small village on the shore of lake Garda as capital?"

Rachele listened quietly, after Guido finished his tirade she simply said

"As a lawyer, you have to support upholding their laws."

That morning Guido was not in the mood to be silenced.

"And yet I am active in the resistance, actively contributing to their downfall. Anyway, look at page six."

Rachele opened the bundle to page 6 and read, "members of the Jewish race are to be considered foreigners; they belong to an enemy nation." The law continued stating that the state would requisition all their assets, and members of the Jewish race could even be arrested.

"Well, we have moved on from 'Italian citizen belonging to the mosaic faith,[2] my only concern is Gabriele's parents. They are the only ones in my family that are still openly living where they used to live, or at least that is what Emma tells me."

"Are you worried?"

"I am mad, or better, Rachele Modiano Mendes is worried and mad. Rina von Moden Conti is not affected and has other things to worry about. I shall discuss these rules at home this evening. Keeping things well and truly separate has become the secret of survival."

Venice

Anita was on her way to see Samuele and Fiamma Mendes. So far, Samuele had been adamant that Venetian Jews would outlive and outlast the current restrictions; his wife and children could not convince him otherwise. They had lost all their help, so Anita and Maria took turns 'visiting them' and helping them do the heaviest chores around the house. It was a long and familiar walk from San Giacomo Dall'Orio to Fondamenta del Ghetto. Samuele and Fiamma were still living in a large Venetian merchant home with a (now) empty warehouse and offices on the ground floor, the main home on the two floors above, and a huge attic that was used as a warehouse when they were running a business from there.

Anita had just crossed the bridge over the Canal Grande and turned right towards Canal Cannaregio when she stopped to get something warm. She noticed that the newspaper's front page featured the action plan of the Republican Fascist Party. She controlled herself, but her eyes fell on: "Members of the Jewish race are to be considered foreigners…". She was about to run back home and talk to Roberto, but decided to see what was happening at his parents' home and continued walking towards Fondamenta del Ghetto, noticing at least two other posters along the way. When she arrived at the home of Samuele and Fiamma, she pulled the cord that rang the bell and waited. Fiamma opened the door, smiling; obviously, she had not read those posters, and nobody had discussed them with her.

Anita decided not to mention them until she talked to Roberto. After refreshment and a chat with Fiamma, she got on with her work.

She was busy cleaning the stairs when she heard somebody open the back door; she turned around alarmed and relaxed when she saw Roberto walking in. She stopped what she was doing to tell him about the posters. He had seen them as well, and he was here to make the umpteenth attempt to talk to his parents. He only had to convince his father. His mother would not move without him. Anita went back to her work, and he went straight to see his father. He found him where Samuele had spent his mornings for most of his life, in his office. Now it had become his study, and he was reading a book about the Most Serene Republic of Venice.

His door was open; Roberto knocked at the doorpost to announce his arrival. Samuele lifted his head and smiled at his youngest child.

"Good Morning, Roberto.. What brings you here today? Your mother is somewhere in the house with Anita. It is kind of her to come and help us. She has become like another daughter to us."

Roberto was making a considerable effort to control his emotions. He wanted to get some sense of reality into his father's mind. He had brainwashed himself to stay calm, no matter what.

"Good morning dad; Anita has been one of us for years, dad. I shall see mum later. Have you been out this morning?"

"I got dressed and came here. I don't like the weather; I have no reason to go out."

Roberto was still trying to sound calm and matter-of-fact.

"If you had gone out, you would have seen posters stating that we are now considered foreigners and enemies of the country. Dad, they will confiscate our assets."

Samuele's reaction was almost explosive.

"Foreigners? Those puppets of the Germans cannot tell us we are foreigners! We can prove our presence in Venice since 1490; where were their ancestors in 1490?"

Roberto steeled himself not to lose his temper. He tried not to sound patronizing, with mixed success.

"That is not the point. Worse things may come; they round up Jews in other countries. A month ago, they rounded up Jews in Rome! You and mum need to leave here and go somewhere else where they do not know you. A friend of a friend is in touch with the convent of San Lazzaro degli Armeni; you can hide there."

Samuele was not easily convinced.

"Hide? Look, I am reading this book about the history of the Republic of Venice. Do you know how many times the Venetian Senate imposed restrictions on Jews? And yet, Jews have always outlived and outlasted them. The city needed us. Your ancestors ran one of the subsidized pawn-brokers in the Ghetto. This time will be no difference; I see no reason to go."

Roberto was still trying not to lose his temper; he could not hide the frustration in his voice.

"Dad, this time is different. We have heard that Germans rounded up everybody they found in Rome, not just men they could send to forced labour. They took old people, children, everybody, and that was after asking them for gold in exchange for being left alone."

Samuele would not change his mind.

"Rome is not Venice; it is more complicated to round up people here."

Roberto was beginning to lose his temper.

"There are boats; there is the bridge.[3]Venice is not the bubble you think it is."

Roberto was surprised to realize that it was his father who had enough.

"We have to agree to disagree. I have told your mother many times she can go; I will not."

Roberto controlled himself a few minutes longer.

"Dad, you know very well that Mum will not leave without you. Speaking of mum, I am going to see her; then I have to go."

Roberto stood up, walked towards his father, kissed him on the forehead, and left the room, looking for his mother and Anita. As he was climbing the stairs to the first floor, his frustration came out. He kept banging his fist on †he handrail. Anita and Fiamma heard the noise, stopped what they were doing, and went to the landing. Fiamma smiled.

"You know, that poor handrail is not responsible for a difference of opinion between you and your father."

Roberto smiled at his mother; he was not mad at her.

"Good morning, Mum; this is not just a difference of opinion. I am very worried for both of you. Do you know that 'The Republic' has decided we are foreigners? Not only foreigners but enemies of the state! A month ago, Jews were rounded up in Rome. I am very worried about you, and actually, I am also worried about myself. I think I am the only one of your children left in town; you are my responsibility."

Roberto kissed his mother on the cheeks, and they all moved to the sitting room. Anita left them alone to go back to what she was doing; She had plenty of opportunities to speak to him alone later in the day.

Fiamma was trying to reassure her son. She was also determined to make her point.

"We are not your responsibility; we are still capable of making our own decisions. You do not have to come if you think it is too risky. Anita and Maria come regularly, Sofia Mondani drops in almost every day, and they could be the link between you and us."

Roberto was calmer now; he was giving up any hope to change his parents' minds.

"It is not that. I am frustrated because I cannot convince Dad that this time is not like when the Venetian Senate forced Jews to wear a sign or certain clothes or stop contact between Jews and non-Jews. This time is different; they are rounding us up and taking us away."

Fiamma sounded very calm but also very determined.

"You can only try. As I said earlier, your father is capable of making his own decision."

Roberto made one last attempt.

"And you?"

"It is my decision not to go anywhere without him. We have been together for fifty years, and I have known him longer than that. He was the good-looking young man I saw from my window, and I could not believe my luck when my parents suggested I marry him. I still cannot believe my luck. So, no, wherever he goes, I go. If he stays, I stay."

"Can you at least try to talk to him?"

"I will, but do you think he will change his mind?"

Roberto smiled and stood up.

"Well, I need to go. Roberto Cunin[4] has work to do, and he cannot be caught hurrying up. After all, he has a weak heart; it is the reason he is not in the military."

Fiamma stood up and hugged her son.

"Well, tell Roberto Cunin to be very careful. I am fond of him."

"He knows."

Roberto kissed his mother on the cheek, shouted, "I'll see you later, Anita," and left. He felt very fortunate that there was nothing wrong with his heart. He was so mad at his parents that Roberto Cunin could have a heart attack before reaching the vaporetto stop. He left by the back door, walking through familiar narrow lanes, constantly checking that nobody followed him. He had calmed down by the time he reached the main street and got lost among all the other people going about their business of the day.

Stra

Rachele had tried to concentrate on her work today. She had to prepare the text of paperwork exonerating various people from military service; she had the rules in front of her and was trying to prepare exonerations for a variety of reasons. It might raise unwanted questions if all the men of military age walking around the village suffered from a weak heart. She had no idea whom those exemptions were for; the printer would fill all the details when he forged the actual document. A few days earlier, she had prepared a template for him with the details of a fictitious person.

Her mind would regularly go back to the 18 principles of the Republican Fascist Party Guido had shown her in the morning, especially to principle number 7: "*Those belonging to the Jewish race are foreigners. During this war, they belong to an enemy nation.*"[5]

Every time she caught herself thinking about it, she would think of her parents-in-law still in their home in Venice and her brothers. Daniele, had sent his wife and grown-up children to Switzerland, and Michele, whose wife and daughter were in Switzerland, but his sons were not, they had stayed in Trieste because "They had to do something to make sure they had anything left after all of this." Several people she had got in touch with for work in the past few weeks knew Michele. None of them told her what he was up to or what name he was using, but all of them knew who he was. Also, nobody had heard anything from her brother Ricardo, who lived in Milan. According to Enrico, nobody had reported him in Switzerland, but they may be hiding somewhere else. She still did not know how Enrico knew.

These thoughts were distracting her, and she had to take twenty exemptions to the printer by the end of her day so he could prepare twenty fakes of excellent quality.

She met her deadline despite the distraction. At the end of her day, she got on her bike and delivered the texts hidden in a legal document that had to be re-typed and bound. She decided to check if Emma was still in her workshop; she wanted to talk to her alone; if they ended up being late for the curfew, they could take a long way home, the way that was all inside the estate.

Emma had already closed shop, so she biked home the quick way, trying to figure out whether she would discuss things with Gabriele during their evening walk or wait until she could talk to Emma. She arrived home. Her sons were playing in the garden. Diana was sitting outside with Mila; Anna was cooking and talking to her father. Gabriele was sitting at the kitchen table updating the family ledger and figuring out the state of their finances. Emma was nowhere to be found. Gabriele sensed her presence before he saw her. Anna told her that Emma had just come home and was preparing Diana's work for the following day. Her husband smiled at her, and Rachele decided they were not in any immediate danger for that evening. She relaxed, losing herself in Gabriele's smile. She would talk to Emma in the morning.

6 December 1943

Venice

They had come the previous night. They rang bells and banged at doors. The Germans were still confused by the peculiar systems of Venetian addresses, so some were missed or were too low on the list. Samuele and Fiamma lived in what used to be the second and final extension of the Ghetto. They heard the noise, switched off the lights, opened the curtains, and watched. Samuele was almost frozen to the window; his son was right after all. They did not come for them; for whatever reason, they had been spared. In the morning, they wondered how they could tell Roberto, who must have known who was still around.

When Maria came, they opened the front door and let her in very quickly. They told her to go away and tell Anita what had happened the previous night. Fiamma was defiant, Samuele was petrified. He kept saying that his youngest son was right, but perhaps they had no use for an old couple.

Maria's husband was a well-known socialist, so they had many unwelcome contacts with black shirts, secret police, and, more recently, German officers. That had made her always alert to her surroundings. Samuele and Fiamma were aware of that, so they trusted her when she said she had noticed nothing out of the ordinary on her way to them. Fiamma realized that she had to bring back some normality to their day for her husband's sake, so she announced she would go shopping for food. Samuele was panic-stricken and insisted that Maria had to go along. Maria accepted and reassured Samuele further, saying that she would show her papers and tell them that her mother had forgotten hers if they stopped them. Samuele was reassured and told them to hurry and use the back door. Samuele hugged his wife as if it were the last time he would see her; Fiamma put her coat on, grabbed her shopping bag, made a joke about being optimistic, and left with Maria.

Maria's company and a relatively successful shopping trip had restored Fiamma's mood; they were almost back home. They were about to turn left into Fondamenta del Ghetto when they saw a group of men in uniform outside Fiamma's home. Fiamma froze; Maria had the sense of dragging her on; they kept walking and crossed the bridge into the Ghetto Novo, then the other bridge into the Ghetto Vecchio. When they reached the banks of Canal Cannareggio, they turned left and walked into a café. Maria was sure that the owner had recognized Fiamma because he looked surprised and concerned seeing them, then he brought them something warm and refused to get paid.

Maria convinced her she should not go back home, but go somewhere safe. She was even prepared to take her home with her to Castello, sticking to the story that Fiamma was her mother. Fiamma composed herself and insisted she could go to Paolo and Sofia Mondani. They were Gabriele's best friends, and Sofia and Anita were in touch. She also gave Maria her house keys and asked her to go and check what had happened. Maria told her she would do so and tell Anita later.

Fiamma felt strong enough to go on her own, but Maria insisted on going with her at least until they reached the market; she would then go back and see what happened. They boarded the vaporetto in silence; when they got off, they made an effort to look like two women perusing the market's stalls. At some point, they parted company. Maria went to tell Anita what had happened, give her Fiamma's keys and then go back to Castello; Fiamma walked to the Mondanis. Once she was alone, she did not want to draw attention to herself. She fought back the tears, but was getting more anxious and more desperate with each step. She finally reached the building where Paolo and Sofia Mondani lived; pressed the doorbell; she couldn't pull back her finger.

Sofia opened the window to check who was ringing so desperately when she saw Fiamma she immediately realized that something had gone wrong. Instead of buzzing the door open, she ran down the stairs and opened the door herself, calmly pulled Fiamma inside, hugged her, and whispered that she was safe, she had just to keep it together for two more floors, and then she could let it go. She took Fiamma's arm and led her up the stairs, gesturing her to be silent. Once they were inside and closed the door behind themselves, Fiamma collapsed, she started crying, and all she could say was.

"They came when I was out shopping for food with Maria. I saw them take him away; he looked defeated and old. Maria pulled me away; I did not know where else to go."

She kept repeating it as Sofia hugged her; Sofia only had a vague idea of what she meant.

Finally, Fiamma stopped crying. She seemed to be calmer now. She told Sofia what had happened, starting from the previous night. She also mentioned how they thought they had not come for them because they were old, their Jewish neighbours were younger, and they had teenage children. Had she felt that they would have come for them in the morning, she would have told Maria to go away. Instead, she had agreed to go shopping for food with her. When they returned with what they found, they saw them take

146

Samuele away; he looked old and defeated. He did not look up or back at the house, but followed them.

Sofia kept making reassuring noises; she now had a better idea of what had happened. She had to wait until Paolo came home from the hospital to go out and tell Anita. Roberto would appear at some point; Sofia was sure he would find out relatively quickly. She reassured Fiamma that she was welcome in their home for as long as she needed. She could use their son's bedroom; it was far away from the entrance to the flat and had a storage room with a door usually hidden by a screen where she could hide in case of real trouble.

Fiamma realized she was still holding on to the shopping bag. Sofia took the chance to suggest they prepare lunch just to distract her. Fiamma had not noticed that they had been sitting in the living room for over an hour.

Fiamma insisted they cooked what she had bought; Sofia was happy to oblige. She had not been out that day yet. Lunch was a bit late for both women. Fiamma kept talking about Samuele, how they had celebrated fifty years together the previous week, and how she would have gladly gone wherever they were taking him. She was strangely calm as she told stories about her long married life. Sofia made all the right noises and laughed at the right moments; she was very concerned and could not wait until the evening when her husband would be back. Paolo surely would know how to make sure Fiamma was all right. He had known her since he was five; she had been Aunt Fiamma ever since.

Fiamma had grown silent; Sofia did not know how to start another conversation. The doorbell broke the silence. Fiamma jumped up, and Sofia showed her to her son's bedroom before going to open the door. As she was leaving the room, she told Fiamma that if any stranger came in, she would say that Fiamma was her mother, Marianna, visiting from Murano.

Sofia was relieved to see Anita come in with a large bag. Anita had followed Fiamma's instructions to Maria. She went in from the back door. She had ignored the front door but had noticed seals; obviously, somebody had their sight set on that home. Everything in the house was neat and tidy. Fiamma remarked Samuele must have been in the study downstairs when they rang. Anita had gone to their bedroom, found a large bag, and put Fiamma's clothes inside. She then quietly locked the door as if it were her own home. Anita thought Fiamma needed spare garments and brought them here. She had not spoken to Roberto, but she was sure that if the Mondanis were happy to keep Fiamma for a few days, Roberto would come up with a more permanent solution. Anita knew he did not trust his parents to know where he was living under his 'new' identity, so she did not mention he was not home when Maria arrived. Sofia and Paolo were aware of the situation, so Sofia had figured out why Anita had not spoken to Roberto yet. In her distressed state, it did not occur to Fiamma that the other two knew how to reach her youngest son.

7 December 1943

Venice

Roberto had a very troubled night. The previous night, when Anita and Elsa told him what happened, his first instinct was to go to the Mondanis. Anita insisted that it would have been dangerous. Fiamma was in a safe place, with people that were fond of her. Gabriele often said that Paolo was almost like another son to his parents.

Once he woke up, he thought he was better off seeing Paolo first. He had to figure out an excuse to visit him. He did not know who else lived in the building where the Mondanis lived; curious neighbours might decide to talk to the police or exchange information for a cup of sugar, or real coffee, or money.

He got out of bed and got ready for his day; he mentally rearranged his commitments to make time to see Paolo; he decided he would go to the hospital pretending to be his cousin. A few years ago, when Paolo and Roberto gathered they were members of the same clandestine group, they had devised that system to tell the other one that they needed to talk in private as soon as possible. The other thing he had to do was to find a way to tell Enrico and check with him if Gabriele and Rachele could take Fiamma.

Stra

Emma was used to various women from the estate visiting the workshop when she was there, so it did not surprise her when she heard knocking. She was surprised when she opened the door to find Countess Contarini, who had a message from Enrico. Emma closed the workshop and followed her. They walked into the sitting room, and the Countess told her that Enrico would be with her once he finished a phone call; in the meantime, she had organized mint tea. She left and came back with a hot teapot and three cups. Emma wondered whether the Countess would join Enrico to have tea with her or who could be the third person invited to this unexpected meeting. Enrico appeared, excused himself, told Emma that they should wait ten minutes for her mother. Countess Contarini left the room saying that she might organise a fresh pot of tea

149

because it might get cold by the time Rachele arrived from Stra

Emma wondered why her mother had to be there and what prompted Enrico to ask her mother to come. She also noticed that the Countess was beyond her usual polite and hospitable self and acted in a very considerate way, as if she were ready to hug her at any moment. She was not paying any attention to Enrico's small talk; the doorbell startled her; she hoped it was her mother and that everything would be revealed.

Neither Enrico nor the Countess moved; she noticed that her father and the Count followed Rachele into the room. Now she was really worried. The Countess was sitting between her and her mother, and the Count and Gabriele sat on the other sofa. Enrico cleared his voice and started talking.

"The reason we asked you here is that I have something to tell you, and I thought it would be easier to tell all of you together. Emma, you are here as a representative of your siblings. The three of you will decide with whom to share what I am about to say."

The Countess held Emma and Rachele's hands

"As Emma and Rachele know, I am in touch with Roberto, and my parents are in touch with Paolo and Sofia Mondani because Arrigo and my brother married two sisters. So, this morning I found out through the grapevine that the SS rounded up Jews in Venice. They took Samuele Mendes, Fiamma escaped arrest thanks to a lucky chance, and sought refuge at Paolo and Sofia. She arrived there yesterday in a very distressed state."

Rachele was the first one to recover

"How is she?"

"Roberto has not seen her yet; all we know is that Anita saw her yesterday and brought her clothes and other things she managed to retrieve from their home. I am not sure how. At the moment, we do not know where they took Samuele. A colleague is trying to find out more."

The Count continued

"We were thinking of asking Paolo and Sofia to come and spend a few days in the country with us and bring Paolo's aunt with them. As Gabriele knows, Paolo does not have an aunt in Venice; most of his extended family is in Bologna."

Emma added,

"And I have heard uncle Paolo called my grandmother aunt Fiamma several times."

Enrico continued

"We do not know when it will happen. We are not even sure that this is how Mrs. Fiamma Mendes will arrive here, but she will, and she will be safe. Meanwhile, we are also trying to find out what happened to Samuele Mendes."

Gabriele looked utterly deflated. He kept mumbling that all his children had told him to leave, but his father was too stubborn. He also worried over his younger brother and hoped that Anita and Rachele's parents would take care of him.

After a while, Rachele stood up thanked everybody for their consideration, hospitality, and for letting them know. They had to go home and at least tell Anna and Diana and together decide what to tell Leo and Davide once they were back from school. The Count and the Countess insisted they would walk with them for part of the way. Gabriele accepted their offer, and the five of them left the room.

Venice

It was very convenient that Paolo was a cardiologist. He was the one that had signed the certificate stating that Roberto Cunin was exempt from military service because of a weak heart. So, they had agreed for the sake of noisy neighbours that Roberto was a patient who could not get an appointment at the hospital, but had to talk to Professor Paolo Mondani very urgently. When Paolo opened the door, Roberto kept saying how grateful he was that Professor Mondani had agreed to see him at home. Since he was supposed to have a heart condition, Paolo walked down to greet him and make sure he took his time on the stairs. In reality, Paolo did that because he had a vision of Roberto running up the stairs and wrecking the cover story they had agreed on earlier in the day.

When Roberto made it to the second-floor flat, he hugged Sofia, and when the door was closed loudly, Sofia disappeared and quickly reappeared with Fiamma, who started crying again when she saw her son. They stood in the middle of the hall, silently hugging each other for a while. Paolo and Sofia had withdrawn into the living room to give them some privacy. Roberto pulled himself together and walked into the living room with Fiamma. Sofia hugged her and sat down next to her. Roberto became very pragmatic.

"I do not know where dad is, but I know that somebody is trying to find out. He could be in any of the three locations where they have brought the Jews they arrested. Paolo and Sofia have agreed to keep you here until they will take you to Gabriele and Rachele. The owner of the place where they are staying suggested it. Although, I do not know when you will be able to go there."

Sofia was surprised that Roberto did not see fit to tell his mother where Gabriele and Rachele were.

Roberto stayed another half an hour; then Paolo reminded him that the 'consultation' with his doctor had already lasted over an hour, and he had to get to Campo San Giacomo dall'Orio before the curfew. He hugged his mother and Sofia, thanked them, and left. Paolo walked down with him to make sure that "his patient" did not overdo the steps. Once they were on the street, Paolo reassured him that Fiamma could stay as long as she needed.

12 December 1943

Venice

Fiamma hardly slept. She had got used to being in Paolo and Sofia's home; the bedroom she was using had been her refuge, a place where she could think of her husband and cry or smile. Samuele had always been on her mind in the few days since he was arrested. She kept thinking of fifty years of marriage. She was desperately hanging on to the thought that she might see him again, but she was afraid she would not.

It was the day Paolo and Sofia would take her to the country and ultimately to Gabriele and Rachele. Roberto had been quick to arrange her false identity; she was now Franca Monti, married to Sandro Conti, who had been reported missing after an air raid in Verona.

She was ready and packed when Sofia knocked at her door. They had some breakfast and left for the station.

Stra

Anna and Emma were in the kitchen preparing breakfast. When somebody knocked at the kitchen door, they were surprised to see Countess Contarini carrying a basket with eggs, flour, and milk instead of Giuseppe. Anna took the basked and invited her in; she apologized for the state of her family coming in for breakfast on a Sunday morning.

The Countess told her that as long as she could hold Mila, she would be blind to everybody's appearance.

Rachele appeared dressed for her morning walk, followed by Gabriele and their two very sleepy sons wearing dressing gowns. They had not expected to see the Countess sitting at the kitchen table playing with Mila. Gabriele immediately checked that Leo and Davide were presentable; Rachele greeted their guest a bit loudly to warn Diana that they had company.

Countess Contarini apologised for the morning intrusion; she had come to invite them to lunch; they had guests that would be delighted to see them as well. When Rachele was reassured that it meant all eight of them, they accepted. The Countess played a bit longer with Mila, then left.

Journey from Venice to Stra.

Paolo was used to addressing Fiamma as "Aunt," calling her Aunt Franca required practice. In the end, he decided that just calling her aunt was the best way to avoid tripping on a first name. Sofia was more concerned with Fiamma's state of mind. On the way to the vaporetto and when they arrived at the station, Fiamma looked very deflated, following them like a puppy but not being in the moment. Once they were sitting in their compartment, Fiamma mentioned she had read about trains being attacked by fighter planes; she told them she would stay on the train and tempt fate if it happened to them this morning. That statement concerned Sofia even more. She started talking about Count and Countess Contarini. They had a large estate; they would eat very well today. Their hosts had insisted they stay for lunch before going to Gabriele and Rachele.

The Count and a farmer met them at the station. Fiamma remarked they used to travel by horse and cart when she was a child; she remembered it from their visits to her uncle in Padua. Paolo noticed Fiamma had come alive talking about her childhood memories. He hoped that time with some of her grandchildren would help her come to terms with her husband's arrest.

Stra

Rachele and Anna had baked biscuits and a cake. They hoped that the Contarinis' cook would not get offended, but they felt they had to contribute to lunch since the Countess had invited all eight of them. Gabriele had already warned Leo and Davide to behave, or else. Emma, Anna, and Diana were wearing their best winter clothes, and they wrapped Mila in a blanket.

They arrived just when the other guests were in their rooms to recover from the trip, so they were led to the less formal sitting room. The room still had some toys left by the Contarinis' grandchildren when they fled to Switzerland. Leo and Davide were taking advantage of the toys, and Diana was busy entertaining Mila when the door opened. The Countess welcomed them and told them that Paolo Mondani had brought his aunt Franca with him. She stepped aside, and Fiamma appeared. The children shouted "Grandma" and ran towards her; Gabriele was glued to the chair and could not move; Rachele stood up and helped her husband. Mila was surprised by the noise; she looked at her sister to decide whether to smile or cry.

It took five minutes and a few threats to calm the children. Emma and Anna took their younger siblings away from their grandmother; Leo and Davide went back to the toys. Diana and Anna sat on the sofa playing with Mila. Gabriele approached his mother, and they both started crying. Emma apologized to the Countess; her family had ignored their hostess. The Countess told her she did not expect anything else, and that Enrico wanted a quick word before lunch. For a moment, Emma and the Countess stood side by side, surveying people inside the room and in the hall. The Countess whispered "in the winter garden" to Emma, and she slipped out.

Rachele hugged her mother-in-law, excused herself, and left the room to join Paolo and Sofia in the hall. She hugged them both, thanking them for all they did. Paolo replied he was touched that Fiamma thought of them when she was in such distress; he thought of her as his honorary aunt most of his life. He was genuinely fond of her. They would have gladly hidden them both if only somebody had convinced Samuele.

Emma walked across the large hall to the veranda, the Contarini's winter garden. She found Enrico looking outside. Roberto had specifically asked him to discuss his grandfather with Emma. She would make the best decision about what to tell her family.

"It is unusual to see fog in December; I have always loved fog; It made me feel protected. Anyway, your grandfather is in the same school Roberto attended as a teenager. Samuele Mendes is with other men who are there without a family. The Catholic wife of somebody who shares a room with him reported he is not eating.

Enrico paused to study Emma's reaction to what he had told her until then, before telling her what Roberto has recommended.

"Your uncle suggested you do not to share this today. Your parents and your grandmothers should just enjoy the relief that he is safe, if not exactly in safe hands."

The idea that they knew her grandfather's whereabouts reassured Emma.

"I suspect uncle Roberto must be upset. He had begged Grandpa to leave Venice several times, and we did too before we left, so did uncle Emanuele and I know that Aunt Miriam begged my grandparents to go to Switzerland with them."

Emma went back to the playroom. Anna was the only one who noticed that she had gone and come back.

Chapter Eleven

January - February 1944

14 January 1944

Stra

Gabriele and Rachele were still keen to make Friday night special. Friday nights and their morning and evening walk were the only things their current life had in common with their life in Venice. Fiamma, Rachele, and Anna started planning Friday night dinners on Wednesdays, figuring out a menu based on what they could find in the shops and saving flour and eggs to bake a cake. Since they had fled Venice for the countryside, the food situation had improved, but it still required careful planning. Rachele only worked three days a week, so on Friday mornings, she was helping Fiamma and Anna in the kitchen. Gabriele was at the main house; he had moved from 'helping Count Contarini with admin' to 'doing the admin for Count Contarini.' Emma was at her workshop near the farmers' homes.

When they heard somebody knocking at the front door, Fiamma ran to her room; Anna and Rachele looked at each other. Anna unlocked the back door and stayed in the kitchen; Diana wrapped Mila in a blanket and left from the backdoor walking towards Villa Contarini. Rachele opened the door and found a black shirt and two German officers.

One of the German officers told the black shirt to translate that they were looking for Captain Rodolfo Contarini and his family; Rachele answered in German.

"They are not here; we rented this house when we escaped the air raids in Verona. I am Rina Conti, and I live here with my husband, children, and mother-in-law. My husband, Giuseppe Conti, works for Count Contarini as a bookkeeper, and I work for Avvocato Guido Orlando in Stra, three days a week."

"Your German is perfect."

"I was born in Trieste; my parents met in Vienna. My mother was the daughter of a Turkish diplomat, and we spoke German at home. I was born an Austrian. Do you want to see my papers?"

"It is unnecessary; I will leave you to your cooking. Heil Hitler!"

"Goodbye."

Rachele watched the two Germans and the black shirt go back in the car. She smiled at the German officer and waited to close the door until the car had reached the main road. Once she closed the door, leaned on it, breathed a sigh of relief, then went back to the kitchen where she found Anna; she smiled at her and sent her to fetch Fiamma. As she waited for her heart to stop beating so fast, she realized that speaking German without an accent had made all the difference. The German officer thought she was one of them. Therefore, he did not want to see the papers. She was also too young to be the Countess and too old to be Captain Contarini's wife.

Anna, Fiamma, and Rachele had gone back to preparing Friday night dinner when they were surprised by Enrico and Giuseppe knocking at the back door.

"Is everything all right?" asked Enrico. "When Diana and Mila appeared at the house, my mother sort of took over and sent us here to see what was going on. She also told my father to keep Gabriele where he was at all costs. They will be released from their temporary captivity once we go back and report. We heard the car leave, and we were not sure what we would find. "

Anna was covered in flour; she pointed to her mother, saying she had answered the door. So it was up to Rachele to comment.

"They came looking for your brother and his family; I ignored the Black Shirt man and answered in German. I told them our cover story. When the German officer asked me why I was fluent in German, I told him part of the truth. I was born in Trieste; my mother was the daughter of a Turkish diplomat, and my parents met in Vienna and added that I was born Austrian. All of which is true. I omitted what was not in my interest to say."

Enrico smiled; he was beginning to get the measure of this unusual upper-class lady.

"Well, done. Interesting that they came here looking for my brother; they did not come to the house. I can go back and tell my mother to release your family from captivity. Words have probably reached Emma as well. Giuseppe's wife was under strict orders to keep her at the workshop or take her

160

to the main house if she insisted. Maybe we should start keeping the gate closed and have somebody move into the gatehouse."

Later that evening, the family was less relaxed than usual. Rachele gave Emma her Sabbath blessing[1]-before dinner. She sent her to sit in the dark by the window in the sitting room to check that no unexpected visitor arrived while Fiamma was lighting the candles and saying the blessing and Gabriele was making kiddush, the toast that welcomes the Sabbath.[2] They did not want any more surprises for the day. Gabriele also announced that Rachele would deal with the Germans as much as possible from that moment on. Her sounding just like one of them might save the day again.

The Contarinis were not celebrating Sabbath, but the conversation at dinner was all about the Germans coming to look for their eldest son, Rodolfo, and his family. Unbeknownst to his parents, Enrico had already organized a message to reach Rodolfo's sister-in-law Carolina, whom he knew was visiting her uncle in Bologna. She would know how to send a message to her sister in Switzerland, who could warn her husband that they had come looking for him. Enrico's mother could not understand why he was not worried until her husband mentioned that 'knowledge can bring peace of mind' and left it at that.

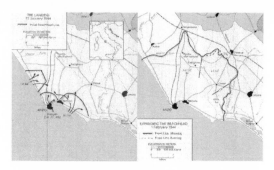

Figure 7 - Landing at Anzio and consolidating the
beachhead (images courtesy of US Army Center
of Military History)

21 February 1944

Stra

Emma was spending more and more time as a courier,
moving people from one place to another. Today she was
supposed to go to Venice to deliver papers to Mrs. Toffolo,
where she would also meet one of her "parcels" who would
be delivered to the dentist in Rovigo; by now, they had
become friends. She had to pick up somebody from somewhere near Ferrara and bring him (or her) to Venice for the
first time. A full schedule. Since her grandmother joined
them, she had started transforming herself into Elena
Giadrossi at the workshop with the help of Diana. She felt
it was a safe place to do it. Given everything else that was
going on in the building where her workshop was, she was
sure that those living in the two houses nearby had developed selective blindness.

Venice

Anita and Esther were getting Emma's room ready. Anita
had still not become used to Rachele's mother, Baroness

Modiano, insisting on helping her every day. They heard the doorbell from the backdoor, they both went to open it, they were expecting Emma's arrival. She walked in, hugged and kissed Anita and her grandmother, followed them to her bedroom, dumped her suitcase, apologized for her haste, and promised to spend time with them later; she had to go to Mrs. Toffolo and back before the curfew.

A couple of years earlier, she would never have expected that Mrs Toffolo would turn out to be a distribution hub for false papers. She was also not aware that her mother had written the text for half of the exemption notice she was carrying. Her honorary uncle Paolo Mondani had written the other half. Mrs. Toffolo was also crucial for her cover story if anybody asked why she travelled to Venice once or twice a week. Emma was carrying a bag full of half-finished clothes and at least one parachute, which would probably be turned into silk shirts.

She left Mrs Toffolo with work for her and Diana; the notes accompanying the work were also a way to conceal information that would be used to prepare false medical certificates, exemption notes, and other false documents.

Once she reached home, she prepared different notes for her sister, prepared the requests for false documents using a different coding system, and burnt the original list she received from Mrs Toffolo. She then joined the others for whatever was available for dinner, knowing full well that it would not be as plentiful as she was used to thanks to the produce of the Contarini estate.

22 February 1944

Venice

Emma woke up in her old bedroom. Before racial laws, before the war, she was just a Venetian teenager like any other. She forced herself to think of the here and now, going through her instructions for the day. Where her collection point was, where she would see the sign that meant she should stay away and the signal that the collection had to be cancelled. She looked forward to seeing the dentist in Rovigo and his wife; they had grown to like each other. She knew they would pamper Elena Giadrossi that night.

She got dressed and went to the kitchen to see who was awake and if there was anything available for breakfast. She knew that the previous day's food shopping had not been very successful and therefore there would not be much this morning. In Stra, they were very fortunate to have eggs, milk, and flour delivered to them every morning with a smile. She gave her baby sister credit for that. There were not many children in the Contarini estate, and Mila had been the centre of attention of many a farmer's wife or mother.

Emma joined Anita and her grandparents for a hot cup of mint tea; Anita was growing mint in vases in the kitchen to make sure they had something decent to drink in the morning.

Emma was in a good mood after her hot drink. She hugged everybody, kissed on the cheek her sleepy uncle Roberto, who had just appeared in the kitchen, and left. When she got to the Lido, her 'parcel' that day was a couple; when the couple appeared, she was surprised to see it was one of her older Trieste cousins and his wife. They reacted very well to be introduced to 'Elena' and, much to Emma's relief, they did not indicate that they knew her very well. They simply said that they were running away from Trieste and had travelled south to be closer to the front line and possibly cross it with the help of local people. Emma suspected that there was more to the story, but she knew she had to take whatever she was told at face value and not ask questions. She could not be tricked into revealing what she did not know, and the least she knew, the better.

They left the shop and walked together to the vaporetto stop that took them to the station; they sat away from other passengers. Their conversation was guarded and generic; they were making an effort to call her Elena rather than Emma, but they were very good at it so far. Unfortunately, Emma had completely forgotten what names they were using; she decided to avoid using any names until they were on the train, and then she would ask if they were alone in the compartment. So far, the only thing they had to do was follow her, and they were both familiar with Venice; Emma did not need to use names.

They were alone in the compartment, but the sound-proofing was non-existent. Emma knew she had to act before they reached Mestre[3] station, so she introduced herself as Elena Giadrossi; her cousin promptly took the hint and introduced himself as Renato Moducci and his wife, Cristina. Emma hoped that the papers they had with them had those names.

The journey to Rovigo was very smooth, and they had no problems going to the dentist's practice. His wife greeted Elena as if she were a long-lost daughter and everybody relaxed a bit. Emma explained to the dentist's wife that she knew her current 'parcel' before the war. They were left alone in the sitting room, and they could catch up a bit; Emma was only half surprised when her cousin told her he would make sure that Roberto could tell her whether they had successfully crossed the front line. They were waiting for the next handler, who was supposed to take them to Bologna. Before she arrived, the dentist's wife came to tell Emma that she had to disappear. Apparently, Emma already knew too many people in the organization, and they had rather not have her meet anybody else. Emma knew better than asking who "they" were, hugged her cousin and his wife, wished them good luck, and disappeared to go to the room where she was supposed to spend the night.

Figure 8 - Map highlighting the location of Stra, Rovigo, and Ferrara

23 February 1944

Rovigo

Emma was busy studying maps and train timetables. She had to go to a Benedictine abbey with a 'parcel,' check with an agent dressed as a monk, and collect another 'parcel' to take as far back as Verona and then go back to Venice. They had to change trains in Ferrara, and two bicycles were waiting for them at Codigoro station. She had to memorize the route to the Abbey. Her cover story was that she was a monk's sister and was going to (or had just come from) the abbey to introduce her fiancé to her brother. She used her concentration as an excuse with her hostess; whatever brew replaced coffee was disgusting, and she could not bear to drink it.

She heard the doorbell to the practice. She hoped it was her "parcel" rather than a patient. They had two trains to catch, and there were few trains to Codigoro. When the dentist's wife came to get her, she was ready to go. Her "parcel" was another Italian, not the usual downed allied airman or escaped prisoner of war.

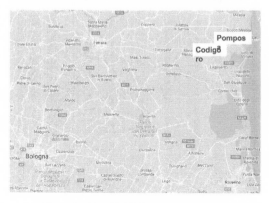

Figure 9 - Map highlighting the location of
Codigoro and Pomposa

Stra

Gabriele was always nervous when Emma was not around; he woke up even more nervous because Rachele told him she had to file documents at the higher court in Padua that day. What Rachele had not told him, or not yet, was that on the way back, she would have messages for Enrico and possibly some spare parts for a radio hidden in a parcel allegedly full of court documents.

Rachele had decided to bike to Padua; she had already surprised German soldiers who stopped her by speaking German and gave the version of her life story she used with the first German officer she had met. She was confident that her papers as Rina von Moden, married to Mr. Conti, would stand the scrutiny of a German officer. Her journey to Padua did not need a cover story. She genuinely had papers to deliver to the higher court. Before leaving the court, she looked for Pietro and told him she had to collect a parcel for Avvocato Enrico. The package was small enough to fit in her bike basket, so she started heading back to Stra. Along the way, a military vehicle with German officers passed her; ten minutes later, she caught up with the car that had stopped by the road. Two of the three officers were talking, and the third was nowhere to be seen. They stopped Rachele and asked for her papers in Italian. They noticed the German-sounding last name. Rachele could not figure out why they stopped her, but she kept calm. She overheard a comment the officer made in German, and she replied in kind; after all, she 'was' Rina Von Moden from Trieste, married to Giuseppe Conti. She gave the usual explanation as to why her German was perfect. The third officer returned and started reminiscing about his childhood summers in Muggia, near Trieste.

The officer offered Rachele a lift; she saw no reason to refuse. They loaded her bicycle (with the parcel) and drove her to the main square in Stra, where her office was.

Guido Orlando happened to look outside from his window and saw her arrive in a German army vehicle and his heart almost stopped. He saw a German officer give Rachele her bike back and noticed that the parcel was still in the basket. The same German officer clicked his heel and kissed Rachele's hand. He could not hear what they were talking about, but Rachele smiled waved at him as the car was driving away. When the car was out of his sight, he could still see Rachele talk to the person sitting by the bike rack. He sat down in the first chair he found and allowed himself to breathe again.

When Rachele entered the office, he was still sitting by the window.

"My heart missed more than one beat! What possessed you to get in the car with German soldiers, being who you are and considering what you are carrying?"

Rachele felt as if her nanny had reprimanded her. She was smiling when she answered.

"They stopped me and asked me for my papers. I think they were bored. They made a comment on the German last name they saw in my papers, and I answered back in German. I gave them my usual explanation why I have a southern accent when I speak German. Meanwhile, the senior officer had returned from relieving himself, started talking to me, and we moved to share memories of our summer holidays. When they offered me a lift, I thought it would have been very rude not to accept. I just hope that the valves hidden at the bottom of the package did not break."

Rachele's explanation did not reassure Guido Orlando; he did not change his tone of voice.

"The valves, the blank court papers, and everything else that was underneath the first ten pages of legitimate court documents! I think this calls for a glass from the precious bottle of brandy I have in the office. I have not yet recovered from seeing you in a German army vehicle!"

On the way from Rovigo to the Abbey of Pomposa

They had reached Ferrara in time to catch the train to Codigoro. They were asked for papers. Emma's 'parcel' told them he was an army doctor, and they were on their way to see his grandmother in Codigoro. He wanted to introduce his fiancée to her. Emma immediately saw the advantages of delivering an Italian 'parcel'; he could do the talking!

When they arrived at Codigoro station, they had to go to a café where they found two bikes that Emma would return the following day. The café owner gave Emma a map with directions. They drank some water, had something to eat, then started towards the Abbey.

Since they moved to Stra, Emma had become used to riding a bicycle and walking, so a seven and a half kilometres bike ride was not worrying her. Her travelling companion was less fit than she was, and they stopped several times along the road, especially where they could sit. Whenever they met people, they stuck with the story of the fiancée meeting family members for the first time, only this time it was "my brother, the Benedictine friar." They finally arrived within sight of the abbey. Emma had become annoyed by the 'freewheeling' cover her 'parcel' was using; she was very meticulous in sticking to the agreed story all the time. She pointed out that he may be used to these things, but he was the 'parcel,' and she was the courier. She had instructions on what to say and do once they were at the abbey.

Emma pulled the chord to ring the bell. When the door opened, she told the friar who opened it they were there to meet Friar Francesco, who was expecting them today, and whether they please bring the bikes inside. The door opened to a cloister; they were told to leave the bikes by the entrance and wait for Friar Francesco. Emma's "parcel" pointed out that now that they had arrived, he also had his instructions; he also explained to Emma that Friar Francesco was British special forces fluent in Italian. When Friar Francesco appeared, the 'parcel' looked around and spoke English.

"Good afternoon, I am …."

Friar Francesco replied in Italian.

"I know who you are; the fewer names, the better. Your pickup will arrive tonight."

He then turned to Emma.

"I hope somebody told you that your next 'parcel' arrives here during the night. There is a room for you where relatives usually stay; if you wait here, I shall come back to show you where it is." he then turned to the man - "you will use my bed in my cell. You'd better try to catch some sleep now; you need to be very alert tonight."

Emma thought that Friar Francesco looked familiar. She wondered where she saw him. Her problem was that it would be challenging to compare somebody who looked like a Benedictine monk to anybody she had seen before. Yet there was something in his voice, but she had just been told he was English. And yet…

When he came back to take her to her room, she remembered. He met him at the wedding of Arrigo Mondani; he was somehow related to Carolina, his wife. She did not quite remember the connection, but she was sure he was Jewish because the family sat at their table, separated from the others and with their menu. She would not have thought that the young man she met six years earlier was English. She remembered her sisters noticing him as well. Maybe this friar reminded her of him. Perhaps it was not him. She realized that whoever he was talking to her.

"I am sorry. I did not pay any attention to what you were saying; I was in my world. I apologise."

"Not a problem; I said that a fireplace warms the room. I'll help you start the fire, but you should not keep the fire going when you sleep. One of the ladies from a nearby village will hopefully come and start the fire before you wake up. Don't be alarmed if you hear somebody walk into your room first thing in the morning. They have the keys. You should be able to leave in time to catch the 1100 train from Codigoro, connecting with a train for Verona. However, if there are any problems tonight and things get delayed, you may have to spend another night here. I hope somebody warned you of that."

"Yes, they did." Emma thought that the more he spoke, the more he reminded her of Roberto Sonnino; however, she was reluctant to ask a direct question.

"We'll feed you; we are quite lucky with food here. Technically, you should be eating alone, but I will come and sit with you for a bit since I am not a real friar. A colleague of mine will prepare your last 'parcel' to be passed on to somebody else tonight."

"You speak Italian very well, to be British."

"I am not British; this is a long story, probably for another time if you come back here. Ideally, for the time when this complete nonsense is over."

Something clicked on Emma; she stopped him from trying to light the fire and whispered,

"Wait, I may be wrong, but you sound familiar. Five years ago, when Arrigo and Carolina got married. You are connected to Carolina Rinaldi; you are Roberto...."

"...Sonnino, yes. The long story is why they know me here as Rupert Henson-Brown, and I am wearing a Royal Air Force uniform under the habit most of the time. How do you know me?"

"Your family and my family were sharing one of the 'kosher' tables at Arrigo and Carolina's wedding. I remember your name because my youngest uncle is also called Roberto."

"I remember now. You looked a bit different."

"Maybe that is what a blonde wig and padding on my hips are supposed to do."

Roberto laughed

"Wait a minute; you are one of three sisters. Your family name sounds Spanish; I remembered two young girls and two children. Are you Emma or Anna?"

"I am Emma, Anna is my immediate younger sister, and the one you did not mention is Diana, who thought you were extremely handsome. We need to go back to being

Elena Giadrossi and Friar Francesco. That's what we are supposed to do, but I am definitely asking my boss to come here more often. It is nice to talk without pretending."

"Likewise, it is nice to be with someone for whom I am Roberto again; I am getting pretty fed up with Rupert."

Meanwhile, the fire was lit. Dinner was at seven in the dining hall, three doors down.

24 February 1944

Pomposa Abbey

Emma was beginning to like the countryside. She missed her room in Venice, not overlooking a canal and therefore very silent in the morning. Waking up to a different sort of silence, she was surprised to find the fire burning. She was grateful for the warmth in her room and wondered who had come and lit it without waking her up. She turned into Elena Giadrossi, with blonde wigs and padded hips, and went to the dining area, not expecting breakfast but hoping to see Roberto again. She liked the brief exchange they had the previous evening as he was helping her with the fireplace and the conversation they had later at dinner. It was the most relaxed she had been in a long time.

A friar came in with warm milk and white bread made by the monks. Later, Friar Francesco and the new 'parcel' appeared and sat down on the other side of the table.

"Good morning. Did you sleep well?"

"Yes, and I woke up even better when I noticed that somebody had come and lit the fire without waking me up."

"Well, that was a way to put my training to good use. You did not lock the door; when I came to wake you up, you were sound asleep. I let you sleep an hour longer; by the time I came back to wake you up, you were already having breakfast. So I went and woke up Paolo here, and we came to join you."

Paolo smiled and greeted her, speaking Italian with a German accent. Emma was not expecting that accent. Paolo explained he grew up in Zurich and studied Italian there. Unfortunately, he learned it from a German-speaking teacher and therefore gained a German accent that never went away.

They had to be in Codigoro early enough to return the bicycles and take the 11 am train to Ferrara. The friars had organized some food for the journey. In Ferrara, they had to take a train to Padua and change. This differed from previous instructions, but a bridge on the other railway line had been taken down by an air raid three days earlier.

Until Padua, their cover story was that Paolo was a pilot who had a bad landing and had just recovered from a wound in the neck and had problems speaking. On the train to Verona, Paolo was supposed to ignore her and be a German doctor.

Emma realized that she liked Roberto because she was almost paying more attention to the sound of his voice than to the instructions. Luckily, she always could follow her train of thought and hear what somebody was telling her, a skill that often got her out of trouble whenever she was caught daydreaming in school.

25 February 1944

Venice

The journey to Verona had been uneventful. Emma was not comfortable spending the night in the home of people she had never met. This time she had no choice, since she couldn't hope to return to Venice or Stra before the curfew. Her hosts had tried to do their best to feed her with the limited provisions they had managed to find. In the morning, they gave her messages to take back to Venice. Her hosts had no idea she knew whom they were talking about, and Emma did not volunteer the information.

Now she was back in Venice. Before starting on what turned out to be her most extended set of deliveries yet, she had decided that she would spend some time in Venice to be with her grandparents and Anita. She had to be careful, though, not to be seen on the terrace or in the rooms facing San Giacomo dall'Orio without her wig, just in case a neighbour saw her. She delivered her messages to Anita and went to see Mrs Toffolo for the bundle of work that was her cover story to travel between Venice and Stra.

Esther (or Elsa, as she insisted on being called) was a very strong woman with a very sweet side to her personality. She did not know what her granddaughter was up to and had too much sense to ask. Emma enjoyed her company. They talked about Stra, her siblings, and her parents. She also asked how Fiamma was doing; she was aware that nobody knew whether her husband was dead or alive. Davide joined them after a while until Anita came to tell them it was time for dinner; she and Ginevra had found great fish in the market this morning. They did not buy it with ration cards, but it was worth it.

Emma helped Anita clear up. She mentioned she met somebody familiar, a young Jewish man who was also a guest at Arrigo Mondani's wedding a while ago. She might have mentioned him a lot because Anita asked,

"Did he make such an impact on you at the wedding or when you met him in the past few days?"

Emma thought about it and smiled.

"I shall let you know when I see him again."

Chapter Twelve

March-April 1944

13 March 1944

Venice

Emma's underground activities gave her a chance to wake up in her bedroom from time to time. This morning, she enjoyed the familiar noises of her home, so different from the house in the Contarini estate where they were staying now. Today she was very happy; she had another of her preferred trips. Deliver a parcel to Rovigo, pick up another one to take to the Abbey of Pomposa, and then come back with whatever orders she received there. Had she been able to share more with her sisters, they would undoubtedly be teasing her. She could hear Anna asking her if she fancied her 'friar' and Diana chastising their sister and smiling at her. All of this would have happened if they had been still in Venice, living openly and with no war. They were not still in Venice, they did not live openly, and there was a war. Time to get up and get on with the task at hand. Emma reluctantly got out of bed.

This morning, her pickup point was near the station; it was a doctor's practice. She knew what to do, what the receptionist was supposed to say. Her nerves were her friends, keeping her alert. She was confident that she could figure out if somebody followed her and lose that person in the narrow alleyways and doorways between San Giacomo dall'Orio and the Ponte Degli Scalzi. The doctor's practice was close to the railway station on the other side of that bridge.

Luckily, everything worked out all right. Emma was now on the train with another downed airman with a bandaged head and his jaws (not so tightly) bandaged. The bandages were the apparent reason he would not speak. The pleasant surprise was that she was supposed to take him directly to the Abbey.

Stra

Gabriele had counted the cash they kept in the suitcase under the bed before picking up Leo and Davide from school. After lunch, they gathered around the large table in the dining room; he was working at the family books, Leo and Davide were doing their homework, Diana was working. Mila was sitting on the floor, playing with cubes Countess Contarini had given her for her birthday. Anna was in the kitchen working at her first commission as a baker, the cake for the Contarinis' wedding anniversary.

Gabriele reconciled the cash he had counted earlier in the day with what was in the book and started forecasting their financial future. He was quite pleased with what he saw. Before they left Venice, he had carefully planned their finances, withdrawing cash from their bank accounts before their assets were confiscated. He gave Anita money to cover two years of her salary and cover Maria's wages for the same period. They almost had two years before either he or Rachele had to earn any money. They had also been fortunate that Count Contarini paid Gabriele for his work on the estate more than enough to cover rent.

Gabriele felt he could relax about the family's financial future, at least in the medium term. He and the Count regularly listened to the BBC from the privacy, and the soundproofing, of the Count's study. Abruptly, Diana interrupted his train of thoughts. She had a clear view of the road from where she was sitting, and she had seen her mother in a car with German soldiers. As per instructions, she grabbed Mila's and ran for the Contarini's villa. Leo and Davide followed her.

Anna continued baking; Gabriele was alarmed but closed the book, put it away safely and go near the front door, ready to tell Anna to run. Once, he heard the car on the gravel. She saw one German officer picking up Rachele's bike from the back of the car and talking to Rachele, smiling. He waited rather than open the door; Rachele looked too unfazed to be alarmed. He saw the German officer click on his heel and kiss his wife's hand and then go back in the car. Rachele opened the door and warmly waved goodbye to the German officer. Gabriele kissed her on the cheek, waited until the car left the driveway, and closed the door.

"Since when did you become friendly with a German officer? You gave all of us a heart attack."

Rachele smiled as she took off her jacket.

"I am not exactly friendly with a German officer. He was one of three people who stopped me some time ago. One of them made a comment in German I was not supposed to understand, except I did. I replied to them in German, and the conversation started; after all, my identity card says

'Rina von Moden' married to Mr. Conti. So I told them I am from Trieste, my parents met in Vienna, and my mother was the daughter of an Ottoman diplomat, and I was born an Austrian."

Gabriele smiled; he had reasons to be proud of his wife once again.

"All true, except you omitted other details such as you are Jewish and two of your brothers ran away to fight for Italy during World War I."

Rachele smiled back.

"Of course, I did. Anyway, they offered me a lift back to work. It shocked Guido Orlando when he saw me arrive in a German Army car. The content of the parcel I was carrying in the basket of the bike was enough to get me arrested and shot. It turned out that the German officer is the son of an officer of the old Imperial Army and grew up in Trieste. So we started reminiscing about summers in Trieste. I was obviously cautious not to mention where my home was or other things that could identify my family. Today, he saw me coming home and decided to give me a lift. I could hardly say no."

"Well, you gave all of us a heart attack. Diana ran to the main house with the children, and Anna stoically continued working on her first paid commission as a baker. I think it will not be long before somebody discretely comes here from the main house to check if we are still here."

Gabriele had hardly finished speaking when Anna appeared from the kitchen with the Count and a farmer who saw how they were.

Gabriele smiled, looked at his wife, and told her to explain what had happened. Later he walked back to the big house to retrieve the younger children and apologise for causing alarm.

Abbey of Pomposa

Emma and her parcel arrived at the abbey with no significant issue. The bandaged head was convincing enough that nobody queried her when she told them that her fiancé, a pilot, was going back to his parents to recover from severe burns. Emma was happy to be back at the abbey, nothing to do with the building or the cloister's atmosphere, however pleasant. A lot to do with the pretend Benedictine friar, who was part of the British special forces, but, in reality, was a Jewish young man from Bologna. She was more than aware she felt very warm inside when Friar Francesco smiled at her. She was grateful for the short days that prevented her from reaching any safe destination before the curfew, and just had to spend the night.

As usual, Roberto lit the fire in her room and told her she would meet her for dinner in the guest refectory. Emma admitted to herself that somehow she was sort of feeling better when he was around.

Emma felt very relaxed at dinner. The conversation flowed freely, and they did not just discuss the war or what they were doing; at the end, they walked around the empty cloisters. The friars had all retired to their rooms, and nobody was around. It was a nice evening of late winter with some early signs of spring. They walked in silence for the first half of the cloisters, then he invited Emma to sit on the low wall by one of the pillars.

"I know this is highly irregular. Even if we have recognised each other from our previous lives, I should call you Elena, and you should call me Friar Francesco, but... as long as we remember to do it in public, we shall be fine. I love talking to you in such a relaxed way, and do not have to be careful when I am with you. I love it."

"I know exactly what you mean. I love not being Emma Conti or Elena Giadrossi for a few moments."

"Once this is over, we shall spend a whole day as Emma and Roberto. How easy it will be to find you in Venice?"

"Well, it seems we are sort of connected already. You told me you were at Arrigo's wedding because you were almost family with Carolina. So you could ask Carolina to find out where I live from Uncle Paolo, or you could ask her sister, Angelica. We are staying in the home her in-laws built for her and her husband. Angelica and the children had to flee to Switzerland because of some involvement of her husband with the kingdom of Italy in the south."

"You gave me too much information; you are lucky that the British trained me to keep quiet under interrogation."

"Well, you have to find me. How else will we spend a whole day being just Roberto and Emma?"

"Indeed, it almost sounds like you really wanted to be found."

"Of course, I do. I enjoy talking to you."

"It may not be the last time you come here. Both the parcel you took here last time and the one you picked up for delivery to Verona spoke very highly of you. I think you will be asked to pick up more parcels from here. You are one of the best couriers of this "parcel delivery service." They all praised how you keep absolutely cool in tense situations and how you never stray from the cover story. "

"Happy to be of service and happy to come here again, but if you can find me after the war, I can find you. I'll hold you to that day just being Roberto and Emma."

"Great. Now, I have to let you go to bed. I have a different sort of delivery to collect in the middle of the night. I hope to see you tomorrow morning. By the way, no parcel for you tomorrow morning. You can go back to Venice. Your cover story stays the same."

"Well, good night 'Roberto/Rupert/Friar Francesco."

"Good night, Emma/Elena."

Emma stood up, kissed him on the cheek, and felt she was waltzing back to her room.

Roberto had something urgent to do, but he had a huge grin on his face as he was getting ready to meet a British submarine off the Adriatic coast in the middle of the night.

2 April 1944

Stra

The family had gathered for breakfast in the dining room. It was the day the kitchen was dedicated to making unleavened bread for Passover. The previous days, when the kitchen was thoroughly cleaned, were familiar and vital for the family. They represented some sort of normality and a sign that the family kept its values even during these exceptional circumstances.

Emma, Anna, Rachele, and Fiamma were busy preparing matzot with Diana keeping time to make sure that the entire process would last 18 minutes. Leo kept going back and forth from the kitchen, hoping to lay his hands on any matzah[1][1] that had been rejected because it was not within the time limit. It was definitely not like any other year, but it was nearly enough to reassure Gabriele that they could still be a Jewish family, even in hiding. That was very important to him. He was also hoping that now that they were in the country and getting more ingredients, his wife, his mother, and his daughter could find a way to make some of the Passover biscuits he loved. Gabriele thought one could live in hope, especially during stressful times.

He could hear the women in the kitchen talking as Diana was shouting the passing of time when Enrico appeared in his dining room. The noises from the kitchen had covered any noise he had made coming in.

"I need to spend some time in your loft. Toni's wife came to tell us they have all been forced out of their home and are kept in the courtyard at gunpoint. Black shirts and Germans are looking for 'rebels' and specifically for my brother. My father thought they might see through my false exemption certificate and sent me here to hide in the loft. This house and the villa have a separate entrance from the rest of the estate, and they may not come here."

Gabriele told Leo to go with Enrico and then make sure that he neatly pulled back the curtain, hiding the door to the loft. When Leo returned, he told him to watch his younger siblings and told the women in the kitchen that they should stop what they were doing. They could continue another time; he did not know how long they had to get ready for an inspection. Fiamma wrapped the unleavened bread in clean and ironed tea towels and put it in a cupboard that had been scrubbed clean. Emma and Anna started cleaning the table, and Diana got ready to run with Mila and Davide; she even thought of a spot in the garden of the main villa where they could hide until they had finished searching the house.

They were almost ready when they heard the car at the front door. Luckily, it was the German officer who knew Rachele as Rina von Moden. Gabriele looked out from the dining-room window and saw him. The German soldiers and some black shirts were getting off their vehicles and ready to search the house. Gabriele just had time to call his wife to open the door with him; Rachele appeared wearing an apron and with flour all over her. She opened the door to find her "friend," the German officer.

He clicked his heels, kissed Rachele's hand, and gave Gabriele a 'Heil Hitler' salute. Diana saw the scene and had an idea. As the German officer explained to 'Gino and Rina' what they had to do and what had to happen, Diana came and told them that Mila was not feeling well and thought she would just be in bed with her. Rina made sure that the officer had understood.

They all gathered in the courtyard at gunpoint. In these circumstances, Rachele was the one to be relied on to keep her calm.

They had finished searching the ground floor; a soldier came to shout that it was all clear. The officer reminded them that a young woman and a sick baby were in one of the bedrooms. Emma thought that the entire scene looked ridiculous; they were all gathered in the middle of the driveway with machine guns pointed at them, and yet her mother was chatting amiably in German with three officers. She knew also that Enrico heard all the noise in the loft, and she did not know how he would react. Fiamma kept saying that, at worse, she would just join her husband, which invariably prompted Gabriele to silence her and remind her they did not know whether he was dead or alive. Emma and Anna were looking at each other, rolling their eyes, but were too worried to say anything.

Then it was over. They walked out shouting in German that everything was in order. The four soldiers that were aiming machine guns at the group lowered their weapons. The German officer kissed Rachele's hand and apologized for the inconvenience. He asked one of the soldiers coming out of the house if they had woken up the baby, and they reassured him they did not. Everybody got back on their vehicles and left.

Nobody moved for a few minutes; then, they started walking back to the house. Once they were in, with the door closed, Diana appeared, holding a smiling Mila who did not know what happened but had enjoyed being in the big bed with one of her sisters. Diana explained what happened in the bedroom:

"Mila did not like the dark, so she kept whining. When the black shirt and the soldier came in, I told them I thought she had measles and a high temperature and could they please not open the curtain; I was ready to pinch her if they started opening the curtain. They looked under the bed, in the wardrobe, and they knocked on the wall looking for openings, but they did not open the curtain."

Enrico appeared as Diana was explaining. He kissed her on the forehead and thanked her; he also kissed Mila on the forehead; she rewarded him with a big smile and a chuckle.

Enrico had just left to walk back to the main house when they heard noises coming from the open gate and then the sound of something sliding on the gravel. Gabriele and Rachele rushed out to find Guido Orlando, the lawyer who, technically, was Rachele's (or Rina's) boss. He was embarrassed. He had fallen off his bike due to his muscular issue on his left leg, a problem that exempted him from military service even during a war. He could not get up. Leo, who was watching from the living room window, thought he looked like a bird with a clipped wing. Rachele was aware of the problem and rushed to help him, asking Gabriele to help her help her boss.

Once they had managed to get him up and checked that nothing was damaged beyond his pride and trousers, they helped him inside. Once he was sitting down, Gabriele apologised, saying that the strongest thing they had to give him was mint tea, and he went to make it. Rachele was not sympathetic.

"Whatever possessed you to tale the turn into the garden so fast that you ended up falling on the gravel?"

Guido's voice was very apologetic.

"Well, somebody knocked at my door and told me they were raiding the Contarini estate, looking for rebels. I immediately thought of you and your family, and I wanted to warn you or check that you were all right, depending on my timing."

"Yes, they came, and we are all right. But we were also lucky."

"What do you mean by 'lucky'?"

Then Rachele told him that the same German officer that gave her a lift and almost gave Guido a heart attack was the commanding officer for the raid. Emma came in with the tea and told him her version of the event, having caught the end of her mother's tale. She did not mention why they did not want the loft searched, and Guido did not ask.

By then, Guido Orlando had recovered. He told Rachele that she had to go to Padua the following morning to collect court documents. Rachele knew that they did not have an active court case in Padua. The parcel she would collect had something else inside, but she appreciated plausible deniability. She simply asked if she had to collect them from their usual contact.

Gabriele came to invite him to lunch. They would share whatever they had. They were lucky enough to have a supply of fresh eggs, milk, and real flour every morning, and they also had vegetables from their garden. Anna was making a vegetable soup to calm down. If Guido Orlando stayed, they would also share something that usually came out when they needed to be cheered up, and they definitely all needed to be cheered up.

3 April 1944

Padua

Rachele had come relatively early; she wanted to beat the rush because she did not want to sit and wait long. She approached the desk of the court officer they knew and found a lady sitting there.

"I am looking for Leonardo Natali. My name is Rina von Moden and I work with Avvocato Orlando in Stra. This morning, Avvocato Orlando informed me I had to collect court papers."

"Do you know the details of the court case?"

Rachele smiled, trying to get the court officer on her side.

"Avvocato Orlando came to knock at my door fairly early, and I was more concerned with getting my children ready for school than with listening to him. The only thing that registered was that I had to come here to collect something. Leonardo usually has a parcel prepared with Avvocato Orlando's name on it."

The lady sitting at Leonardo Natali's desk excused herself, stood up, and went to a storeroom. Now, Rachele was anxious that something had happened to Leonardo and that source of blank official papers might have been busted. Luckily, the lady returned with a sealed parcel with "Avvocato Orlando" written on top.

"I have no idea what they are; Leonardo must have prepared them on Friday."

"Do you know why he is not here?"

"I am not sure, but I was told that I had to take his place for a while."

Rachele thanked her and left the building in as normal a way as she could. She was sure that somebody would stop her at some point; maybe they found out about Leonardo's extra-curricular activities and had him arrested. She went back to where she left her bicycle, tipped the attendant, put the parcel in the basket, and started on her way to Stra. She couldn't wait to begin her journey back to Stra.

Nobody stopped her along the way. When she turned into the square, she saw an unusual car parked near the front door of the building where Guido Orlando's office was. The owner of the café on the opposite side of the square gestured for her to go inside. She left the bike just outside the café, locked it, took the parcel, and went inside. He pointed out that whatever was happening inside that building, she was better off waiting until the car had left. They had been there longer than an hour.

Rachele sat at a table with her parcel and ordered whatever they used as a coffee surrogate. She waited a while and then saw three men get back in the car. Her boss was not one of them. The owner of the café was not convinced that it was entirely safe for her to go; he shouted at his wife to come and mind the store for a while. He and Rachele left and crossed the square; Rachele left the bike in the usual rack, tipped the attendant in advance, picked the parcel, and went up to the first floor, followed by her escort. They did not notice anything strange on the door, and when Guido Orlando came to open the door smiling, they both relaxed.

The owner of the café asked if Guido knew anything about the vehicle. He said that he had heard people run up the stairs, went to look outside from his window, and noticed the car. They had gone to the second floor, where one of the town doctors had his practice. The three of them looked at each other and went up one floor to inspect.

The doctor's receptionist was busy picking things up from the floor; one of the cabinets was overturned. The doctor came out of his study, saw the visitors, and shook his head.

"Thank you for checking. They found what they were looking for."

He then took Guido Orlando aside and added,

"I create a file for every fake exemption certificate I sign; I try to build a back story. This time it saved my life."

Guido and Rachele went back downstairs as they had something urgent to discuss. The café owner stayed and helped.

Once they were back in the office, Rachele told Guido what happened at the court in Padua. He told her she should discuss it with Enrico, but somebody would need to check before using the content of the parcel. Rachele suggested asking Umberto De Antoni to come and look at the package before they opened it. Guido left to fetch the police detective. When her boss returned with company, Rachele repeated what happened in Padua; Umberto was concerned.

"I am trained not to believe in coincidences. I wonder if there is a connection with the raid to the Doctor's practice upstairs. I haven't heard of Leonardo Natali being arrested. Either Enrico or I would have heard. Let's just assume it was not a coincidence. It is safer."

They opened the parcel and looked at each piece of paper inside. There was a copy of an old case on top and then many blank sheets of paper with the court letterhead. They looked at each of them and found nothing wrong. They put each of them against a window next to an old one, and again they saw nothing wrong. Umberto suggested they should wait until he spoke to Enrico. Guido suggested they did not use them until one forger had checked them. They were much more trained in spotting differences. Nothing would happen until Umberto or Rachele had spoken to Enrico and reported back to Guido. They put the package in the safe. Umberto went back to the police station, and Rachele went home.

Chapter Thirteen

April 1944

11 April 1944

Venice

It had been almost five months since Rachele's parents had moved in, and Anita was growing fond of them. She was getting used to being treated as their equal, especially by Esther. Baron Modiano spent a lot of time by himself in what used to be Gabriele and Rachele's study; his wife kept very active. She occasionally went out, although she was reluctant to leave the safety of home and fully participated in the life of the household.

Davide Modiano had become less of a recluse in the past few days. He had embraced the role of the Patriarch in the Passover celebrations or in the way they could celebrate Passover, given that they were not supposed to be Jewish.

Anita's musing on the members of the household stopped when Roberto walked into the kitchen, clearly not fully awake but fully dressed.

"Do you have any message for my brother or Rachele? I meet Paolo Mondani later this morning, and he could pass any message on to Sofia, who would call Countess Contarini. I have no idea what code they use, but, as you know, they manage to pass on messages with a surprising level of accuracy."

"None really; I would like to know how everybody is doing, but I think Emma, sorry, Elena Giadrossi, is due to appear soon, so I might just ask her."

"Do you have any idea why my niece is so eager to end up at the Abbey of Pomposa these days?"

Anita smiled

"None I would feel free to share. I think you can tell whoever is running that operation that they should not worry."

Stra

Emma was stunned when she walked into her workshop to find the pile of clothes on the floor. There were a lot of uniforms and three parachutes. She did not know how they got there, but she never did. They were not there the previous night, and they had to be hidden quickly before "the wrong people" saw them. She needed help and knew that those upstairs in the barn could not be seen in the courtyard during the day. She went to look for Silvia, Giuseppe's daughter. She could trust Silvia simply because her husband was hiding in the loft of another outbuilding in the estate. She had a similar vested interest in keeping quiet.

When Silvia saw the pile, she had the same reaction Emma had. Only she expressed it, wondering if there was anybody left wearing an Italian military uniform. There were at least forty full uniforms on the floor, representing a wide range of ranks in all three forces.

The two of them set out to fold all the uniforms, divide them by size, separate jackets from trousers. Then Emma took them into the warehouse behind her workshop and put them in the back end of very deep cupboards. Meanwhile, Silvia cut all the strings of the three parachutes, folded them in a pile that made them almost look like bedsheets. They had just finished putting the three parachutes away when a strange car appeared in the courtyard. Emma and Silvia looked at each other and immediately started acting as if they were discussing adjusting some clothes for Silvia's children.

A middle-aged gentleman got off the car and knocked at the door where the estate manager lived. Emma and Silvia looked at each other; Silvia said he was likely to be from the official food provision office to check that the estate was not cheating on the quantity of food staples sold through official channels. They kept working until the car left.

They were discussing how they could dye all that material when Enrico appeared. Silvia was not sure what was going on in the barn, but she knew enough to know that she was better off not knowing, so she left.

Emma discussed with Enrico what she found when she opened the workshop. Enrico had something to tell her, but he was reluctant to do so. Emma cut to the chase after too much small talk.

"Enrico, what is going on? What are you trying to find words to tell me?"

Enrico sat down where Silvia had been sitting when he arrived; he looked at his shoes for a while, then looked up with a serious face.

"Your honorary uncle, Paolo Mondani, has found out what happened to your grandfather putting no one at risk. He used his role as a doctor to ask questions in various places. We know that Samuele Mendes was taken to a transit camp. Unfortunately, by the time the German authorities that run the camp decided to allow Paolo to visit as his doctor, it was too late. He found out that Samuele had been transported to Germany when he arrived. We are not sure what it means, but some of our people in Verona related horrible stories about people on freight trains with only tiny windows open. They were not even using the wagons used to carry animals. I do not know what happens once they get there, but it can't be good. How old is your grandfather?"

"Grandpa Samuele is in his mid-seventies; I think he is 74. I am sure he'll be very passive. My grandmother tells me that the last words she and Maria heard from him the day he was arrested were all about how wrong he was and how he should have listened to his children. My grandmother saw him being taken away and described him as looking defeated and accepting his defeat. I need to find a way to tell my parents without my grandmother listening and probably let my father decide whether to tell Grandma Fiamma."

Emma stopped working and started crying. Enrico never knew what to do when a woman cried. The only thing he could say was that he had to go and that he would send his mother to see how Emma was doing. His mother was far better at dealing with tears than he was.

Venice

Only Venice could have a hospital with unique seventeenth centuries frescoes. Roberto Cunin was waiting to be seen by his cardiologist, Prof. Paolo Mondani. Paolo had been working at a clinical history for his honorary little brother since Roberto Mendes had joined a clandestine anti-Fascist political party. He knew he might need an excuse for his exemption from military service.[1] So now there was an entire file for Roberto Cunin, down to fake test results, dating back to 1938, when Roberto was 20. Paolo had also provided 'real/fake' certificates stating why he was exempt. The certificate had granted Roberto an official letter from the office of the Navy in Venice stating why he was exempt from military service. The only risk was if Roberto was ever caught running since according to Roberto Cunin's medical file running for more than ten minutes would cause his death.

Paolo's receptionist informed him it was his turn. When he walked into Paolo's office, he knew from his face that he did not have good news.

"Paolo, your secretary left a message with Anita saying that you had your test results and had to see me. It cannot be the tests I never took. What happened?"

Paolo told him what happened to Samuele Mendes. Roberto breathed a deep sigh and sat in silence for what felt a long time.

"I have to tell my mother."

"As far as I know, Enrico is supposed to tell Emma away from the rest of your family. She will be the judge of how your mother is told."

197

"Poor Emma, the war has catapulted her to adulthood earlier than expected. She is only 20, but she has been through a lot."

Paolo could not hide his pride.

"Well, if I can say something in praise of my honorary niece. I understand she is highly valued in the organisation."

Roberto eagerly joined the 'we are proud of Emma' club.

"They say she is one of our best couriers. She never loses her control, and she has behaved wonderfully during a few sticky situations."

Although it was not a competition, Paolo was not prepared to be outdone in the 'pride front.'

"Well, she's my niece. Daughter of my closest friend, my honorary brother. Your brother and Rachele are exceptional people that have exceptional children."

Roberto could not help but smile in agreement.

Paolo stood up, hugged him, invited him to dinner, and took him to the door like any other patient. To make everything more believable, he instructed the assistant to organize an appointment for tests the following month.

Abbey of Pomposa

Roberto Sonnino loved being on the top of the bell tower at sunset. When his predecessor started in the Abbey, he found a spot for the radio just under the top where the bells were. He had acquired the habit of being there 10 minutes before the time agreed for the Radio transmission to enjoy the view. He particularly loved being there during the sunset or sunrise, and always felt lucky when he managed that.

The other reason he was always climbing up to the top before using the radio was to check that there were no unusual vehicles around the abbey (an indication that somebody had intercepted the radio or suspected its presence). He did not want the Germans to intercept his communications. That evening he was informed of a "human delivery; " the next time a Royal Navy submarine appeared off the coast, he would have to pick up special force lieutenant Algernon Crawley. Roberto smiled; he knew he was none other than Rodolfo Contarini, one of the 'fabulous four' that left Switzerland around six months earlier, travelled to Gibraltar to be trained, and flown to the United Kingdom for further training. He had to make sure Emma would deliver him wherever he had to go. Rodolfo would love to hear how his family is doing. Roberto trusted her and was happy to have a reason to see her again.

18 April 1944

Venice

Emma had grown to love the opportunity to go to the Abbey. She loved the place and had also admitted to herself that she was growing fond of a certain young Jewish man who was a British Special Forces agent with an assumed name who was pretending to be a Benedictine friar. Somehow, someone had decided to accommodate her, and she was getting more and more trips to the Abbey. Her uncle told her it was because she was one of the best and had proven that she could be trusted. Her uncle was also smiling each time he said that. Emma still had not decided whether he was proud of his niece or had a chat with Anita and was aware of her interest in another Roberto.

She was on her way to collect the parcel she was supposed to take directly to the Abbey, from where he would continue south. She hoped she was given a different cover story this time; her last name was not typical of the abbey area. All her cover stories were based on meeting in-laws or introducing her fiancé to a family member who was a friar at the abbey. It was time to think of something new.

This time, Mrs Toffolo's workshop was her pickup place. It was unusual, but not a surprise; Emma did not like unusual. She knew the area very well, and was confident she would quickly figure out if there was anything odd, out of place, or otherwise, "not right."

She soon found out why the pickup was at Mrs Toffolo; she had to change into a voluntary nurse uniform. Her cover story was complicated. She was supposed to take a former naval officer, who had been badly burnt, to the abbey, where he would complete his recovery and later be taken south. Her 'delivery' appeared, and she could hardly see his eyes; his face was bandaged, leaving only eyes and mouth and part of the nose visible. One of Mrs Toffolo's assistants explained to him in French that Emma was his escort to the next staging post. Emma put the uniform on. Her dress was neatly folded and put into a larger overnight bag, and off they went.

Abbey of Pomposa

Rodolfo was beginning to feel claustrophobic. He had been there three days, waiting for a courier to take him to Verona. He did not understand why they could not let him go alone. Roberto kept telling him it was the protocol. They were given a British identity, so they would be British prisoners of war, not traitors if the worst happened. Travelling around Northern Italy accompanied by a local was part of their cover. The day had almost arrived, though, one more night, and he would leave the abbey, a beautiful place, but not why he had spent all this time away from his family.

As usual, Emma was on time. Personal feelings aside, Roberto loved the idea that she would ring the bell precisely an hour and fifteen minutes after the train arrived at Codigoro. He was surprised to see her parcel with such an extensive bandage. Emma saw his surprise and smiled and told him that 'her parcel' could not keep his mouth shut. 'The man with a bandaged face' had no clue what was said and made some noise. Roberto took them to the refectory; he spoke English to the man and told him to sit down. Emma left them alone to go to what she considered 'her room at the Abbey.' He started 'unwrapping the parcel.'

"Thanks, my jaws were beginning to hurt. Where is the young woman dressed as a nurse who took me here?"

"She has gone to freshen up in her room, I think."

"Great, I'd like to thank her. Do you know if she speaks English?"

Roberto did not like the tone of the voice of his new guest.

"It is part of our system that you have as little interaction with her as possible. She only knows the cover story. It is for your safety; she can't share what she does not know."

Meanwhile, Rodolfo had appeared in the refectory, in civilian clothes. Roberto asked him to take their guest to the men's guest bedroom on the other side of the cloisters and explain how meals worked.

With everybody gone, Roberto decided to see if Emma was all right. She had already changed out of her nurse uniform and was trying to light the fire. He jokingly bent to stop her.

"That's my job."

"I know, and it is not even that cold, but I like the atmosphere of this room with a fire."

He was pleased by the sense of familiarity In their interaction.

"I understand. Did you have a fireplace at home?"

"I think there was one in the living room when I was a child, but it was taken out at some point. I remember that by the time the older of my two brothers was born, about 12 years ago, it had already been taken out."

He lit the fire. They both sat on the bed, looking at the fire and enjoying being close to each other. After a while, he broke the silence.

"When all of this is over, we'll spend an evening by the fire somewhere. I promise."

Emma looked at him, smiled, mentioned something about promising, kissed him, and stood up to leave the room. Roberto sat for a few minutes, surprised by the kiss, then he stood up, walked towards her, kissed her, then they left the room holding hands.

When they entered the refectory, Rodolfo was there. He was not expecting to see them holding hands and could not help to ask Roberto if he had behaved in a respectful way, given he was wearing a friar's habit. Roberto laughed told him he thought so, but he had no idea how friars behaved.

They sat down; Roberto introduced Emma to Rodolfo; Rodolfo was surprised he used their real names. So he had to explain, setting aside all the cover stories. He sat where he could watch the door and started updating both Emma and Rodolfo.

"Rodolfo, since you insist… Elena Giadrossi, meet Algernon Crawley. He will travel tomorrow under the name of Sergio Carli; a name he will drop once he is in Verona. In reality, he is Rodolfo Contarini. When we realized we had met before, you told me you and your family were staying in a house in the Contarini estate."

"Wait a minute, what house? Is it a house with its own gate and drive…"

Emma continued

"… with a back door that leads to a wood and a path that leads to your parents' house. I think we are staying in your home, or at least we are staying where your wife and children used to live before they were whisked to Switzerland. By the way, I am aware your wife gave birth to a girl. Congratulations! A few weeks ago, we were held at gunpoint by the Germans and the Black Shirts because they were looking for you. Now I appreciate why."

Emma told him the tale of how her sister's Diana quick thinking had stopped them from finding the door to the loft where his brother was hiding. Enrico had managed to escape from their parents' home before they got to where he was hiding. Rodolfo laughed and added that his wife was responsible for the curtain covering the whole wall. She wanted to hide the door to the loft!

They were so relaxed that they had forgotten who they were and where they were. They stopped laughing when an elderly friar appeared and told them they were noisy, and should be more careful since, officially, they were all there under assumed identities.

Roberto felt duly reprimanded, thanked the friar carrying a tray with dinner, stood up, picked the tray, left three plates on the table, and left the room to take the fourth plate to the parcel that had arrived with Emma.

By the time he came back, Emma was telling Rodolfo about his parents, how his mother had fallen in love with her baby sister, and how generous they were towards them, allowing them to stay rent-free for Emma's father helping the Count with the administration. Rodolfo commented that given how bad his father was at administration, he was sure that Emma's father was 'doing' rather than 'helping.'

When Roberto sat back at the table, he had turned into Rupert. He became all professional, discussing their cover story and telling them where Emma had to take him and how they should remember to call each other Elena and Sergio.

Emma wished them good night. She did not want to spend the night in Verona, so tomorrow, they had to catch the 9 am train from Codigoro if she had any chance to be back in Venice before the curfew. She had checked the timetable when she was at the station earlier that day.

Rodolfo waited a reasonable time to make sure that Emma had gone to her room and could not accidentally or intentionally overhear their conversation.

"So, let me see if I got things right, Friar Francesco. You are developing an interest in a young Jewish woman whose father is Carolina's father-in-law's best friend and whose family is currently staying in my home under a false identity. She also happens to be one of the best couriers in whatever organization she is part of, so you can reasonably request that she is the one to 'deliver' and 'pickup' from here."

"I think that you have got it right so far."

"You are getting too close."

"Actually, not as close as I would love to."

Rodolfo felt he was Roberto's surrogate big brother. Roberto's parents and his sisters lived with Rodolfo's wife in a big house in Switzerland. They were part of the same team. They both had real/fabricated British identities.

"Leave the level of closeness you wish for after the war. You should concentrate on other things, and you should be careful not to use your real names around anybody else."

"You are not anybody else. Your wife is part of my family. You are like a big brother, or better, a big brother-in-law."

"You know what I mean. Now I need to go to bed; as Elena Giadrossi said, we leave early in the morning."

An elderly friar approached a figure barely illuminated by a tiny lamp.

"You know you should not eavesdrop, young lady."

"I know, but I had a feeling they would be talking about me."

The elderly friar smiled.

"At least, did you like what they said?"

"Oh, yes! I liked it very much, and I will sleep so much better. Could we keep this between us?"

"Only if you invite me to the wedding."

The elderly friar went back to the section of the abbey reserved for the friars. Emma went back to her room. Their presence had gone unnoticed by Roberto and Rodolfo.

19 April 1944

Abbey of Pomposa

Emma and Rodolfo had practiced calling each other Sergio and Elena during breakfast. This time, their cover story was that they were husband and wife; he was an air force pilot going back to his base after recovering at his parents' home. After they left, Friar Francesco received a visit from an elderly friar in his room.

"Roberto, I was surprised when I recognized you as my friend Mario's son, but I was even more surprised when I noticed you liked one courier so much that you kept asking for her. Well, let me reassure you of a couple of things. Number one, she is very good. Number two, she has also developed an interest in you. How do I know? I caught her eavesdropping on your man-to-man conversation last night. She was hiding in the right spot, not to be noticed by a casual passer-by, but close enough not to miss a word. By the way, I have already been invited to the wedding."

Having said what he wanted to say, Davide Soave (also known as Friar Giosuè) left the room smiling. Roberto sat there for a while with his mouth wide open.

On the way to Verona

Emma and Rodolfo were supposed to be married to have a relatively open conversation about family. When they were changing train in Ferrara, Emma had whispered to him they could talk about his family if they acted as if it were hers until Padua. From Padua to Verona, they would then talk about her family. They were travelling first class. They had a relatively empty compartment, and Emma kept her voice low because they could have been overheard if somebody wanted to eavesdrop on their conversation.

Emma was updating Rodolfo about his parents when the conductor opened the compartment door, asking for their ticket. Immediately behind her, a black shirt appeared and asked Rodolfo why he was in civilian clothes. Emma was about to answer when she remembered that, this time, her 'parcel' spoke perfect Italian with a local accent.

Rodolfo gave him the entire cover story. He had contracted an infection, and after a month in the hospital, he had been sent home for another month to recuperate. Unfortunately, he was advised to stay away from his children. His immune system was fragile, and he did not need to pick up anything from his young children, so he spent a month at his parents' home in Codigoro, where his father was one of the local doctors.

When the conductor and the black shirt had left, Emma took a quick trip to the restroom. She checked that the black shirt was asking questions to people sitting in the other compartments. He was looking for something, but it had nothing to do with them. When she returned to where Rodolfo was sitting, she told him what he had seen. Rodolfo's only comment was that he could see how she got the name of being one of the best in her organization. Emma thanked him. She also told him that if black shirts had been waiting for the train in Padua, they would have stayed on and continued to Venice. She knew that people in Verona would have been there the following day if they had not appeared during the agreed timeframe.

Venice

Emma did not see anybody suspicious waiting for them at the platform in Padua, so they had continued to Verona. After delivering Rodolfo, she rushed back to the station to catch the train that would have taken her back to Venice and then to her old home before the curfew.

Once she arrived home, she removed any trace of Elena Giadrossi (blonde wig, padded hips, and suitable clothes) and spent some time with her grandparents. She then joined her grandmother to help Anita in the kitchen.

When they were in the kitchen, Anita and Esther kept mentioning how cheerful and relaxed Emma looked. Once they had sorted the food, Anita sat at the very long kitchen table, pulling up two other chairs.

"Now, sit down and tell two poor old ladies what happened to you. Something nice has happened, and we need to hear nice things; you know it could damage our health if you keep us in the dark."

Emma smiled and sat down. Twenty years of dealing with Jewish parents had trained her to recognize the preamble to inquisitive questions.

"Anita, you have spent too long with Jewish mothers; you are sounding like one."

"Well, I keep saying that you and your siblings are like my children, so… stop any diversionary tactic and let us know what is going on. Your grandmother has class, and she is not asking directly, but she is as eager to know as I am. I am sure we are not past sending you to bed with no dinner if you don't co-operate."

Emma was amused, but she knew when to give up.

"I cannot remember the last time you threatened to send me to bed with no dinner. There is a young Jewish man that is interested in me, and I am interested in him. I cannot tell you anything more, but I am sure that you and my parents would approve if you knew whom I am talking about."

Esther Modiano looked at Anita, burst out laughing, and said,

"I told you. Now we need to tell everybody that dinner is ready." then she got up and left the kitchen.

Anita did not get up. She turned to Emma.

"Jewish?"

"Jewish!"

"Italian?"

"Italian!"

Emma could not stop laughing, got up, and followed her grandmother. Anita complained she had not finished, but in the end, she smiled, shook her head, and got up as well.

Chapter Fourteen

September–December 1944

Figure 10 The Gothic Line–southernmost line
represents the extent of the allied advance by 12
September 1944, the other line represents the
German defence "The Gothic line" - Courtesy of
ibiblio.org

11 September 1944

Stra

"Rachele's German officer" stopped by. He had written
about Rachele and her family to his wife. He was being

transferred back to Vienna, and wanted to photograph them. They all dutifully stepped out and stood by a well in the garden. Emma and Anna were not exactly enthusiastic. Nobody was. Fiamma kept saying to her son that she did not care if she died; she would join Samuele. Rachele was worried. Emma, Anna, and Diana were too busy watching out for another German car or, worse, a truck to smile. Leo did not want to be there. Davide insisted on being photographed with a goat he had rescued, and Mila was not happy with that man in uniform.

Nobody was laughing or smiling. The German Officer promised them he would be back in two days with a copy of the photograph.

Once they were back in the house, Emma rushed to the Contarini's villa, looking for Enrico. She bumped into Countess Contarini almost halfway and told her the story of the photograph. The countess was alarmed; her immediate reaction was to protect the children. She decided there and then to suggest to Gabriele and Rachele that Diana, Leo, Davide, and Mila would move to her home for a few days until the German had come back with the photo or with reinforcement. She did not know that Rachele's main concern was that somehow the friendly German officer could access Trieste city records and figure out that there was no Von Moden family in Trieste, nor had ever been one.

Emma came back with Enrico, who had added his mother's plan. Diana would be replaced by Silvia and her son, whose only task was to run to the main house to tell Enrico that they were arresting Gabriele, Rachele, and whoever else was in that house at that time.

13 September 1944

Stra

Emma did not know what her parents had planned for Rosh HaShanah; she knew it would be something special. She knew she could count on her father for that. She would be missing it. Elena Giadrossi had to go to Venice for a delivery. She was annoyed to miss being with her family in the next few days, but she was thrilled because she might see Roberto again. As she was getting ready, she remembered the German officer and the photograph; she'd better make arrangements to turn into Elena Giadrossi somewhere else. She had to organize a larger suitcase to fit her blonde wig and the padding around her hips. She had no problems with her cover; she was genuinely going to Mrs Toffolo to get work, only it was work for Diana, not for her.

Emma was almost done packing when somebody knocked at the front door. Her grandmother went to open it; that was one arrangement they had planned. Fiamma would open the door to give Anna, Emma, and anybody else who was in the house time to run away. So Fiamma opened the door and found the German Officer who had come by bicycle. She smiled at him, and he saluted her. Then, in his halting Italian, he asked for Rina von Moden. Fiamma did not know who that person was, but somehow she figured out he meant Rachele. Without mentioning any name, Fiamma told him she was still working, and if he wanted to talk to her or her husband, they would be back after 6 pm.

The German Officer told her he would not be in Stra anymore by six pm. He gave her an envelope with two copies of the photograph. He said to her she should "say ciao" to Rina and the rest of the family, saluted her

(Fiamma noticed it was a traditional army salute, not the *"heil Hitler"* she was expecting), got back on the bicycle, and left.

Fiamma closed the door and stood there holding the envelope. Anna, Emma, and their guests joined Fiamma in the hall. The only thing Fiamma could say was 'he left' and gave Anna the envelope. Anna opened it, and there they were. Two copies of a very nice photo of the whole family, except nobody was smiling.

Emma voiced what was in everybody's mind, saying that it was just a photo. They were not going to be arrested and deported after all.

5 December 1944

On the way back from Pomposa

Emma was not comfortable travelling alone. Her senses were alert in a different way. When she had a "parcel" to deliver, she was constantly aware of her surroundings. Danger meant people in German uniform or wearing all black, the uniform of the Fascist militia. When she travelled alone, she was constantly aware she was a young Jewish woman (Emma Mendes) pretending to be a Catholic woman (Emma Conti) who was using an assumed name (Elena Giadrossi) because she was active in an underground movement. The focus was not on making sure that the "parcel" arrived safely at the next staging post. The focus was on her safety. It unsettled her. She would hide behind a book to read and refuse to engage with fellow travellers.

The train was crossing the river Po; Emma was aware that the bridge was a target for the Allied Forces. She was very nervous when the train slowed down. There had been no announcement of disruptions at Ferrara station, so Emma was not expecting to get off the train to continue her journey in another way. However, she was very surprised when she noticed they had stopped to give precedence to a train with anti-aircraft guns, a German military train travelling north. She had to remember to tell her uncle or Enrico about it. It might be a sign that the Germans were retreating or simply moving around equipment. She was relieved when the train started moving again. She touched her handbag, where the ticket, her papers, and a few other personal items were keeping company to a gun she never had to use. She counted on her blond wig, her padded hips, and her nerves to protect her.

Stra

Rachele was trying to concentrate on her task. She did not know what her eldest daughter was up to. She believed in plausible deniability and was always relieved when Emma was back. She was happy that the war was not going well for the Germans or the Fascists. The front line getting closer had made travelling more complicated and risky. She put any thoughts of Emma away. She had to prepare a plausible text to allow a forger to prepare a fake travel permit for a commercial van, something necessary to have access to the dwindling supplies of petrol for civilians. That was the only thing she had to know, and she had no problems with that. She had a copy of the relevant rules on her desk and was trying to figure out a reason generic enough to be used in as many situations as possible, but strong enough not to be questioned. If the wrong person would come into her room, she had prepared an application for a travel permit so she could say she was working at figuring out the best way to apply for one. She did not hear Guido

Orlando approaching her, and she was startled when he spoke.

"I need to go to the police station; the Fascist militia brought them a young man who claims he is not fourteen yet and therefore too young to serve in the military. We may need a falsified birth certificate."

Rachele stopped what she was doing and started putting things away in a hidden compartment of the desk behind her. As she was doing it, she said that it would be better if she went with him, just in case they had to retrieve his birth certificate. Guido did not notice her smile until she pointed out that she did not say where she would go for his birth certificate.

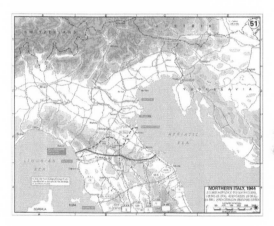

Figure 11 - The dotted line represents the extent of the allied advance by December 1944 - Courtesy or Wikimedia Commons

Venice

Roberto had to be somewhere else; he did not give many details. He simply asked Mario Modlich, aka Baron Davide Modiano, and Anita to listen to the BBC for him at a

215

specific time and take notes of every single message to the resistance; they should also remember to report any news they had heard.

When somebody listened to the BBC in Roberto's room, somebody else was making noise in the kitchen. Anita and Baron Modiano had been busy transcribing messages that made little sense to them, yet they knew that possibly one of them could be important for Roberto. When it came to the news, they were less focused on what they heard until the newsreader said that the allied army had entered Ravenna. Anita was comparing the notes she took with the one Baron Modiano took, so she wasn't paying much attention. It was Baron Modiano who jumped up from his chair.

"Anita, they are in Ravenna. They are getting closer. I must tell my wife."

Anita lifted her head; she asked him to repeat what he had just said. After hearing it for the second time, she thought of Paolo and Sofia. She had to make sure they knew they were indeed getting closer. Meanwhile, Baron Modiano had left the room. He knew he was not supposed to listen to the BBC and that, in Venice, sound travels very fast; he whispered to everyone he met that the allied had reached Ravenna.

Anita picked up the phone, called Sofia, and simply asked if she knew whether there was anything left at the fish market, their code to arrange a meeting. Sofia replied she did not and could check in about forty minutes. Anita did not know whether Paolo was with Roberto or at the hospital; she had to make sure that Sofia heard the news.

Stra

Gabriele was in Count Contarini's study, going through the November books with him. Gabriele did not know whether the Count was active in an underground movement or not. He knew his children were. As usual, Countess Contarini came with mint tea for both of them, saying aloud that she thought they would like a hot drink. When she was inside the room, she whispered that there was nobody within earshot she did not trust. It was her way of telling her husband that they could turn the radio on and listen to the BBC. They ignored the coded message to the resistance; they were not for them. When they heard the news about Ravenna, they looked at each other and smiled. The smile turned into a huge grin, and then they stood up and hugged each other, very unusual for both of them. The Count went looking for his wife; they came back with the keys to the cellar. She then told both men to figure out a reason to celebrate. They did not trust everybody; they wanted to celebrate but could not be seen to celebrate a victory against the Axis.

* * *

Rachele and Guido Orlando left the police station with the boy. The boy really was 12. Guido offered to walk him home. Umberto De Antoni had given both of them a letter to explain why they were potentially in breach of the curfew. On her way home, two black shirts and a German officer stopped her. As usual, she ignored the black shirt and spoke German. The officer asked her to show the letter from the police to the Italians. Once again, he thought that Rina von Moden was one of them and whispered a derogatory comment about the Italians. Rachele smiled at the German. The black shirt gave her the letter back, and she was on her way. When she reached home, she was relieved to see Emma. It took a few seconds to realise that everyone had a huge grin. Gabriele came out of the dining room, kissed her on the cheek, and told her they were getting closer. Rachele immediately figured out who "they" were. Maybe, just maybe, she might allow herself to think of going back to Venice.

15 December 1944

Abbey of Pomposa

The Abbey was now close to the front line. Things had definitely changed; it took longer to get there. The train from Ferrara to Codigoro had become less reliable, the café where Emma used to get the bikes had been closed, and she was now collecting them from the station. Slightly more dangerous because now there were German soldiers permanently posted in what used to be a barber shop near the station. Emma did not dare ask whether it had been requisitioned and what had happened to the barber. She knew she should not linger or talk too much, just in case somebody might recognise her later. These days, she was much more aware of the gun in her handbag and was grateful to Silvia, who had taught her how to use it. She had no intention of using it, but it was a reassuring presence. Her "parcel" was an Italian who could have been her father. She did not know why he had to cross the front line. She did not want to know; their cover was that they were father and daughter visiting an uncle at the Abbey. They were stopped three times between Codigoro and the Abbey. Emma was wondering whether this stretch of the road not very far north of the front line was still safe. The abbey finally became visible in the mist. Emma was relieved; it had been a very slow journey.

Roberto had been waiting for her by the main visitor's entrance; he was in the atrium when the real friar let them in. He smiled at Emma, greeted the "parcel," and took them in. Emma thought he knew precisely who her "parcel" was. She had decided not to find out. She went to her room, hoping that somebody would shortly appear with a drink of hot milk and honey to relieve the cold she was feeling in her bones.

* * *

Emma was not sure whether to take her "Elena Giadrossi" uniform off; she did not know whether the "parcel" would join them for lunch or whether he would be on his way to somewhere else by then. The short winter days meant she was spending more time at the Abbey; even if she were willing to bike back in the dark, there was a curfew and no train from Codigoro. Somebody had lit the fire in her room, and she was very grateful for that.

Roberto knocked at the door. He carried a tray with the hot drink she was craving; he put it down on a table near the window overlooking the cloister. They moved away before they hugged; they were both aware that a young friar would not have embraced a young woman.

"I have good news and disappointing news. Yesterday, troops from New Zealand entered Faenza. The disappointing news is that the Allied high command has decided to pause the Italian campaign till the end of the winter. We are still on the wrong side of the front line. Tomorrow you are going back with messages for Renato and Sandro to that effect; we shall give you two Christian bibles with the new codes for them."

Emma wondered whether he was aware she knew Sandro was her uncle Roberto; he must have known that Renato was Enrico Contarini. She knew too much, and it could be a considerable risk for the organisation if she was caught and tortured. She had better be very careful and not get caught. She smiled and asked if he had messages for anybody else.

Chapter Fifteen

March-April 1945

10 March 1945

Abbey of Pomposa

Roberto was sure his days as Rupert Henson Brown, also known as Friar Francesco, were coming to an end. Winter was almost over; the Allied Army would soon restart the Italian Campaign. Surely, it was a matter of weeks.

He couldn't wait to say goodbye to 'Friar Francesco'; he also couldn't wait to have a proper day with Emma. A day when both of them were free to be themselves without pretending to be anybody else. He could not wait to ask her to marry him. Meanwhile, it was an unusually foggy day. He was frustrated he could not get on top of the church's bell tower attached to the Abbey and lookout for a young woman with a blond wig (at least he knew it was a blond wig) riding a bicycle with a man riding next to her. Emma was always very precise, but today she was understandably late. No matter how well she knew the road, visibility was so bad that she had to proceed with caution.

He was halfway down when he bumped into Davide Soave, his commanding officer. They were both British Special forces. Davide was smiling; he told Roberto not to rush. He did not want to kill himself just now when things looked about to go back to normal. Irrespective of the future, the present was too nice for him to have a disastrous fall. He kept teasing Roberto until they both heard the bell at the visitor's entrance. Davide smiled.

"Go, your secret is safe with me… although I am not taking any responsibility for the real friars!"

Friar Francesco opened the door and greeted Elena in a professional way. He took care of the "parcel" and showed him the room where he was supposed to wait until it was time to go to the meeting point. The front line was so close now that the Abbey was the last staging post before the crossing; an old fisherman would take him to Rimini, on the other side of the front line. Friar Francesco told the "parcel" that he'd better sleep; he would not have much time to sleep that night.

Friar Francesco went to the room Emma normally used. He had to start the fire; it was part of their ritual. He knocked at the door, Emma opened it. Roberto was happy she had got rid of her Elena Giadrossi persona; Emma was all business.

"I think this may be the last trip; there is not a single crossing of the River Po standing. The train stopped on the north bank of the river, and we were ferried in an old barge, only to get on another train on the south bank. The road bridge is also gone, and I could not see any others; I wish I had told my parents I would wait out the end here. It will be complicated to go back."

"You can stay here; we have ways to send a message to your parents."

"No, I'd rather go back. I am concerned, though."

He could not comment on the last statement because Friar Giosué knocked at the doorpost to announce his presence.

"Sorry to interrupt. Roberto, you might as well introduce me properly since she already invited me to the wedding," said Davide Soave with a smile.

"But I haven't asked her yet!"

Then he turned to Emma

"No, don't say anything. I have it planned in my head, and I want to do it that way and most definitely not here and not when there is still a war going on. Emma, meet John Bennett, or better, Davide Soave. The head of operations here."

Emma did not know what to say. She knew Roberto had practically proposed to her, and she was not supposed to react. She shook the hand of the friar; Davide Soave was smiling and was still teasing Roberto.

"I will not congratulate you because your parents must be the first to do so, and he hasn't asked you yet! Anyway, the reason I am here is to see if you are willing to accept a travelling companion on your way back. We are winding down here. By the time we have closed up everything, the allied army will surely be close enough to Bologna for Roberto, or should I say Rupert, to reach Bologna to protect his family home. It was part of the deal we all signed with special forces. I need to reach Verona and take the place of somebody else you are familiar with, who shall also make sure that his family is fine."

25 March 1945

Stra

Enrico appeared, bringing the usual provisions and some great news.

"The allied army will start moving soon. Their only barrier is the Po river; it won't be long before they arrive here."

Fiamma, who opened the door, smiled but was not enthusiastic. Enrico followed her to the kitchen, dropped milk, egg, and flour on the table, hugged her, and repeated.

"The allied will start moving soon; now there is the largest plain in Italy between them and us... only the river Po is a barrier... they won't be long."

He was not getting the reaction he expected from Fiamma. When Gabriele appeared, still half asleep, he repeated the announcement, and the response was closer to what he expected. When Anna and Emma appeared, Enrico got his reaction; they both smiled, hugged each other, hugged their grandmother, and hugged him.

Gabriele reminded them to calm down; he did not want Leo and Davide to share the news at school; nobody was supposed to know. He did not want any attention to be drawn to his family. He did not want anybody to think that they were listening to the BBC, although he suspected that at least half the town was tuning in to the news in Italian broadcasted by the British.

Enrico collected the biscuits and the pastries that Anna had prepared for his parents. He took Gabriele aside to tell him that his parents had suggested that they move to the main house once it was apparent that the Germans were withdrawing. They thought it would be easier to defend the villa and a couple of the farmhouses from a withdrawing army that probably might be hungry as well. Some of his men would move in. Gabriele saw his point and accepted his offer. He would discuss the details with Rachele; he asked Enrico to let him know when they should move. Enrico left, and Gabriele went back inside. It was the first time that Enrico mentioned 'his men.' Gabriele had more sense to ask who his men were and what they were doing.

Venice

Roberto and Anita were having their morning conversation over mint tea. He told Anita that another member of Rachele's family would arrive shortly. He would call her asking for him and giving his grandparents assumed last name, Modlich. She was supposed to tell him he was not at home. The call was his notice that he would arrive the following day. He would use the door in the courtyard to avoid being seen by anybody in the Campo.

Abbey of Pomposa

Friar Francesco was in the prior's study. He rarely inter-acted with the leaders of the abbey. Since he arrived a little over a year earlier, he mainly dealt with Davide Soave. He was used to dealing with other friars, but it was the first time the boss summoned him. The prior was not a tall man. His beard, the glasses he was wearing, his authorita-tive voice, and the kind expression on his face gave the overall perception of somebody who had to be listened to.

"I am not sure what to call you. Do you mind if I call you Rupert?"

"Rupert is fine."

"Rupert it is, then. You may or may not be surprised to know I listen to the BBC. I know that the allied army will be on the move soon. Tell me, do you think we are in any danger from the withdrawing German army? Do you think we offer refuge to families who live nearby? You know, open the door of the abbey to protect them? After all, it may be a matter of weeks."

Roberto had no more information than the prior; he wished Davide Soave were still here; he could only offer his opinion.

"My orders are to stay here until the allied armies have entered Bologna and then reach Bologna and report to the British Army there. We need to figure out when they make a breakthrough on the road from Ravenna. We are outside of the main routes to Germany; the abbey may be at risk from German soldiers retreating or from desperate black shirts with a bad conscience that are trying to flee north to save themselves."

The Prior took his glasses off and closed the book that was open on his desk.

"When we agreed to host your operations here, we did it because we hoped it would give us the information we needed to help people in the area. I should inform the parish priests that the abbey is open to old people, women, and children until the allied army has reached us."

The prior stood up, and Roberto took it as a sign that the meeting was over.

"Before I go, let me apologize if I have done something that might have been interpreted as not respecting you, the habit, or anybody else in the abbey. It was never my intention."

The prior smiled.

"Don't worry; we did not expect that a British soldier following the Anglican church had any idea what to do. Nobody has reported your behaviour to me without praising you."

The prior's smile reassured Roberto.

"By the way, I am not a member of the Anglican Church."

The Prior interrupted him in a conspiratorial tone.

"My dear young man, that is the story I told everybody. Would you like the friars to think that I lied to them?"

The Prior opened the door, still smiling. Roberto left the room, puzzled.

Stra

Emma had gone looking for Enrico. She knew Elena Giadrossi would have nothing to deliver, and she wanted to discuss how she could help with other things. Enrico was in the pergola by the tennis court, cleaning a motorcycle.

"We have everything organized, but we could still use your help. Your father probably shared my parents' idea of moving everybody in the main house and the two farm-houses closer to it. My father maintained that this place has seen many armies and that his grandfather told him that was what they used to do in the old days to protect people and animals. That is why the bigger farmhouses and the bigger stables are relatively close to the main house. "

He stood up, puts the rags he was using in a basket and started removing grease from his hands.

"You can help organize the move. The moment we know that the allied army has reached the river Po is when we need to have everybody here. You, Clara, and Toni will coordinate moving people. Your family comes here, but there are six families and a lot of animals to move. We have no idea how long it will be for."

10 April 1945

Stra

Leo was tall for his age; he could easily pass for a sixteen or even eighteen-year-old, yet he was only thirteen. Gabriele was worried that he would be mistaken for somebody older and forced to join the black shirts or a 'rebel' group. Davide was two years younger, but equally tall for his age. Gabriele and Rachele decided they would not go to school anymore.

Rachele was riding her bike back home; the road had never been so busy. Full of any sort of car or vans, they were going towards Padua and probably continuing to Verona and then the road to Germany. A lot were German military vehicles, but many more were cars with people that were running away. Rachele could not help thinking that, this time, the Fascists were running for their lives. She reckoned things would get worse.

She finally made it to the gate, opened the small pedestrian gate with her keys, pushed the bike in, closed the gate, and breathed a sigh of relief. The road had never felt so dangerous; the garden had never felt so safe.

She found her family very busy. They were getting ready to move to the main house. The Contarinis were worried that some elements of the German army had already started withdrawing from the area. They were even more concerned about what the black shirts might do during the last days of the war. They figured that a hungry and defeated army was less dangerous than a desperate militia whose members felt they had nothing more to lose. Therefore, they would try to settle scores.

The plan was that young men would move into the first floor and the attic. Fiamma had decided to stay. She thought that if anybody came to the house, the sight of an elderly woman opening the door would either discourage them or give the men time to organize a response or hide.

Emma was busy giving directions to Leo and two other young men who were supposed to take luggage to the main house. Davide was making sure that Mila stayed out of the way. Anna, Diana, and Gabriele were busy packing, so Rachele joined them.

Venice

The phone call Roberto announced a couple of weeks earlier finally arrived, and Alessandro Modlich appeared at the door in the morning. He was a young man in his early twenties with red hair and blue eyes. He warmly greeted Anita and then spent most of the time with his grandparents.

When Roberto arrived home, he announced that he and Alex would be in his room until dinner. Once the door was closed, he was all business.

"We can speak freely here; there is a canal where the window is, and there is no other external wall. If we keep the window closed, nobody can overhear us."

Alex had kept it together until that moment. Once the door was closed, he let himself go. His posture, voice, and restlessness were clearly showing how worried he was.

"We have problems in Trieste; representatives of the Slavs have stopped co-operating with us. We understand they had orders from Tito, the commander of the Yugoslav partisans, or there was a strong suggestion that they did. We are concerned that there might be a race between the allied army and Yugoslav partisans to get to Trieste first. My father thinks the Slavs might turn against Italians to prove that the city was never Italian to begin with."

Roberto was concerned by the political situations, but he was more concerned over any risk for Rachele's family.

"Who is still in Trieste? Where is your family?"

Alex started counting with his hands

"My sister, Paola, is in Switzerland with her husband. My older brother Max's family is in Switzerland; my father is determined that my brother gets out of town. We have been very active in the clandestine Italian political parties. The Slavs might have our names on the list of those who need to be silenced. We are also afraid that they might give up some of the Jews that are active in the Italian resistance."

Roberto was trying to be as reassuring as he possibly could

"I am sure that nobody will kick you out of here, and I am also sure that this would be a nice place for your brother as well, but how can we help?"

Alex had shared something that had been bothering him for a while, so now he sounded calmer.

"There is not much you can do from here. In theory, if we kick out the Germans without the help of the Slavs… but I do not think it is likely to happen. We just need to hope that the allied armies arrive in Trieste before the Slav partisans."

Ginevra De Antoni knocked at the door and opened it without waiting for an answer.

"Anita tells me that there is somebody at the front door looking for 'Avvocato Roberto Cunin'"

"That is the sign for me to leave; I'll see you tomorrow. Anita would know how to reach me."

Roberto picked up a briefcase and ran to the back door. There he found Esther, who told him she had been watching and there was nobody in uniform in the courtyard.

He left and managed to reach the fish market from a long route. A route that he hoped would easily allow him to check whether he was followed. He then rang the doorbell of Paolo and Sofia Mondani. He pressed the bell three times in quick succession and three times resting his finger on the bell for a while. A sign that he was in trouble, but he thought it was safe to be there.

Sofia buzzed him in, and by the time Roberto had climbed the four flights of stairs, Paolo had already opened the door. He walked in, and the door was promptly shut. He leaned back against the door and almost whispered.

"They came asking for Roberto Cunin. Thank heaven, Anita opened the door and made sure somebody could tell me while she was stalling. "

Paolo pulled him away from the door and into the living room.

"I am not surprised; this morning, we were told that our daughter-in-law Carolina died during interrogation an undetermined number of weeks ago. We did not know she had made it back to Venice. So we were not aware that she had been arrested. They must have got some lists to have arrested her and come looking for you. Fortunately, I never introduced myself as Paolo Mondani; I always borrowed Sofia's last name. Paolo Taiman was safer. I just do not understand why now, when things are about to come to an end, and it is not a nice end for them."

26 April 1945

Stra

The last five days had been exciting for the people in the main house and tense for everybody protecting them and those in the two farmhouses nearby. Gabriele, Rachele, and Count Contarini were glued to the radio. The allied army had reached Bologna. The allied army had reached the Po River. They were coming; this will end soon.

Enrico's men were more concerned about the German army withdrawing. A few weeks ago, they would have seized the opportunity to attack them; now, they were more focused on protecting their homes. Leo and Davide had insisted they joined other boys from the estate. They were taking messages from 'the core of the castle', the three buildings full of people that had to be protected, to other buildings in the estate.

Emma was collecting information brought to her to update a large map of the estate. She was not sure whether Count Contarini knew what he was doing or if he enjoyed playing the general of his little private army. Nothing much was happening other than roads jammed with vehicles going north.

Suddenly, Davide burst into the big room.

"Mum told me to tell you she heard on the radio that the allied army crossed the river Po yesterday; they may be here soon."

Emma decided it had to be reported, so she told Davide and a couple of other boys to tell the others. Countess Contarini and Anna appeared a few minutes later, asking if she had heard. The excitement was palpable. The end had begun.

Venice

Sofia and Anita had made a point of bumping into each other at the fish market every day since Gabriele and Rachele had left Venice. Sofia knew how to reach them, and Anita knew what was happening in their home. It was a perfect system to update each other.

If one of them had to talk to the other one, she would tie a red ribbon on the handle of the shopping bag. This morning, Anita had the red ribbon, so they warmly greeted each other, and then Anita followed Sofia home. When Paolo heard Anita's voice, he told Roberto that he could come out of the bedroom. Anita had an important message to pass on.

"I have distressing news, and probably you have heard the exciting news. Alex's brother, Max, arrived last night just before the curfew. One of his father's closest friends had disappeared. He had a Slav last name, but he was very active in a clandestine Italian political party. Max Modiano thinks it is the beginning of the Slavs trying to get hold of

Trieste. So he sent his sons to Venice; he stayed there to protect his home and business. Alex has been listening to the radio non-stop; this morning, he told me the exciting news that you probably have heard yourselves…"

Roberto hugged Anita

"… the allied Army has crossed the river Po. They are coming, Anita. It won't be long now!"

29 April 1945

Stra

Everybody in the main house woke up very tired and still very excited from the previous night's celebrations! The allied army had crossed the river Adige, the last natural obstacle between them and Stra. They would soon be here. Everybody from the main house and the two farmhouses was out celebrating. At some point, Enrico rushed in to tell them to be quiet; some German might still be around, they were not out of trouble yet. Nobody had seen an American or British Soldier as yet.

They had little food left, but the animals they had managed to cram in the two stables could still give them milk and eggs. Maria, one of the estate farmers' wives, came with her bag of flour, and she and Anna went to work baking. The Countess, Diana, and Rachele were busy preparing a big table in the garden of the main house. They were sure they would celebrate today. Emma was still in the Count's study with the large map; the most unsuspected people were phoning to tell her what was happening in their area. The café owner in Stra main square said to her that there were still some black shirts around, but they were preparing to run away. Similar calls were coming from shops and private homes until somebody rang from a village on the road from Padua; Emma could hardly hear what she was saying.

"They are here; they are here. They arrived this morning from Padua. They are here. It's over; it's over. Tell Ettore that it is over. They are here. I am calling from the Post Office of Ponte di Brenta. Tell Ettore they are here; they should be with you in the next couple of hours."

Emma dutifully put a mark on the map with the hour of the call, opened the door, and shouted for her brothers. Leo appeared.

"Go, tell everybody that the allied armies have arrived at Ponte di Brenta; they should be in Stra in a couple of hours. Tell everybody we are celebrating today."

She then called the café owner in the main square in Stra and simply told him "Ponte di Brenta." He screamed, called his wife, and told her to watch from the window of their home upstairs. The moment she saw them, he would open the café

Emma could tell when one of her messengers had reached a group of people because she could hear shouting and celebrating. The Count and Gabriele ran into the study smiling; the Count was getting the key for his special cellar; he could not care less if they drank all the wine. Soon Rodolfo will be home and Angelica with the children, including the granddaughter born in Switzerland they had never met. Gabriele took Emma's face in his hands and shouted that they would go back to Venice soon.

Venice

Anita got up early to be ready to go out as soon as the curfew was lifted; she had her morning meeting with Sofia.

They had a quiet celebration when Alex and Max told them the allied army had crossed the river Adige; they were concerned they might be overheard. This morning, Anita was hoping to get more news from Sofia. After all, Paolo and Roberto should have had their own information network.

News travel fast in Venice, so when Anita met a total stranger on her way to the market who told her that stalls were practically empty, but things would improve soon. The allied army had now reached past Rovigo; they would be here any time.

Anita was getting excited; another total stranger told her she had heard that they were approaching Mestre. Anita could not believe that people felt free to exchange information about the allied army with total strangers.

She met a very excited Sofia who told her to forget about shopping, Paolo and Roberto were expecting her. She followed Sofia; once she was inside their home, Paolo hugged her.

"We just heard from Emma; they have reached Stra. They made it; they are free. We'll see them soon."

Roberto ran into the living room. "They are on the outskirts of Mestre; I need to be ready to go outside my parents' house and claim it back. They are here; they are here."

30 April 1945

Stra

It was the morning after the day before. Emma and Diana were busy opening the hems of everybody's coat to fish out their original identity cards with their real names. Leo hugged Mila saying, "We are called Mendes again. Mila, you will soon be called Mendes too." [1]

Venice

Everybody had gathered at Paolo and Sofia; they were cramming their terrace on the grand canal to watch the parade organized by the City. Several *vaporetti* were full of allied soldiers, and the whole town was filling the banks of the Grand Canal. It was over.

Roberto was not there with them, as he promised his mother he was outside their home to see who was living there and trying to get it back. He found the main door open, walked in and saw footprints of boots on the walls of the entrance hall. His father's study completely ransacked, the warehouse that had been used as an impromptu Jewish high school for his niece and her friends destroyed. They even removed the shutters. He was afraid of what he would find upstairs; when he got there, he was relieved to see that the place was a mess. People had left in a hurry, but there was not a lot of actual damage to the furniture. His parents' bed was broken, which put a smile on his face. They had taken with them all they could; bed linen and some other transportable items were missing. Overall, the home could be quickly restored. He tried his key on the backdoor; it was still working, so he bolted the big front door from the inside and left.

The old Mendes home could still be used. When Gabriele and Rachele returned to Venice, some people living in their flat could be housed there. His parents would be happy to have company. Having done that, he had to look for his fiancée, the woman he had wished to marry for years, but because she had a non-Jewish grandfather, they could not get married. The civil servant in charge of upholding the racial laws in 1939 would not allow Roberto Mendes, 100% Jewish, to marry a woman who was 75% Jewish. That did not apply now. Marrying her was part of rebuilding his life.

Now he could join everybody celebrating and dancing.

Chapter Sixteen

May-July 1945

6 May 1945

Venice

After the celebration, everybody felt free and relaxed; the next step was to rebuild their lives. Roberto Cunin and Carlo De Antoni's first step was to use their names again. Whereas a few years earlier, they would have introduced themselves as Roberto or Paolo, they were now stressing their last names to mark their re-acquired freedom.

After Roberto secured his parents' home a few days earlier, nobody had gone in. That Sunday morning Paolo, Sofia, Anita, Roberto Mendes, Paolo Morpurgo, Gaia Morpurgo, and their children Emanuele and Deborah met outside the home of Samuele and Fiamma to organize a major clean-up.

Paolo Morpurgo and his family would move in until they decided what to do with themselves. If Alex and Max Modiano needed somewhere to stay, there was room for them as well.

Roberto knew the state of the place, but the others did not. They wondered how on earth boot print could be so high on a wall. When Paolo Mondani walked into one of the big rooms of the ground floor, where all the samples of printed silk were kept ages ago, the state of that room moved him to tears. They used that room to dump everything that had to be thrown away. Paolo and Roberto started from Samuele's study, and the others moved to the first floor to begin cleaning the home.

Paolo and Roberto talked about Samuele as they cleaned up his study; whoever had occupied the house probably burnt the books on the lower shelves during winter. Wood was hard to come by in Venice. Paolo and Roberto talked about the immediate future as they cleared up. Paolo was very fond of his friend's parents; he felt the Mendeses were also his family.

"You need to talk to your siblings and decide how to find out what happened to your father. Emotional issues aside, I am sure there are some legal implications to consider."

"I'll ask Rachele when I see them next Sunday. They are not sure when they will move back to Venice; Gabriele is eager that Leo and Davide finish school if it reopens. They plan to stay till mid-June; Count Contarini is not happy to lose his administrator."

"What about your other siblings, Emanuele, Miriam, and Raffaele?"

Roberto stopped what he was doing. He stood there holding a cupboard door they had found in the room that did not belong to any piece of furniture in the room.

"Miriam is still in Switzerland; I do not know where Emanuele is, and I wrote to Raffaele in Canada yesterday."

Paolo came out from under Samuele's desk, stretched his back, and picked up the broom before continuing.

"As you know, I am very fond of your parents, and I know them very well. Since I lost mine, they are the closest things to parents I have. So, I am here if you need me, especially if you need to convince Gabriele of anything. Sofia, Anita, and Esther have decided that we let you go alone next Sunday; once you have reported how easy it would be to go as a group, we'll have our outing to Stra."

They had moved to inspect what was left of the shutters of the two windows. They had to be very careful not to fall into the canal, so the conversation stopped.

Stra

The Mendes were using their last name again; they had gone back to their temporary home after the celebration and discussed what to do next. This time, Gabriele and Rachele discussed it with their older children while Fiamma kept Davide and Mila occupied.

The initial decision was to wait until mid-June to allow Leo and Davide to finish the school year. The Contarini had no problems; they thought it was unlikely that Angelica and the children would come back from Switzerland before the end of June, but even if they did, there was plenty of room for them in the main villa. Gabriele presented the family's financial situation.

"We still have our Swiss bank account, most of the gold, and have not touched the jewellery, but it would probably be worth less now because there is not much cash floating around. We have not paid rent because I am helping Count Contarini with the estate admin. We paid Anita and Maria until April next year, and our cash reserve could probably last us till December. We are not in a hurry to earn money."

Rachele had contacted her old boss to see if she could get her job back, but she would love to open her law firm. Once they were back in Venice, she might suggest to Alvise Cantoni to work together. Rachele also saw herself primarily working for the family in the following months. There were assets to reclaim and, hopefully, some compensation for those who had been racially persecuted.

Emma and Anna said they were too old to go back to school. Emma loved making clothes. She wanted to continue doing it, so she would ask Mrs Toffolo if she could have her job back; Anna wanted to become a master baker and maybe open a kosher patisserie. Diana said she wouldn't mind trying to see if she could study independently and sit for an exam one or two years later. In this way, she would catch up with her contemporaries. In the meantime, she wanted to ask Mrs Toffolo if she had a job for her as well.

Gabriele did not know what to do. He thought that book-keeping was a sort of stop-gap way of earning money and was surprised at how good he was at it, but he was not sure he wanted to consider it a long-term professional choice. He agreed with Rachele that the extended family might need him, and he'll use the next couple of months to see what he could do. He had no intention of going back to his old job. He felt betrayed by the city he loved.

13 June 1945

Stra

They had spent three days packing and cleaning; they had dinner with the Contarinis the previous night. Anna, Fiamma, Rachele, and Emma were cleaning the kitchen after breakfast. Diana was getting Mila ready, Leo and Davide were helping Gabriele get the suitcases and bags downstairs.

They made it. They survived. What will the future bring? They were using their names again; will they go back to their old lives or something else?

Each one of them had hopes, concerns, and doubts.

They were talking about something related to what they were doing or talking about going back to Venice as if it were something abstract, not a collection of unanswered questions related to the beginning of rebuilding their lives.

They were waiting for Giuseppe to come with horse and carriage; the front door was open as they had been taking suitcases, bags, and boxes outside. They were not expecting a car, so when one appeared in the drive, Davide rushed inside to call his parents without waiting to see who had just arrived. Count Contarini, Enrico, and Roberto Mendes were surprised until the Count pointed out that for the past couple of years, an unexpected car had meant trouble, and eleven-year-old Davide reacted the way he would have reacted a few weeks earlier. They did not have to wait long for Gabriele and Rachele to appear.

Roberto told his brother he had organized a boat at Marghera. He and Giuseppe would take suitcases, bags, and everything else to Marghera; Gabriele, Rachele, and the children could just board the train with very little luggage. Enrico was here to help him load everything, and the Count was taking them to the station, taking as many trips as necessary. Giuseppe appeared with horse and cart, with Countess Contarini as a passenger.

It was an emotional goodbye. They were invited back to visit a month later once Angelica and the children had arrived back from Switzerland. Emma, Anna, and their brothers were the first to get to the station. Once they were alone, Davide brought his sisters back to reality.

"When do you think I'll be able to see my old school friend?"

The first one to recover was Anna.

"I do not know; it all depends on where they have been in the last couple of years and when they are coming back. You'll probably see them again when school starts or when-ever they come to Synagogue.

Venice

Anita, Esther, and Davide were very excited. Paolo and Gaia Morpurgo, their children, Alex, and Michele, had moved to Fiamma's home. Anita and Maria had cleaned the flat more thoroughly than during Passover cleaning. Esther kept asking them what she could do to help, and after the third time telling her they had everything under control, they gave her something to do just to get her out of the way.

Roberto called once the train was on its way to Venice. Anita, Esther, and Davide left to meet Fiamma, Gabriele, Rachele, and the children at the station; Paolo and Sofia joined them. Paolo pointed out that they were the first members of their extended family to come back to Venice.

It was a very emotional reunion. The large group started walking home. Later, Roberto arrived with their things. Gabriele was surprised to find a few extra bags with food. The Contarini estate had provided eggs, flour, vegetables, and "milk for the children" one last time.

As Anna was making pasta and Anita and Esther were taking care of dinner, Gabriele and Rachele slipped out for their evening walk. A habit they were eager to start as soon as possible. They enjoyed being back, back to Venice, back to an old routine they loved. They walked in silence for a long time, taking a roundabout route to Rialto, through Campo San Polo, through narrow streets and bridges over narrow canals. Everything was familiar and new at the same time. When they reached the Grand Canal, they stopped in silence for a while, in full view of the Rialto Bridge. As they were walking back along Calle del Tentor, they were stopped by an acquaintance who told them how happy she was to see them because she thought they were all dead. Somehow, both Gabriele and Rachele found it funny; they managed to keep a straight face until they parted company, then they got the giggles, and then they started laughing.

They had reached the end of their walk. Gabriele looked at his wife before he opened the door of their 'real' home.

"Tomorrow we unpack properly, Friday we prepare for Shabbat, and from Sunday we start looking for the pieces to put together. Hopefully, we can find all of them."

23 June 1945

Going to synagogue for most members of the Jewish community in Venice was a sign of normality. It was the outward sign that you were getting your old self back, and you did not have to hide anymore. The Mendeses had gone back to having Saturday lunch at Fiamma after synagogue.

Being in synagogue was also a way of finding out about others, those who had already come back and those who would not come back. Gabriele was pleased to see Alvise Cantoni and his son Franco. They had come to the Spanish Synagogue to meet Gabriele, Rachele, and their children. The Cantonis were safe; they were in Asolo[1] with false papers. At the end of the service, Alvise and Franco talked to Rachele and Emma; Gabriele and Diana spoke to one of Diana's former schoolmates and her parents. When they started moving towards Fiamma's home Roberto joined them; he had been to the Levantine Synagogue with his fiancé. They had just crossed the bridge into Campo del Ghetto Novo when Roberto took Gabriele aside.

"Alberto Levi was sitting next to me in synagogue; he told me he managed to escape from the place in the Giudecca where they took him, the same place where Emanuele and his wife were taken. He told me they were shot as they tried to escape with him and a few others. He did not know what had happened to their children. He was taken in by a woman who lived nearby who just opened the door and told him to get inside. He was pretty sure Emanuele and his wife were dead."

"Can we wait to tell everybody else? Is there a way to find out what happened to their bodies?"

"The first thing I can do is ask if anybody has heard of bodies floating in the lagoon; other than that, I do not know what else to do."

"Let's wait to tell others until we know something more. Do we know what happened to Mario and Paola?"

"Not yet, no. As you know, I have been checking with the Red Cross, but they have not come back to me with any news of them, our father, or of Miriam's husband, Michele."

"It's still early days; let us not give up hope."

Leo and Davide joined them after they crossed the second bridge into Fondamenta del Ghetto. Gabriele and Roberto quickly changed the subject.

Leo was talking about his upcoming Bar Mitzvah[2] and wondering whether he could learn everything he was supposed to know in four-month

02 July 1945

Rachele and Alvise Cantoni were still excited at the idea that they were going back to their professional life after more than six years. They had not got used to it yet. A week earlier, they had decided to start their legal practice; they knew they had a lot to do to help other Venetian Jews regain their homes or other assets confiscated by the "Republic" at the end of 1943. They gave themselves six months to see if they could make a go of it.

They had decided to work from Gabriele and Rachele's study until they could afford to rent premises, but they had nowhere to see clients. The temporary solution was a café near the Rialto bridge; the café had a room for people to play cards or other games in the afternoon and evening. So they had the space in the morning if they needed it. They had just finished a meeting with a client when Gabriele joined them.

"Alvise, Rachele, the extended Mendes family is now your client as well. I have been to the bank where mum and dad had their money. It is all in joint names, and they have been difficult because there is only mum; they want to block the accounts. Mum needs the money. Also, Miriam called Sofia Mondani to tell her she and her children were coming back. She was thrilled to know that we were safe and in our homes. She needs access to her old home."

"Was it in her name? Did Samuele buy it the way he did it for us when we got married?"

"I think he did."

"Gabriele, the bank should not be a problem if the accounts had both names. Otherwise, we need to know what happened to your father; first, we need to check with the Red Cross. Who is the bank manager?"

"I am not sure; I have the feeling that it is a party faithful that has not been dismissed yet or somebody inexperienced who has just replaced a party faithful."

Alvise turned to Rachele.

"We need a secretary, somebody who can also run errands."

"We can't afford one."

Gabriele looked at Rachele and smiled; Rachele nodded. The silent conversation puzzled Alvise until Gabriele spoke.

"I am trying to re-start my bookkeeping business until I know what to do. So far, I only have two clients, Mrs

Toffolo and Count Contarini. I can be their bookkeeper and your secretary and bookkeeper. Alvise, I think Rachele has the chance to earn more money faster than I do. It is in our interest that I support her rather than trying to develop work that will not give us enough money to live on once our savings have run out. We have known each other for a long time; I think it can work."

Alvise's body language told his friends that he was considering the idea.

"What are your current commitments?"

"I go to Mrs Toffolo's premises one morning a week, and Count Contarini has asked me to pay him a visit once a month for a while until Enrico can manage the administration of the estate with no help."

Alvise liked the idea.

"Franco and one of your daughters could help when you are not around. Thank you for your offer, Gabriele. We do not need to ask Rachele's opinion; I think she gave her approval during the silent conversation you had before you shared your idea with us!"

10 July 1945

It had been a very hot and humid day, but the whole of the Mendes clan was at the station. Miriam and her children were due to arrive from Switzerland. Journeys were not predictable; works to repair the railway lines damaged by air raids, mines, and other acts of war had barely started. Miriam managed to find a phone at Padua railway station to confirm that they were about to catch a train for the last stretch to Venice. Sofia Mondani had informed Fiamma and Anita, who had told everybody else. So the whole family was at the station; the group included Alex and Max Modiano. Max's wife was in the same refugee camp; she had decided to wait until she heard from Miriam before starting the same journey with much younger children.

The train arrived, and people started pouring in from the platform. Fiamma, Gabriele, and Roberto were looking for Miriam and her children. Enrico had grown a lot and was now carrying one of the suitcases. Miriam dropped the other to wave, but it was Gloria, nine years old, that made everybody teary, shouting "Grandma, Grandma" before she started running towards her grandmother.

After a long time hugging Miriam, telling Enrico that he now looked like a man and Gloria that she had grown up a lot, the group started walking towards Campo San Giacomo dall'Orio. Alex and Max carried the suitcases; nobody wanted to spoil the moment by bringing up what happened to Michele Bolaffi, Miriam's husband. Today it was time to celebrate.

Rachele and Paolo Mondani were keeping count.

"Now that Miriam is back, we are left with Michele and Emanuele's children, Mario and Paola. Somehow, I do not think that Samuele made it."

Chapter Seventeen

July-August 1945

16 July 1945

Diana was busy taking a dress apart. Most of the work at Mrs Toffolo's workshop started that way. Focusing on rebuilding their lives had replaced the survival instinct that made most people live for the present; there was a reason to plan and save now. Also, the material was not readily available. Diana was happy because re-cycling old garments implied taking them apart, something usually done by the apprentices. She had work; she was still not sure whether to go back to school. In the meantime, she was happy commuting across the Giudecca canal with her sister.

Emma was busy working out how to cut a piece of material. It was one of the few new dresses being made in the workshop. She was trying to figure out how the finished dress would look like so she could place the paper pattern in the appropriate position before cutting. There was no margin of error once she started. The client made very clear to Mrs Toffolo that it was a unique piece of silk, something they found in her grandmother's home. Emma wondered if it had come from her grandparents' company or indeed from the ransacked warehouse.

She was so concentrated that she did not notice Mrs Toffolo approaching until the tap on her shoulder startled her. Diana lifted her head to see what happened and smiled when she noticed that the source of her sister's shock was Mrs Toffolo being behind her. When Emma left with Mrs Toffolo, Diana went back to her work. Mrs Toffolo led Emma into one of the fitting rooms, but did not go in. Emma was surprised to see Sofia Mondani sitting in what looked like a small sitting room with many mirrors.

"Aunt Sofia, what happened? The only thing Mrs Toffolo told me was that someone wanted to see me for something complicated, but nice. I had no idea it was you."

"Well, it is complicated, and I am sure it is nice. As you know, Carolina's family is very close to a Jewish family. They act as one large family. They call themselves the Rinaldi/Sonnino Clan. A young man called Roberto Sonnino, a member of the same clan, would like to have your address and phone number. Angelica, Carolina's sister, told me he was very persistent. He even rang them in Switzerland, asking Angelica to contact us. He was sure that Count Contarini knew how to reach us. My question to you is, do you want this young man to have your address and phone number? Whatever you say will stay between us two; I have an arrangement with Angelica that she'll tell Roberto Sonnino whatever you wish to tell him."

Emma smiled and felt very light inside.

"Aunt Sofia, I'll be thrilled if Roberto Sonnino has my address and phone number."

"So, how did you meet Roberto Sonnino?"

"Well, we met at Arrigo and Carolina's wedding, and we sort of recognized each other when we met last year, despite using different names. We had a moment alone in the same room, free from prying eyes and ears, so we relaxed and had a conversation between Emma and Roberto instead of using our pretend names and identities. Something highly irregular, I know, but it was very nice. We then had reasons to meet again, and again, he told me he had ways to find me after the war. I am glad he wants to see me."

"Just glad?"

"Well, let's leave it at "glad" for the moment. I'll let you know what happens once I see him without the risk of being captured and deported or shot. Thank you very much for coming and being discrete."

Emma hugged Sofia and saw her out; she hugged and thanked her again as Sofia was leaving. Mrs. Toffolo appeared once she heard the door close, her face asking many questions. Emma decided to share something with her.

"Mrs Toffolo, during the war, you and I have been involved in activities we are not prepared to discuss; well, during those activities, I bumped into a nice young man I had met before. He found a way to find me, and my honorary aunt came to ask my permission to give him my address and telephone number."

The smile on Mrs Toffolo's face was wider than the Giudecca Canal itself.

"And you gave her your permission. Well, just remember, we will make your wedding dress! In the meantime, this stays between the two of us!"

Emma went back to the cutting room. When Diana asked why she looked so happy, Emma answered that she had figured out how to cut the dress.

28 July 1945

Three months since the end of the war and services in Synagogue were still an opportunity to find out what happened to old friends. There were a few new faces, most of them wearing a uniform, and they were immediately noticed. The "Mendes group" included some new additions. So Gabriele, Roberto, Paolo and Emanuele Morpurgo, Alex, and Max Modiano were sitting together with Leo next to his father. They noticed that somebody new was not wearing a uniform, an unusual sight.

During the reception that followed the service, they noticed that the stranger was talking to Alvise Cantoni. Alvise approached them with the stranger, introduced him, and told Gabriele and Roberto that he would be around if he needed them. The two brothers looked at each other; both puzzled by Alvise's remark. The stranger introduces himself as Daniele Voghera.

"I was in the same transport from the transit camp to Germany as your father Samuele; I saw him die. When we got on the train, he started talking to me and told me his name was Samuele Mendes, from Venice. Your father died not long after we boarded the train; he managed to tell me to come and find his family and tell them. After we reached Verona, we stopped because the railway line was attacked. The train could not go any further, so they shunted us to a siding, and they made us change trains. Some of us tried to escape; I used to run competitively at University, and I could still run pretty fast, so I escaped. Luckily, when they started shooting, they did not catch me. An old man who had heard the shots took me in; later, I joined a group run by a British man who could speak our dialect."

The last sentence gave Roberto confidence that they could check this stranger's information with Rodolfo Contarini. He must have been the British man who could speak the dialect. Gabriele was shocked and went looking for Rachele. Roberto thanked the stranger, invited him to lunch, provided he would not tell the story to his mother.

Rachele heard the story from Gabriele; she excused herself.

"It is not that I am not supportive, but I am also the family lawyer. I need to talk to that man and ask him if he is ready to sign an affidavit to take to court; it will help your mother's finances. I hope you understand."

Rachele joined the stranger, Roberto and Alvise. When she heard that her brother-in-law was already discussing the affidavit, she returned to her husband, hugged him, and decided they had to go for a short walk before joining the others for lunch. She told Anita to make sure that all the children would make it to Fiamma's home in time; she and Gabriele would join them later.

29 July 1945

Gabriele and Rachele were out for their morning walk. It was one of the elements of 'normality' they had some control over. They knew they were not the only ones rebuilding their lives after the war. Hundreds of thousands of others had lost their homes, lost family members, were being demobbed. Jews who had survived the war without being arrested or deported were taking back control of their names. No hiding, no pretending.

The little things in life were necessary for their sense of self; their moments to themselves every morning and evening were very close to their heart. Gabriele, Rachele, and thousands of other Jews were trying to cling to some elements of who they were before racial laws, the war, false identities, etc.

They had left before breakfast; they stopped in a café halfway through Calle del Tentor for coffee. Real coffee was still scarce. They enjoyed it in silence. When they left the café, they started talking about their children's future; soon, the conversation moved to themselves. Rachele wondered if Gabriele would mind being her secretary for a bit longer. Her old boss had approached her, but she felt funny going back to her old job. A lot had changed since she lost it because she was Jewish. They needed to get work other than what they were doing on behalf of other Venetian Jews. She and Alvise were not comfortable asking for money when they were helping other members of the community trying to navigate the bureaucracy to regain their confiscated assets.

Gabriele reassured her they did not need to earn money for the next four months, and he was putting away whatever he was making from Mrs. Toffolo and Count Contarini to see how long they could extend their self-sufficiency.

Diana woke up determined to figure out what to do with herself. The previous day had given her a glimpse of the life she remembered before everything else began. She knew that before the war, the general expectation was that she would have continued going to school and maybe go to University as her mother did. Her older sisters had made their decisions; she had to make hers. She had discussed the possibility of studying towards an exam that would allow her to start the following year at the same level as non-Jewish students her age. Her time in Stra had made her aware that non-Jewish teenagers had lost years of schooling as well, but she did not fancy the idea of being two years older than her classmates. So, she knocked at Emma's door to ask her if she could get her books for the last two years of her schooling, the same books Diana would have had to study to sit for that exam. She was surprised to find out that Emma had already gone out.

Emma had told her parents that a friend she had met during her undercover work had recently got in touch through Sofia Mondani and arranged for a visit. They would spend most of the day together. Emma had not lied to her parents; she had just been very vague about who this friend was. Gabriele thought it was due to the habit of keeping other people's identities a secret and did not pay any notice of it. Rachele noticed Anita's reaction to what Emma was saying and wondered what happened in Venice when they were in Stra, but kept her thoughts to herself, planning to ask Anita later.

Roberto Sonnino had said he would call the Mondanis as soon as he had any idea when the train would arrive in Venice. The journey from Bologna was still disrupted and required many changes from train to bus, so the arrival time was not predictable. Roberto would try to ring from Padua; the line between Padua and Venice was not damaged and, therefore, predictable. Emma was now having a hot drink on the Mondani's terrace. She was a few vaporetto stops away from the station. Uncle Paolo did not miss that opportunity to tease her.

"We are your parents' closest friends. Your father and I have known each other since we were five, so you know I will not keep this visit a secret from them. But... I am your honorary uncle, so I will only answer a direct question from your parents; I will not volunteer any information."

"Leave the poor girl alone; she is nervous."

"Thank you, Aunt Sofia, but don't worry, I am used to Uncle Paolo teasing me. I am nervous because I am not sure whether the same sparkle will be there. There was the war; we were both doing something dangerous; we were thrilled to use our actual names when we were alone. Let's see what happens when we see each other."

"But what would you like to happen?"

"I sincerely hope that when I see him in normal clothes, I react in the same way, and hopefully, he will too."

"Well, let me be the first to ask to be invited to the wedding."

"Uncle Paolo, you are not."

Emma told her honorary uncle and aunt what happened when she was caught eavesdropping. She had just got to the end when the phone rang; Sofia went inside to answer it. She came back to the terrace and confirmed that Roberto was in Padua and he would be in Venice in less than an hour. Paolo looked at her, smiling.

"Go. If you take two steps forward and one step backward, you might just make it."

She smiled, kissed him, and left. After she had gone, Paolo remarked he had seen a genuine smile on his wife's face for the first time since they had the news that their son had died of typhoid fever in a Prisoner of War camp in Kenya.

Emma took the vaporetto to the station to ensure she was there on time before the train arrived. She reached the end of the platform when the train was coming into the station.

When she saw him in the crowd, she realized that the sparkle was still there on her side. She also noticed that when Roberto saw her, his face lit up.

11 August 1945

Synagogue had not become a habit yet. The whole family enjoyed the old Saturday morning ritual of getting ready, having breakfast, and going to synagogue in groups. The groups had developed because the age of the Mendes children had changed. Gabriele, Leo, and Anna were the first to go; later, Rachele would go with Emma, Diana, and Davide; Anita would take Mila an hour before the end.

The second group arrived; Davide sat with his cousin Enrico Bolaffi, Miriam's son, between his father and their uncle. The rest took their usual seats in the women's section. The extended Mendes clan in Venice was in Synagogue present and correct, including the Modianos and Morpurgos that temporarily stayed with them.

An elderly lady walked in with a boy and a girl. She did not know where to go. Visitors were still an unusual oddity, and the person who sent her and the little girl to the women's section thought it was strange to have a tourist in Venice now when people had not started travelling yet.

The three newcomers had arrived relatively late, during the end of the silent prayer, and very few people looked at them. The boy wanted to sit near somebody specific, but knew enough to wait until the silent prayer was over. Leo noticed the newcomer; once his father had finished praying, he mentioned he looked familiar. Gabriele looked at the young man from his seat, reached to Roberto over the head of Davide and Enrico, and pointed him to his brother. They nodded, and they both said in a low voice that he looked very much like their nephew Mario, the son of their late brother Emanuele. Leo overheard his father and his uncle, turned towards the newcomer who was trying to move closer to them, and said loudly, "Mario, come here!". Something similar was happening in the women's section, except that Fiamma had recognized her granddaughter Paola. The lady that had brought them there was surrounded by Fiamma, Miriam, Rachele, Emma, and Anna. They were asking several questions. Diana and Gloria, Miriam's daughter, were around Paola. When Anita arrived with Mila, she was concerned when she saw two ladies crying and all the Mendes women gathered around another person until a lady approached her.

"Emanuele's children are alive and well; isn't it great?"

Anita picked up Mila, kissed her forehead, and moved to join the group.

* * *

It turned out that the lady in question used to be Emanuele's neighbour. She was alarmed by the noise of people banging at doors on the other side of the Canal; she saw a family being taken away. She did not know them, but she remembered the posters she had seen on the street wondered whether they were Jewish. She immediately thought of Emanuele's family, rang their doorbell, and when Emanuele opened it, she explained what she saw and offered to take the children. His wife knew the people arrested, so she quickly told the children to follow their neighbour and gave this lady a key to their flat to go back later to take the children's clothes. She also told the children that whatever they might hear, they should be away from the windows until the following morning. A few hours later, the lady got the children's clothes and other things.

She then started spreading a story that her nephew and niece from Verona had joined her because her sister had lost her home in an air raid. She had come to Synagogue because she thought that a few months after the end of the war, she might have been able to find some of their relatives.

* * *

In the best Mendes tradition, there were three more guests for lunch. On the way to Fiamma's home, Alex Modiano asked Rachele if he could come and talk to her. He was not sure what to do with himself. In 1938, he could not start University because of the Racial Laws. He was not sure what he wanted to do; the situation in Trieste was still confused. He was torn between going back to University in Italy, going to the Holy Land, or applying for a visa to move to the United States. They agreed that he would have lunch in Campo San Giacomo Dall'Orio the following day.

16 August 1945

It was another happy day in what had become the extended Mendes/Modiano/Morpurgo clan. Max Modiano's wife and their children were arriving from Switzerland. That had caused some nice problems and shuffling around in the two households since Miriam had not got her home back yet. Anita directed assorted members of the combined households to make room for the new arrivals in Fiamma's home since Mario and Paola were moving in with Gabriele and Rachele. By early afternoon everything was more or less sorted; children would have to share rooms, Alex would go back to the room Roberto used when he was hiding as Roberto Cunin in Gabriele and

Rachele's home Samuele's study had a double bed in it. In the end, almost every adult had some private space. Hopefully, it was just for a few months; Max and his family would move back to Trieste once things had settled there or decide where to go if they settled in the wrong way.[1] The news of people who had survived genuinely excited Fiamma; she had stopped staring into space thinking of her husband, at least for that day.

They all went to the station to support Max. They all needed to know that somebody else had made it through the night. Rachele was keeping count of those who had not reappeared yet or given any news of themselves. Michele Bolaffi, Miriam's husband, and two of her siblings, Sarah and Ricardo, and their families. She also knew that those who had stayed in Trieste - Michele, Celeste, and Daniele - had survived that specific nightmare but were not entirely out of danger yet.[2]

They all walked to Fiamma's home; before crossing Ponte delle Guglie, they started debating which route to take until Max pointed out that maybe the shortest route would do, even if it was not the most scenic. There was a relatively minor celebration for the newly returned. They wanted to give Max some moments of privacy with his family. They had been reunited after almost two years. The cooks in the clan had organized a large celebratory meal for the following Saturday. That would give them a day to make sure they could find the ingredients they wanted to cook. As Anna put it, they did not have Giuseppe coming with flour, eggs, and milk every morning.

17 August 1945

Given the chaos at home, Rachele had decided to have a meeting of the still informal law practice at Caffe Florian.

It was an unnecessary luxury, but she felt they deserved it. The firm comprised Rachele, Alvise Cantoni, and now Roberto Mendes. Gabriele was their secretary, and Alex Modiano had decided to work as their assistant and general dogsbody while deciding what to do with himself.

Fellow Jews trying to recover their assets still provided most of their business, and they did not feel comfortable charging for that. Although, as Gabriele reported, one of their clients, who had been the first to recover a sizeable property successfully, paid them what he could, and a couple of others had promised free products. They were also making good progress in the recovery of Miriam's home; Roberto suggested they could help the people who lived there, refugees from Pola, find another accommodation, and that would speed up Miriam going back to her home.

The really exciting news was that Alvise and Rachele got their first 'real' clients. An old client had come back to Rachele for a complicated contract, and a family had contacted Alvise for a difficult will made even more complex by one of the heirs still reported missing. Roberto suggested Alex could be in charge of logging who works at what. Rachele and Alvise looked at each other and smiled; Alvise remarked that it almost felt like being in a real law firm, not just a bunch of people trying to rebuild their lives.

Chapter Eighteen

September-December 1945

03 September 1945

Diana had spent most of her Sunday looking at her sister's pile of books. She loved the idea of learning to make clothes, but she also loved the idea of teaching. To teach, she would have to continue her education. When she woke up, she knew what to do; she would discuss it with Emma on her way to Mrs Toffolo. On her way to the bathroom, Diana could hear the breakfast noise from the kitchen; now that Mario and Paola lived with them, breakfast was even noisier than usual. They had moved in only the previous Wednesday. They had bonded very quickly with Leo and Davide.

Emma had woken up early and had started her day reading the last letter from Roberto Sonnino. It had become her habit since his first visit to Venice. She looked forward to seeing him the Sunday after RoshHaShanah, her last letter to him on her table waiting to be put in an envelope. She looked at a framed photograph taken before the war and thought of her cousin Carlo arriving in Venice from Germany to celebrate the holiday. He had been a Canadian citizen for a few years, and he had volunteered to join the Army in 1943. He was due to arrive in Venice for ten days' leave. She was looking forward to seeing him in uniform. They had planned a large family meal to celebrate his arrival; he would stay with them sharing the room with Alex Modiano. Emma loved large family gatherings; it was a sign of normality. She wondered whether they would ever stop seeing empty chairs at the table.

Emma and Diana joined the rest of the family for breakfast, and soon they both got lost in the usual morning conversation around the table. The affidavit of the lady who took care of Mario and Paola for almost two years had been accepted. The education authorities of Venice had integrated the record of their schooling under a different name with their past education records, and they would start school with the other children of their age. Everybody was thrilled. Diana got carried away by the atmosphere and announced that she would try to study privately this year and sit for the exam that would admit her to the year of high school appropriate to her age in October 1946. Her parents heard her from the opposite side of the table; they were thrilled by her news. Her grandfather even offered to pay for tutors to help her if she needed it.

On their way to Mrs Toffolo, Diana and Emma discussed the work involved in studying for the equivalent of three years in twelve months, since Diana would have to sit for the exam in September 1946. By the time they arrived at their workplace, they had moved to talk about their cousin Carlo and how much they were looking forward to seeing him. The family had already received a very moving letter from Uncle Raffaele, Carlo's father, and they knew that their father, their uncle Roberto and their grandmother had written to him. They were just curious to see the only member of their family who had fought wearing an actual uniform.

Carlo had received a letter from his father with the family news. He had hitched a ride on a US transport to Treviso. Once he landed, he rang his uncle Gabriele's home, knowing that Anita would be there to answer him. Anita's reaction surprised him; his voice touched her, and she started crying. A worried Anna picked up the phone. When she heard his voice, she screamed at the top of her lungs but quickly composed herself. Carlo told her he was at Treviso airport and would call again from the station to tell them when he would arrive.

He was surprised to find Gabriele, Miriam, and Roberto at the station waiting for him. He had told Anna that nobody should bother, that he knew the way and was looking forward to wandering around Venice. In reality, he wanted to talk to his uncles to figure out how to tell his aunt Miriam that he had news of her husband; they were not bad but were not good either, or at least not good yet.

Carlo decided to enjoy the reunion and leave the heavy-duty conversation to the following day. After seven years, he was just happy to be in Venice; he insisted they walk from the station to Campo San Giacomo Dall'Orio. They stopped in the middle of Ponte Degli Scalzi; he wanted to take a good look at the Canal Grande after so many years. During the rest of the way, he kept interrupting the conversation with a lot of "I remember that!" or "is that new? I do not remember it"

* * *

Emma was concentrating on her work. Cutting was important; she was the only one allowed to cut material other than Mrs Toffolo. Emma was very proud of the trust her employer had in her. They discussed placing the patterns together to maximize the use of the material and minimize waste. She was just starting when she heard the bell ring; although the war was over, an unexpected ring of the doorbell was still an alarming thought. They laughed nervously, commenting that they had been found out. An apprentice usually met at the door people who were expected, but nobody was due to arrive now, so Mrs Toffolo went to open the door. Emma was concentrating on her work, so she did not notice that the apprentice that had left the big room to get buttons had come back and quietly fetched Diana. Diana reached the entrance hall, where a smiling Mrs Toffolo told her to be quiet. Then she opened the door to a fitting room, and Diana saw her cousin sitting there, wearing his uniform and gesturing her to be quiet. Carlo wanted to surprise Emma. Diana hugged him and went back to the workshop to signal when Emma had put down the scissors; Carlo watched from a slither in the door and slowly walked in as Emma was thinking how to approach the following pattern. He softly walked to place himself between the table and the window, obscuring the light in Emma's line of vision. Emma was looking at the material spread on the table, and before she picked the scissors, she lifted her face, annoyed because somebody was standing between her and the window. She was cutting black material with a subtle pattern. She needed all the light she could get. She noticed who it was. Her mouth wide open for a few seconds, then her face lit up, turned into a smile that went from ear to ear, and she shouted "Carlo!" she carefully put the scissors on the table and ran to hug him. Her cousin, better, her honorary brother, had arrived!

It was almost lunchtime, so Carlo told Emma and Diana he would take them to lunch. Usually, Emma would not take a break when she was cutting, but Mrs Toffolo insisted her cousin deserved some of Emma's time; the dress could wait.

Diana declined lunch since she had decided to go back to school, and since it was quite a daunting task to study the equivalent of three years syllabus in 10 months, she had to start immediately. She had brought Emma's Italian literature book from her school days; she planned to eat the lunch she had prepared in the morning and study.

Emma and Carlo walked to a café with a fantastic view over St Mark's Square. Emma insisted Carlo sat facing the water; after all, he was a visitor now.

"I miss Venice. When we arrived in Canada, everything was so different, so exciting. Then, slowly, I started missing the water, and traffic seemed chaotic. Anyway, I am glad I can talk to you alone. I need to ask your opinion about sharing what I am about to tell you with our family. "

Carlo stopped while the waiter was taking their orders, then he continued.

"I am part of the occupying forces in Germany; one of my duty is to deal with Displaced People and help them go back home. To cut a long story short, I visited a DP camp a month ago, and I was told there were Italians in the hospital. So, my commanding officer assigned me to take care of them since I speak Italian. I walked into a ward where severely malnourished men were being treated for several things; I was surprised to hear one of them call me by my name. It was Uncle Michele."

Emma was excited.

"So how was he? I am thrilled to see you, and I miss him as well."

Carlo did not have a happy face reminiscing about the first time he met their uncle.

"I have to tell Aunt Miriam that her husband is alive but weighs around 40 kilos; he survived death camps and a death march. He is being treated for pneumonia; they will release him from the hospital when he is at least 60 kilos. Emma, I hardly recognized him. Do you remember the photos of young Michele Bolaffi and his team of rowers? He is a shadow of that. Somehow, my visit perked him up. I visit him every chance I have. He is making progress, but it is probably a matter of two steps forward and one step backward. He is looking forward to my return to hear all about the family."

Emma had tears in her eyes; she was not making any attempt to stop them. It took her a few minutes to reply.

"I think you should tell my parents and Uncle Roberto first and then have them there when you tell Aunt Miriam. Let's put it in this way; he is alive. Uncle Emanuele and Grandpa Samuele are not. I am sorry, but you need to tell this tale two more times. Also, let them decide how to tell Grandma Fiamma; she is not great. I am sure she will be thrilled to see you, but be prepared to see her suddenly stare into space, lost in her own world. She has been like that since Grandpa Samuele was arrested almost two years ago, and the news about Uncle Emanuele and his wife did not exactly help."

"Now, can you tell me something to lighten the atmosphere? I was so looking forward to spending time talking to you like we used to do."

"Yes, like we used to do in another life. Now look at us, you in uniform and me working in what Mrs Toffolo calls *her atelier.* "

"Paris, beware. Emma Mendes has plans, designs, and scissors."

They started their usual banter from where they had left it all those years earlier. The chemistry was still there. Emma enjoyed it so much that she shared something; after all, she would have already told Carlo in a previous lifetime.

"Well, I have possibly some good news. I met a young man during my undercover work."

"Jewish?"

"Jewish!"

"Italian?"

"Italian!"

By now, Emma had a huge grin on her face.

"Just so you know, you had the same reaction as Aunt Anita; she and Grandma Esther are the only ones to know, although I think my mother and my sisters have guessed something."

"Would I know him?"

"I have no idea; he is a bit older than us and lives in Bologna."

"How much is 'a bit'?"

"About five years."

"Fine, for a moment, I thought it could have been ten or more. I do not think I know anybody from Bologna. So, how is it going?"

"So far, so good. We have met three times as Emma and Roberto, and the sparkle is still there. After you wrote to us, I wrote to him and asked him if he could come here the day after RoshHaShanah; I'd like you to meet him."

"Has anybody else in the family met him?"

"I suspect Uncle Roberto and Uncle Paolo have met him, although not as my boyfriend. We have decided to wait to see each other in our 'normal lives' six times before taking it a step further. I have a feeling there is a ring burning in his pocket, but we have three more times to meet before we talk about the future beyond the next visit."

They were now walking back to Mrs. Toffolo's workshop. In typical Mendes fashion, Emma stopped at the door and told him.

"You know, our lunch is a sign that some things can go back to what they were. You do not live here anymore, you are a Canadian, and you wear a uniform, but you are still like a brother. Today I am happy to be alive; it makes a change from being happy I survived!"

07 September 1945

Anita had just arrived back from Fiamma's home, where she had 'helped' with all the arrangements for the big family dinner. It was RoshHaShanah, the Jewish New Year. Things were back as they were. The family was larger this year. There were empty chairs, but this was something they would have done before the war, before racial laws. They were back; they might all be still crammed in two homes. It was not a problem. The food, the expectation of celebrating the holiday with family, the expectation that those who had been in Synagogue would come back with strangers who had nowhere to go to celebrate the New

Year, everything was there. Paolo and Sofia would join them later to wish everybody a sweet new year.

The Synagogue service had finished. Carlo, in uniform, had been a hit. As usual, there were 'new' familiar faces, people that had arrived back from wherever they had spent the previous couple of years. There were also other young men in uniform; Gabriele invited two American and a British soldier to dinner. Alex Modiano, Anna, Emma, and Carlo were walking with them to Fiamma's home. Carlo was explaining where they were going. Emma and Anna were trying to make them speak Italian. The conversation was very light-hearted; Miriam and Rachele looked at that group and commented that it was a group of young people walking home from synagogue as if nothing had happened. Miriam still had massive mood swings. She was happy that her husband had survived, then suddenly she was worried about his health or concerned about what he had been through.

Gabriele and Roberto were walking behind the younger children; they also commented how normal everything looked. The war seemed far away in time, yet they had been back in Venice for less than four months. Roberto remarked he was very proud to see four young Jews in uniform. Gabriele pointed out that Jews had been fighting as well, only without uniforms and not in a traditional army. Even those who had not been active in any clandestine movement had been fighting for survival.

13 September 1945

Carlo was about to leave Venice; he had confirmed a lift to Germany on a US military plane from Verona the following day and would have to catch a train in the evening to be on that plane. He had photos of the whole family with him for Uncle Michele and letters from Aunt Miriam and their children. His cousins had been reluctant to write, but they both gave him very long letters. Everybody was at the station, a very large crowd for one Canadian soldier at the end of ten days' leave. His grandmother surprised him when she said to the whole group.

"Seeing Carlo makes me realize that there was a reason behind the racial laws. After hearing Carlo's stories, I cried a lot; then I thought what a privilege it was that no Italian Jew was involved in committing those atrocities."

Before getting on the train, Carlo whispered in Emma's ear that he liked Roberto Sonnino

1 October 1945

It was an exciting day as Leo and Mario Mendes and Enrico Bolaffi were going back to a 'regular school' for the first time. Davide and Paola Mendes and Gloria Bolaffi had been enrolled in the Jewish school. Rachele and Miriam thought they were too young for the questions non-Jewish schoolmates would have asked them, and they felt that being with other Jewish children would have been easier.

Another sign of normality, Leo and Mario were in the same class; they were just going to say they were cousins and leave it at that. Other children lived in homes where more than one family was cohabiting, so their classmates would not find it strange that two cousins lived in the same household.

It was also a significant day for Rachele, her very first day in court since January 1939. She was almost as nervous as she was when she tried her first case more than twenty years earlier. This one was also very personal; they had to

273

prove that Miriam and her husbands were legitimate owners, and their residence had been seized for racial reasons. The current occupiers were refugees from Pola; Miriam and Rachele were embarrassed to kick them out; it was almost a case of refugees fighting refugees. Miriam was happy to stay with her mother until the two families from Pola had been rehoused, but she ultimately wanted to be back in her home.

By lunchtime, six children came home from their first day in school, and two ladies came home after a successful day in court. Miriam was grateful; Rachele was thrilled to be back in the saddle. She knew she missed it, but she had not realized how much.

7 October 1945

Travelling was difficult. The last two years of the war had brought many air raids on Northern Italy; both the advancing Allied forces and the withdrawing German forces had destroyed bridges. The resistance acts of sabotage had also hit bridges and railway lines. Once the Slav partisans left Trieste, the allied armies were in control. Michele Modiano started trying to find a way to get his parents back from Venice. His son Max had made the journey with his wife and two children two weeks earlier, and it had taken them a whole day; they had left Venice early in the morning and had arrived in Trieste late at night. His grandson had told him it had been "worse than the journey from Switzerland," he was not prepared to suggest to his elderly parents that they would go through the same experience. In the end, it was his sister-in-law Perla, his brother Daniele's wife, who had come up with a solution. She spoke five languages and worked as an interpreter for the British Army. She got permission for Daniele to use a private boat to travel to Venice to collect his parents and nephew. At the last minute, they had to take Alex off the list. He had decided to stay in Venice until he was sure what he wanted to do next.

Emma was sorry to see her grandparents leave. She had a conflict. Roberto Sonnino was due to be in Venice, and she wanted to spend as much time with him as possible. She had shared her dilemma with Paolo and Sofia, who suggested that maybe it was time to introduce Roberto to her family. They even offered to have him stay with them if necessary. Emma was reluctant to use the phone unless it was necessary, but Paolo and Sofia offered their help, so she called Roberto. She did not know how private the conversation would be at his end, but she was thrilled when Roberto agreed to meet her family.

Roberto Sonnino had arrived in Venice on Friday; he had already met Diana and Anna by then. Emma had tried to be informal in introducing him to people; in the end, Anita lightened the atmosphere. Before shaking his hand, she turned to Emma.

"Is he?"

"He is."

She then took Roberto's hand, pulled him to her, gave him a big hug, and said,

"Thank you for putting a smile on Elena Giadrossi's face; she stopped being so tense after meeting you."

Not everybody knew who Elena Giadrossi was; a red-faced and embarrassed Emma was forced to give a vague explanation to her relatives from Trieste. Her grandmother Esther exchanged glances with Rachele and smiled because she had figured it out!

16 October 1945

In the summer of 1943, when they arrested Mussolini and formed a new non-Fascist government, one of the first acts of the government not connected with the war was to abolish the racial laws. Unfortunately, by then, the Germans had already freed Mussolini. The king and the government had fled Rome to go to Bari, and Italy was de facto divided into two countries. The Kingdom of Italy was south of the front line and what later became the Italian Social Republic north of the front line. The republic was a puppet state of Nazi Germany. So, as the front line was moving north, the racial laws stopped being implemented. As far as the Mendes were concerned, they lasted until the end of April 1945, when the allied armies crossed the Po river. Gabriele and Rachele had managed to save most of their assets. Still, when Rachele unexpectedly became pregnant with Mila in the summer of 1942, she could only see a non-Jewish doctor for emergencies. There was not a Jewish gynaecologist in Venice, only a Midwife. They faced a dilemma that was solved by not stating the name of Mila's parents on her birth certificate.

The first thing that Gabriele and Rachele did after their first weekend back in Venice was to file a petition with the family court to sort Mila's birth certificate and make sure she became Mila Mendes. Alvise had a hard time convincing Rachele and Roberto that he had to run this legal process; they were too emotionally involved.

Today was the day when they were due in court. Rachele had driven Alvise demented, checking all the documenta-tion three times; they had letters from Paolo Mondani and half a dozen of his colleagues. They had sworn statements from two nurses who had recognized Rachele but did not say anything to protect her. Alvise kept saying it was watertight, but they were worried. Emma and Leo were in court because they looked like Mila; Anna, Diana, and Davide were not there because they did not.

In the end, it was an open and shut case. The judge agreed to their petition, and an emotional Anita gave Mila to Gabriele and Rachele. Mila did not know what was going on, could not understand why her parents had tears in their eyes, and hugged her father. Alvise would have to go back the following week, take the original court statement to Venice town hall and get them to re-issue Mila's birth certificate.

When they arrived back at Campo San Giacomo dall'Orio, they found that Fiamma, Miriam, and Gaia Morpurgo had sorted a celebratory meal for everyone.

Mila was confused. She knew it was not her birthday, but Anna had baked two cakes. She kept smiling at everybody until she was too tired and was put to bed.

When one set of celebrations was over, Miriam said she had something important to tell them. She had received a letter from Carlo. Bar any unlikely complication, the hospital would discharge Michele before the end of the month. He still had five kilos to gain. Carlo was concerned that he was too weak to travel, so he had rented a small house for a month and keep him there. They would travel together to be in Venice for the weekend of celebrations in December: two bar-mitzvah on the same Saturday and a wedding the following day.

Enrico Bolaffi, fifteen years old, kept telling everybody in a tone of voice between the embarrassed and the disgusted that his mother had kept saying, "He is coming home, dad is coming home" the whole afternoon.

18 November 1945

Travelling in Northern Italy was still complicated; luckily, Paolo and Sofia Mondani had extended an offer to Roberto Sonnino to stay with them whenever he needed it, provided he behaved himself; Emma was their honorary niece! Roberto smiled as the train crossed the bridge from the mainland to Venice. That strange city was becoming familiar to him; he was inhabiting a sort of halfway space between a visitor and a resident. He could also feel the ring in the pocket of his suit; it was a ring his honorary great-uncle had given him after he told him there was a young woman he wanted to marry. It was a ring owned by his grandmother's closest friend, the sister of his honorary great-uncle. Those two ladies had turned two families into one clan. Emotionally, Roberto could claim it was a family heirloom. The ring felt heavy in his pocket.

When he got to Paolo and Sofia, he showed them the ring, explaining his provenance. Sofia was really touched and hugged Roberto. Their late daughter-in-law, Carolina, was part of the same clan. Paolo said they could almost take the credit for this wedding since Roberto and Emma first met at their son's wedding. Roberto Sonnino knew they had lost both their son and their daughter-in-law. He hugged both of them, looked at his watch, thanked them, drank the coffee, and rushed out, going to Campo San Giacomo dall'Orio to meet Emma. He was planning to give her the ring later in the afternoon.

Although it was only the second time he had lunch with Emma's family, it already included Roberto in the banter between siblings and cousins; he was also surprised by the number of honorary siblings Emma had over her five brothers and sisters. Alex Modiano and Franco Cantoni were both there, and he knew Emma considered her cousin

Carlo like a brother. Lunch was the usual noisy affair around the Mendes table; the Cantonis had been there before because they were also deeply involved in the banter.

Initially, Roberto was not sure how to react when they called him either 'Roberto Sonnino' or 'Sonnino.' Still, when he realised that there was another Roberto in the family, he embraced it, joined the banter, and gave as good as he got.

After lunch, he and Emma went out. It was a foggy day, although the fog was not very thick; it was enough to make everything look out of focus. As they walked, they talked about their plans for the future; they felt they were in their cocoon. Roberto trusted Emma's knowledge of the City not to get lost. Emma decided to show Roberto a nice view of St Mark's square from the Giudecca island, so they started walking towards a vaporetto stop. The ring was really burning in Roberto's pocket by now.

When they got to the Giudecca, they walked to a point where they could see the Doge's palace in the mist.

"Roberto, it looks like an impressionist painting. I love coming here; I discovered this place when I was walking around during my lunch break. Isn't it beautiful?"

Emma had been looking at the view and not at Roberto, so when she turned to him, wondering why he was not saying anything, she found him smiling at her, holding a ring in his hand. They stood there in silence for a while, then Roberto pointed at the ring.

"So, what do you say?"

"You haven't asked yet."

"Do I have to?"

"Well, I'd like to know what I say yes or no to."

"You may say no?"

By then, Emma was laughing.

"I didn't say that. I just want you to ask the question, I think I guessed, but all you are doing is showing me an antique and very precious ring. So, ask the question, and I'll answer."

Roberto was anxious and embarrassed; Emma was not helping by teasing him. He looked pensive for a few minutes, smiled, put the ring back in his pocket, and went down on one knee. By then, Emma had stopped laughing and was aware of people watching them.

"Emma Mendes, will you marry me?"

"Yes, Roberto Sonnino, I will."

Now Roberto took the ring out of his pocket and gave it to Emma; it was not an exact fit, so Emma put it on her middle finger for the moment. Somebody started applauding, but they barely noticed.

"As you know, I am here tomorrow as well. Your parents will know where to take it to be fitted; I am going to talk to them when we go back."

"For all we know, Uncle Paolo, Aunt Sofia, and the Cantonis may still be there."

"I do not care; if they are still there, I dare you to walk in without showing your left hand with the ring."

Emma was partly right. The Cantonis had gone home, but Paolo and Sofia were still there. Roberto was also correct; Emma could not resist showing her left hand. In the middle of noises, congratulations, wishes, Roberto asked

Gabriele and Rachele if he could have a word with them; Rachele suggested the study.

Gabriele and Rachele were sitting in armchairs usually reserved for clients; Roberto was leaning against the desk.

"I am pleased you are both here. My mother would kill me if she found out that I did not include Emma's mother in this conversation. I was raised in a very egalitarian family; my parents are equal partners. That is the model I know, and that is how I hope Emma and I will feel when we are married, equal partners."

Gabriele had a very stern face, but Rachele was smiling.

"I am pleased to hear that. We have been equal partners in our marriage, and that is the example we hope we gave our children. Your parents would surely be proud to hear you say what you just told us; I hope our sons react in the same way."

Roberto was still nervous, but there was something he wanted to say.

"I just wanted to explain to you I have no intention of getting married before I have a sustainable job. Equal partners mean that we both need to contribute to our lives. You probably understand why my plans are still very much in the air, but I wanted to reassure you that from now on, they will be our plan, as in Emma and mine."

The rest of the conversation was slightly more relaxed. When they joined the others, Alex Modiano patted Roberto's back, mocking a very solemn tone of voice.

"As the oldest member of my generation amongst those present in this gathering, let me welcome you to the family. You survived Aunt Rachele's third degree, and she is smiling. You are one of us."

14 December 1945

It was the beginning of a weekend of celebration for the Mendes Clan; many of the Modiano relatives had arrived from Trieste. Emma, Anna, and Diana had remarked several times that it was like the family events they knew before the war and the racial laws. Leo and Mario had received telegrams from Canada, Australia, Palestine. The big dinner organised in the former warehouse of the old Mendes family business was as it would have happened ten years earlier. Carlo pointed out to Emma and Anna that it was only the way everybody was cautious around their uncle, Michele Bolaffi. That was an indication that things were different.

It was the first time that Roberto Sonnino was part of a big family celebration. Davide and Esther Modiano were trying to get a date for a trip to Trieste out of him and Emma. It was a great party. Leo and Mario were very nervous, and Alex and older cousins kept teasing them and reassuring them it was normal.

15 December 1945

It was a packed synagogue, and a packed Mendes celebration. It was not just a bar-mitzvah of two cousins, the first bar-mitzvah since the end of the war. Their uncle would be the groom in the first wedding celebrated since everybody "started coming back" the previous May.

The service had some exciting moments to accommodate the two bar-mitzvah boys and the groom-to-be. In the lady's gallery, Fiamma was in tears because her husband was not there, and she was happy and proud of her son and her grandsons.

Leo and Mario had agreed to share the third call to read the law; Leo would go first because it was his actual bar-mitzvah, Mario would be second because his actual bar-mitzvah would have been a few months earlier.

When Leo was called, everybody stood up; Michele Bolaffi was still weak, but he insisted on standing; Carlo and Alex steadied him and managed to keep him upright for the time necessary to hear his nephew say the blessings. When it was Mario's turn, Carlo and Alex helped him again, and again when it was the turn of Roberto Mendes, the groom to be.

During the blessing of the Cohanim, Gabriele realised he was the oldest male in the Mendes clan, so he took every-body else under his own tallit to pass on the blessing to his younger brother, brother-in-law, his sons, and nephews. He invited Roberto Sonnino as well; he was already part of the family, after all. Emma was thrilled to witness the scene from the ladies' gallery.

It was a great day for the family. A day when everybody thought about the future, even Fiamma: Rachele later remarked to Anita that it was the first time in months that nobody had mentioned war, deportation, survival.

16 December 1945

Roberto woke up anxious. Marrying his fiancée should have happened six years earlier. They were getting married after surviving separation during the war and being re-united only a few months earlier. He still would not believe it. His brother and other male guests met him outside his mother's home to walk with him the short distance to the synagogue, the only woman with them being Fiamma, Roberto's mother. The women were waiting for the bride at the entrance to the Ghetto from Canal Cannareggio. Emma and Diana were part of the team that had made the bride's dress (a present from the Mendes family) and were there to dress the bride. Leo, Mario, and Enrico Bolaffi had the job of standing by the bridge separating the two ghetto areas to signal the men when the women had entered the Levantine synagogue, and the bride was in the room where she would wait for the right moment to appear. Anita tried to control the younger children running around in the Campo del Ghetto.

Carlo explained to Roberto Sonnino that they were following an old tradition of the Mendes family. He did not know where it was from, but that is how they did it.

The wedding was nothing special and everything special, another sign that life was re-starting.

At the end of the reception, Gabriele and Rachele were off for their evening walk together.

"Did you notice that Emma and Roberto went out for a walk as well? Emma took the excuse of walking him to Paolo and Sofia."

Gabriele was smiling; he was thrilled just walking next to his wife.

"Yes, I did, and I hope they keep doing it for all their married life."

Rachele could not stop smiling.

"Today was the first time I realised I survived for something. We are rebuilding our lives. Only the Almighty knows what "normal" will look like in a few years, but we are building it. I wonder if we ever stop counting the empty chairs. I still have no idea what happened to two of my siblings and their family. Also, my sister Barbara, your brother Raffaele, took their family halfway around the world. They may still be here with us if "all that" had not happened."

Gabriele tried to reassure his wife; it was not much effort. He was feeling very optimistic.

"Who knows? They may come to visit us soon when people can travel the world again. In the meantime, let's build the new normality, one brick at a time."

They turned into the empty Rialto market; they smiled because they noticed that Roberto and Emma were walking towards them, their body language just like theirs.

Historical Notes

For several years after Mussolini became Italy's dictator, Fascism had no problems with Jewish Italians or "Italian citizens following the Mosaic faith," as they were called in official documents, laws, etc. Many historians have discussed why Mussolini changed his mind. I like my paternal grandfather's explanation: "He was mad because his Jewish mistress, Margherita Zarfatti, dumped him." Italian racial laws did not have a final solution. Many Italian Jews got a predated baptism certificate, which was enough to be removed from the lists of members of a Jewish community and escape the restrictions and, later, the Holocaust. Before the racial laws, there were Jewish members of the Fascist Party and Jewish dissidents to use a modern word. After the racial laws, very few Jews remained faithful to Mussolini, that loyalty costed them their lives when the Holocaust arrived in Italy.

When Mussolini was an ally of Hitler, he never handed over Jews, either in Italy or in the territories occupied by Italy. In the Summer of 1943, Mussolini was arrested and taken to a hotel in an isolated location in the Apennines.

Italy negotiated a separate peace with the allied forces. The armistice was announced on September 8th,1943. The king and the Italian government fled south of the front line to Bari. On that day, World War II in Italy turned into a Civil War, and the Holocaust reached Italy. In September 1943, the Germans freed Mussolini and re-instated him as head of government of a 'Republic of Italy' that included all territories north of the front line, with the Kingdom of Italy south of the front line. Towards the end of the month, a meeting near Berlin included Italian and Hungarian Jews in the Final Solution. The first roundup of Jews happened in Rome on 16 October 1943. However, in Meina on the shores of Lake Maggiore in September 1943, Jewish guests of a hotel were separated from the non-Jewish guests and later killed by an SS group transferred from Ukraine to Northern Italy. It happened before the decision to include Italian Jews in the 'Final solution.'

85% of Italian Jews survived the Holocaust. Many Jews from Northern Italy escaped to Switzerland, and others found shelter in Convents or hidden by non-Jewish friends or relatives. Others moved and lived as best as they could under false identities, following other Italians who moved to the countryside to escape air raids.

The Italian Front

In July 1943, the Allied armies landed in Sicily, and the new Italian government started negotiations with the Allied forces for a separate peace. On September 8th, 1943, the Armistice between Italy and the allied forces was announced. The Kingdom of Italy, south of the front line, revoked racial laws fairly quickly. while the Italian Republic, north of the front line, passed a law that stated that Jews were enemies of the state, they would be arrested and their assets seized. The relative distance of their location from the front line had become a matter of life and death for many Italian Jews. The allied army reached Naples before the roundup of Italian Jews started, so Naples is the only Italian Jewish community never touched by the Holocaust. The Allied armies advance north was not fast, there were a few very fierce battles, the most famous one being around the monastery of Montecassino, south of Naples, a series of four assaults against the German forces that lasted from January to May 1944. At the beginning of Winter 1944 the advance paused until March 1945.

Acknowledgments

Writing may be a solo activity, but getting a book published is not. To paraphrase a well-known phrase, "it takes a village to create a book".

First of all I would like to thank those who believed in my voice, like Andrea Rosen and my eldest son Eyal, their reaction to the first thing I wrote gave me the courage to start writing this book. Then I have to thank Lynne Halliday, a friend who gave me a well-deserved kick in the backside that prompted me to work on the quality of my writing.

My editor, Richard Arkus, provided the professional view that made it possible to take two steps back and look at the story with some objectivity. He gave me many constructive suggestions.

I also would like to thank Rick Atkinson for allowing me to use the maps of the Italian campaign he used in his book "The Day Of Battle: The War in Sicily and Italy 1943-44", part of his "Liberation Trilogy"

John Arias is the graphic designer behind the cover, he took an image I sourced from the US National Archive and turned it into an oil painting, he also had the patience to guide me through the process of creating covers and why he was asking certain questions.

A special place is reserved for the wonderful creators of the London Writer Salons, Matt Trinetti and Parul Barvishi, their lockdown experiment created a community that made me as a writer and has increased the quality of my life. On May 5th, 2020 I structured this book during my first Zoom session at the London Writer Salons, writing "alone but together" with other writers. Those writers have become my friends and my support group, Katherine Koromilas, Konrad, Jenny Hammerton, Sue Mannin, Patricia Lane, Sofia Koutlaki, Barrie Tankel, Marian green, Claire Upton, Abigali Vint, Lauren McMenemy, Nicolas Laborle, Jodi Hausen, Melissa Wedieman, Patricia Lane and many many others. We wrote together, we supported each other, during the solitary times of pandemic-induced lockdown, we became friends. We look at each other in our "Zoom Squares" and when we finally meet in real life (or, as some say, in 3D), the only thing we do not know about each other is how tall we are. Everything else is familiar.

Daniella Pinkstein encouraged me to keep writing when I had doubts that people might be interested in reading about Jews actively fighting German occupation.

The LWS Gold Members coaches, Kathryn Koromilas, Niamh Mulvey, Eimear Ryan, Anna Wilson, and Parul and Matt, encouraged me, helped me, and overall turned me into a confident writer.

Carole Scott and Tali Sarnetzky supported me in a part of the process that was six galaxies away from my comfort zone. Thank you for helping me without being judgemental or patronising.

Close friends like Alessandro Saporetti, Maria Vittoria Cavina, Alessandra Bellini encouraged me and enabled me to find the consistency and the determination (or the stubbornness???) to continue through several drafts until I felt I could not take it any further. The LWS fellow members of our gold circle and sacred circle provided continuous support, encouragement, and hand holding, and a Zoom-hug when I needed one. Friends like Christian Josso and Nicoletta Iommi, who really wanted to read the manuscript (and reminded me that I forgot to e-mail it to them), made me think that maybe somebody might be interested in what I was writing. My beta readers, who gave me confidence and constructive feedback. Members of LWS who endured my reading extracts from this story through Open Mike and made me realise that I can tell a story.

Last but not least, I need to mention my parents and grandparents of blessed memory, the inspiration for Roberto Sonnino and Emma Mendes, Gabriele Mendes, and Rachele Modiano Mendes, and some of their contemporaries, like Giulia Sermoneta, Giselle Hertisch, Giovanni Di Costola, Maria Jose' Gelmini and many others like Sara Saralvo, who told me their stories and inspired me to pass them on. I hope this book does some justice to their courage and their determination to survive.

Also by Silvano Stagni

A collection of feel-good short stories.

Silvano's blog: https://authorsilvano.substack.com/

twitter.com/authorsilvano
instagram.com/silvanowrites

Notes

Chapter 1

1. This is the name of the exam at the end of the Italian high school; a pass would allow the student to attend University. According to Mussolini's racial laws, Jewish students could only finish high school in Milan or Rome and attend University abroad.

Chapter 2

1. "Avvocato" in Italian means 'lawyer'. If you have passed the Italian equivalent of the bar and you are a practicing lawyer, it is common to use your job as a title. Nowadays, it would be considered a very formal way of answering the phone, and many people would just use their name.
2. Make aliyah, i.e. emigrate to the Holy Land. What is now Israel and what was then part of the British Mandate in the Middle East.
3. Ponte Littorio was the name given to the road bridge that connects Venice to the mainland when it was opened in 1933. After World War II, it was renamed "Ponte della Liberta'" (Bridge of Freedom). The Austrian built the railway bridge next to it in 1846; it was expanded to its current width in the 1970s.
4. The Seder is the Passover ceremonial dinner held in memory of the Jewish slaves leaving Egypt and crossing the Red Sea

Chapter 3

1. General Radetsky - made famous by Strauss with his "Radetsky March" - was a general in the Imperial Army in the 19th century.

Chapter 4

1. In October 1922, Mussolini – who had failed to achieve any meaningful majority at the election - organised a mass demonstration in Rome that prompted the King of Italy to appoint him Prime Minister.

2. Fedelissimo means "Very Faithful," it was the irreverent nickname to refer to those who claimed to have marched to Rome with Mussolini in 1922.
3. Baicoli are typical Venetian biscuits

Chapter 5

1. Germany, The Austro-Hungarian Empire, and the Ottoman Empire

Chapter 6

1. The fascist regime referred to those that were militantly opposing them as "the rebels," whether they were using weapons to fight them or not.
2. Professor Jona was the president of the Jewish Community in Venice.
3. Switching lights, ringing electrical doorbells, using the telephone, are all examples of what observant Jews do not do on the Sabbath
4. One of Venice "sestieri," the six districts of the old City. Castello is the one closest to the Lido and furthest away from Emma's home in Dorsoduro.
5. Racial laws prevented Italian Jews from serving in one of the Italian armed forces, the police, or other paramilitary organisations.
6. The Shofar is a ram horn blown on the Jewish New Year (Rosh HaShanah) and at the end of the Day of Atonement (Yom Kippur), usually in synagogue, but it can also be blown at home.

Chapter 7

1. The artificial canal 'Brenta' was once the primary way to transport goods and people between Venice and Padua; from 1600 onwards, wealthy Venetian families had built grand holiday villas along its banks.
2. Under Italian racial laws, Jews had to have a permission to travel outside the province issued by their local police station
3. After the armistice between Italy and the Allies, the German army – already in Italy – tried to get hold of or neutralise Italian equipment. A few skirmishes ensued, and many Italian soldiers went into hiding to escape fighting alongside the Germans.

Chapter 8

1. In Italian, lawyers are formally introduced with their title "Avvocato" (Lawyer in Italian)
2. Challah is the bread usually baked on Thursday evenings or Friday mornings used to make blessings over bread on Friday night dinner and Saturday lunch
3. Yom Kippur, the Day of Atonement, is a day when Jews fast and gather in prayer to atone for their sins. Even the most secular Jew marks this day somehow. Many Jews spend most of their time in synagogue during the 26 hours fast, going home just to sleep; most Jews go at least once or twice during the day.

Chapter 10

1. Following the 'betrayal' (i.e., The Armistice), the Kingdom of Italy declared war on Germany; the territory of Italy north of the front line became an 'informal republic' with Mussolini as his president. Later in the year, it took the name of "Italian Social Republic." Most Italians called it the Republic of Salo' Salo' is a town on the bank of the Garda Lake that had become the capital of the Republic.
2. [2] The 'legal' definition of Jews in Italy before the racial laws of 1938.
3. The road bridge connecting Venice to the mainland had only been open for 10 years. Before 1933, the railway bridge was the only connection between Venice and the mainland. Called "Ponte Littorio" during Fascist Italy, it is now called "Ponte della Liberta' "
4.
5. Original text" "*Gli appartenenti alla razza ebraica sono stranieri. Durante questa guerra appartengono a nazionalità nemica*"

Chapter 11

1. In the Jewish tradition, fathers bless sons and mothers bless daughters before the Friday night meal. town on the bank of the Garda Lake that had become the capital of the Republic.
2. Kiddush, the toast that welcomes the Sabbath, and lighting at least two candles saying a blessing are part of a Jewish family ritual before Friday night dinner.
3. Mestre is 'mainland Venice', the first important station after the bridge that links Venice to the mainland. Every train stops there.

Chapter 12

1. The Hebrew name of a piece of unleavened bread, *matzot* is the plural.

Chapter 13

1. Following racial laws, Jews were exempt from military service, when Italy joined the war any man aged between 18 and 40 who was not serving in the military or otherwise participating in the war effort, either had a medical reason to be exempt or was Jewish.

Chapter 15

1. Mila was born in the hospital, at a time when Jews could not have access to a regular hospital. They manage to smuggle Rachele in and declare that Mila was the daughter of parents who declined to be named. This is what Leo refers to. Mila would get her birth certificate sorted after the war.

Chapter 16

1. Asolo is a town at the foot of the dolomites, northeast of Venice
2. The religious ceremony that marks the transition out of childhood for thirteen years old boys

Chapter 17

1. Trieste had been occupied by Tito's Army. There was apparent support from the Soviet Union for a part of Italian territory to be handed over to Yugoslavia, including Trieste. That would have meant problems for the Modiano family business.
2. In the summer of 1945, in the attempts to prove that the Slavs were the majority of the population in the easternmost part of Italy, there was a lot of hostility against Italian. A lot of ethnic Italian and Italian speakers fled Istria (now Croatia) and became refugees in Italy.

Made in the USA
Middletown, DE
25 June 2023